MILKSOP

JOHN VAN RYS

 First Printing: 2026
Chicken House Press

ISBN trade paperback edition: 978-1-997584-16-2
ISBN ePub: 978-1-997584-18-6

Library and Archives Canada Cataloguing in Publication
CIP data on file with the National Library and Archives

CHICKEN HOUSE PRESS
282906 Normanby/Bentinck Townline
Durham, Ontario, Canada, N0G 1R0
www.chickenhousepress.ca

For my brother Nick and my sisters Tracy and Wendy

In memory of Melvin and Barbara Knox

Milksop. A person who is indecisive and lacks courage.
Late Middle English: from milk + sop. Literally a piece of
bread soaked with milk, as formerly eaten
by children and invalids.

Definitely not an accurate definition of Evan Mulder,
whatever the bastards claim. Well, maybe not.

MILKSOP

JOHN VAN RYS

The Child is father of the Man;
And I could wish my days to be
Bound each to each by natural piety.

William Wordsworth
"My Heart Leaps Up"

CHAPTER 1

I'm dumped in a farm laneway, a dark tunnel beneath a canopy of trees. That, children, is where my story begins. Standing with a small suitcase held by both hands in front of me, I face four strangers and a large dog with black-rimmed eyes while the sound of a car leaving fades to silence.

Only looking back would I see that moment as a turning aside from the highway I was travelling into the narrow pathway of my life. Even now, as barred sunlight falls across this page, I wonder if such a grandiose idea is just bullshit—my memory playing me, fabricating some pastoral landscape in the mirage that is the past. Is it just a vision to puff up my pride, explain my childish errors, and justify resentments? Am I simply sticking a bandage on old griefs?

It's a story I've never fully told, maybe one I haven't even truly told myself. But now that you're adults and while I, Evan Michael Mulder, *pater familias*, am still of semi-sound mind and mostly intact body, this story I offer as a tiny testament, one thread among many spinning out of the past to make up the lives we've woven together. It's a fabric that frays even as it grows on the loom. As I begin to fray, for that matter, and threaten to become moth-eaten, as my behaviour at my so-called retirement celebration demonstrated. Still, I think our cloth is quite beautiful, if not much larger in the scheme of things than a dishrag or a bandana. Or more important than a snot-rag, if I'm totally honest.

I know you heard the word. Everybody at my shindig must have. "Milksop." I'd like to think Brice, that biggest of all big cheeses, didn't realize the mic was on when he laughed in response to some undoubtedly snide comment from his twerp assistant and used that word to belittle me —me, after forty years of dutiful service. "I'll be some happy to see the backside of that old Mulder milksop." I suspect it was deliberate. I turned red, I know—and then, at long last, I saw red. I'm still embarrassed the four of you had to see it, you and your spouses—sorry, your significant others, or is "partner" the PC term I must use today? For the love of God, when did love become a business transaction? Then again, perhaps in some sense it is, and always has been. Still, why not simply say "husbands" and "wives" and "lovers" when that's what we are? Children, please forgive me my foolish thoughts.

What I'm truly ashamed of, though, is that your mother and Auntie Jo had to witness my juvenile behaviour. That said, I thank God they were there to intervene.

I don't excuse what I did at my bash, but I feel now as if I need to defend to you the little life I've led. I can't bear the thought of you having that word ringing in your ears, wondering if it's true. Children know so little of a parent's life before they themselves were born; perhaps I can give you a glimpse of the shadowy land I travelled from to become your father.

In the end, this is the story of how I fell for your mother. Strangely, it's also a story of a family that was and wasn't my family, someone I loved who was not my lover. What happened took place on a nothing farm in a nowhere corner of the world long ago—1979—the summer I turned 18, the end of a decade that felt like a long hangover from the sixties. It was a dairy farm in Huron County, more than an hour north of London where I grew up, and a bit more than a stone's throw from the shores of what you know is my favourite Great Lake: Lake Huron—

less a lake than a fresh-water, inland sea.

Like many stories, it starts with a journey. Not to some far-flung, exotic corner of the globe or a galaxy light years away, which is the distance usually required for such tales, but just down the road a ways. Sometimes, a small distance will do.

Like some stories, it begins with confession too. You see, I'd royally screwed up in school that winter term in 1979, flunking all my courses. I know. You're shocked. The only way I can explain it is that I'd come to feel aboard a one-man sailboat in the middle of a still sea, the surface like glass. Stuck in the doldrums, nothing filled my sails, and I was rudderless anyway. I thought, *What's the point, really?* None that I could think of.

To borrow the always wise words of Rick and Roger, my life had become a mess. I'd lost the craving for success. Or to use the language of my childhood faith, I was guilty of sloth, that sluggard among the Seven Deadly Sins. The creature bearing its name had become my spirit animal.

Chapter 2

William Lyon Mackenzie King Secondary School. What a pretentious name for a school populated by middle- and working-class kids living in a modest subdivision of bungalows, semidetached homes, and townhouses. WLM-KSS for short, like a vanity plate—this was the calmed sea where I found myself afloat that spring, taking on water, sinking.

WLM-KSS my ass.

By May, I'd quit most everything. That included the track team, though I kept running when things fell apart.

Sometimes after school, never before school anymore. I was having trouble waking up—I never felt fully awake—and started arriving just before the bell or even a few minutes late, sitting still and with my head lowered, staring at the floor in homeroom while over the PA came the recording of the Lord's Prayer and the national anthem, followed by announcements. Our Father... O Canada... burgers and fries the lunch special.

But during school, the need to run often overwhelmed me. Sitting in class, I'd become a ghost. I felt disconnected, and tried to make myself invisible to teachers and classmates. I'd always been quiet, so no one seemed to notice the change—until it was too late. To get away, I started excusing myself to go to the washroom. I'd sit in a stall, silent, while others came and went, pissing and farting and horsing around, taking a quick smoke.

One day, I found etched on a stall wall "WLM-KSS my ass!" The author had captured my feelings exactly. Here was a true kindred spirit, a Diana Barry to my Anne Shirley. It was my *Green Gables* moment, except I hadn't a clue who this bosom friend might be. If I'd been able to find the dude, I would've kissed him. I teared up staring at this poignant graffiti among the dirty jokes and amateur art renderings of male and female anatomy. It became my motto.

The feeling of ghostly invisibility, of classrooms as catacombs, would build to the point where I couldn't take sitting in another class that day. I'd never, ever skipped a class before, but the only relief I could find would be to duck and run, following the circuit around the neighbourhood we'd used for training—five kilometres during which the rhythm and movement of my limbs might, for a time at least, return me to my body, to myself.

I made sure I never skipped the same class two days in a row, hoping I would fly under the disciplinary radar, but then came a time when it wasn't enough. I might go home at lunch and dawdle until my brother Jeff and sister Annalise left for afternoon classes. I went to the basement, a rec room with one small rectangular window near the low ceiling, walnut panelling, and brown wall-to-wall carpeting. I'd spend the next few hours on the puffy sectional sofa my mom had picked out. The fabric was a purple paisley pattern that looked to me the colour of fresh bruising. I'd curl up in a corner or sprawl out on it staring at the white, sound-absorbing tiles on the low ceiling. There, I'd turn on the stereo and listen to rock albums for their raw energy and rage, getting up only to flip records over. As Rick Davies and Roger Hodgson might say, in that basement I became part of the furniture.

Supertramp's *Breakfast in America* had come out that March, and I played it over and over. And it wasn't just Rick and Roger's "The Logical Song" that spoke to me during those dark days. In every note and every word, they seemed to be reaching out to me with messages in bottles, ten in total, sent floating to me on my island, the Alcatraz in which I'd been left alone. I think of that album to this day as a godsend.

One day toward the end of May, I walked into the school, approached my homeroom, and grasped the door knob. I couldn't open it. I couldn't make my hand turn the handle. It was as if I was a magnet, and the negative charge of my hand was being repelled by the negative charge of my homeroom.

Mr. Ashby, my homeroom teacher since Grade 9—I knew he'd be disappointed in me, disappointed and concerned. Trying to lift my spirits, he'd offer me an Ashbyism. Not just my homeroom teacher, he was my favourite math teacher and my running coach. But I just couldn't open the door to face what was on the other side. The banner for pi above the blackboard, running just below the ceiling all around the room, 3.14 going on and on and on. The poster of the Pythagorean theorem, the triangle so crisply labelled, the small squared right-angled corner, everything squared to arrive at the correct answer. On Mr. Ashby's desk, a small model of a lever and fulcrum, and below it on the face of the desk, "Give me a place to stand and with a lever I will move the whole world." Archimedes and Mr. Ashby, two of a kind, so inspirational. They tried.

As I gripped the doorknob, my stomach began to churn. Acid rose to my throat and saliva filled my mouth. My chest tightened so that I could feel my heart beating, beginning to race. I let go.

I turned around and paced the halls, feeling my back-pack straps digging into my shoulders, a weight filled with textbooks and notebooks I'd brought home and once again failed to open. What I was being pulled toward was un-clear; I simply followed the magnet. Walking turned to trotting and then to running. Eventually I found myself at the door to the patio—an area the administration had des-ignated for smoking, and which some students also used for toking. I pushed through the heavy metal door into clouds of smoke as students risked being late for the sake of a few more drags.

I kept running, my knapsack bouncing against my back. I was out of sight of the school when I slowed to a walk. It was a sunny day, still cool but promising to warm up by afternoon. I had no real sense of where I was going or why. I just knew it had to be away, away from the school, away from the person I was there—two-faced in a way I didn't understand and couldn't control.

I found myself walking into the city. It never would have occurred to me to head away from it, into the coun-tryside. I tried to calm my turbulent thoughts by counting my paces up to 100, then starting over again, barely look-ing up from my feet at the buildings I passed, wincing as I was buffeted by blasts of air from the traffic whizzing up and down the road, people busy going about their busy life's business.

At an intersection, I had to look up for the walk signal.

As I waited for the forbidding red hand to change, I saw ahead St. Joe's, the hospital where I'd nearly died, then some months later decided to be born—a leap into life that was possibly the one bold act I'd committed.

The magnet pulled me toward it. As I stepped across the threshold of the main entrance, I felt like an intruder. To the right was the gift shop. For cover, I stopped to buy some flowers. Holding them to my chest, I wandered the halls from floor to floor. I found myself in the maternity ward hearing the sounds of someone in labour. Alarmed, I moved on and found the newborns. I looked through a large glass window at them in pink or blue blankets, sleeping or fussing in their plastic bassinets. Seventeen, almost eighteen years before, I'd taken my first breaths here, crooned and wailed, drank my mother's milk for the first time, filled my first diapers, slept like a baby—not having a choice in the matter.

I had to get away from these tiny, fussing creatures. Soon, I found myself meandering through the cardiac unit and past the burn unit, trying not to see what perhaps the magnet wanted me to see. I caught glimpses of stroke victims, of cancer patients wearing bandanas to cover their bald scalps, and turned away.

Above a set of double doors, I read, "Palliative Care." Clueless what the words meant, I pulled the doors open and walked through. A nurse looked up from a station, smiled, and said, "Can I help you?"

The question lodged in my chest like a needle. How to answer? The sickly-sweet smell of the bouquet I was clutching hit me. "I just brought some flowers."

"For which patient?" She rose and began moving toward me. "It's not visiting hours right now, but I can take them for you and put them in water."

I looked around for some handy answer that might excuse why I was there. The magnet so far had refused to speak. On a door, a clear plastic sleeve held a file that read, "Peter Rubino." I pointed and said, "I'm here for him."

"Is he your grandfather?" Lying, I said yes, and she replied. "Why don't you just step in for a minute. He's stable, but in and out of consciousness from the painkillers. He may not recognize you."

I opened the door quietly—I was surprised how heavy it was—and stepped through into a room that was oddly dim and light at the same time. Perhaps it was because one curtain was open, flooding a patch of floor with sunlight, while the other was closed, casting the bed and its occupant in shadow. I walked to the bedside and looked down at the man, a stranger, mostly bald with a few wisps of hair, skin wrinkled, the back of his hands covered in age spots. His head and shoulders were slightly elevated by the hospital bed. He wore an oxygen mask, and an IV tube ran into the back of his right hand. Machines around him beeped mildly, regularly, with monitors registering squiggly graph lines running from left to right.

He opened his eyes a moment and searched my face, it seemed to me, for some form of recognition. He couldn't find it, and I could think of nothing to say beyond "I brought these for you." He seemed confused and agitated by my gesture. Or perhaps I was the one confused and agitated, projecting it onto him. I wanted to get away but felt propelled by a compulsion I didn't understand; I leaned over and kissed him on the forehead, the skin dry and warm. I placed the flowers on the tray beside the machines.

When I turned, the nurse was in the doorway, her arms crossed. "You can stay a bit longer if you want to."

"Thank you, but I have to go now."

"It can all be too much, I know," she said as she stood aside to let me through. "I'll put those in water for your grandfather. I'm sure looking at them will brighten his days." As she walked into the room to retrieve the flowers, I rushed toward the ward doors and pushed them open, forcing myself not to run through the halls.

I found a stairwell and took two stairs at a time until I reached the very bottom, which I mistakenly thought was the main floor. In the hallway, I found myself instead outside the morgue. A man wearing a surgical mask was just heading in. "Who are you, and what do you want? This is a restricted area."

My backpack felt like a stone, the straps like a straitjacket. "I was visiting my grandfather—it was a bit upsetting—he's dying—and I got turned around and lost." I felt myself tearing up. What for? For a man I'd met for less than a minute? Were these just crocodile tears?

The man sighed through his mask. "I'm sorry to hear that. Just go back up one flight and you'll be on the main floor. Someone can direct you to an exit. This place can be a bit of a maze." He waited for me to turn and go back through the stairwell doors. I started climbing and looked back. He was still watching me.

Outside, the sun seemed much higher than it should have been.

I walked further into the city, counting steps as I went. Downtown, I paused to toss some coins in the hat of a homeless man sitting outside the main branch of the library but didn't stop to talk, though he asked me some question I didn't catch. I passed clothing stores and pubs and restaurants and coffee shops and government buildings and churches and bookstores.

I headed north out of the downtown and found myself in an old-money neighbourhood with large homes, mature trees, and immaculately tended shrubs and flower beds. Unnerved, I felt the windows watching me, lidless eyes.

Eventually, I stood at the stone gates of the university. The magnet had pulled me miles from home. I walked through, feeling myself once again a trespasser. The campus was quiet, it being May. I followed the wide avenue that climbed to a towered stone building, passing many more, some a century old, others cement monoliths built in the last decade.

I felt barred from the buildings, as if they were locked against me and filled with guarded secrets. It looked open, serene and garden-like, but a garden from which I was banned or perhaps a maze in which I might get lost. My heart felt clutched by a claw, a bird's talons. Mr. Ashby believed I was headed here.

By then, exhausted from walking, from thinking and overthinking and not thinking, from feeling and not feeling, I found a bus stop. I climbed aboard and dozed off. When I woke, I'd missed my transfer and found myself in an unfamiliar part of the city, an industrial park. I had to ask the driver how to get home.

CHAPTER 3

That night at supper, the shit finally hit the fan—my mom and dad, my brother and sister, the four blades propelling it around the small dining room of our townhouse, me ducking for cover.

I was taking a gulp of Tang when it happened, grimacing against the taste. My mother sat to my left at the foot of the table, her back to the doorway into our tiny kitchen, my father to my right at the head. Mom loved Tang. She'd made it a staple drink in our house because she was a huge fan of NASA and the Apollo missions, Neil

Armstrong her hero. For her, the future of food was now: dehydrated, freeze-dried, frozen—anything heavily processed—she believed it safer and more nutritious. The processing killed all the bacteria, she said, and the food companies actually added in vitamins and minerals to make it better. That this food tended to be quick to prepare was a bonus, given that she worked all day in the kitchen of the Old Folks' Home.

This night, she'd prepared for us frozen dinners in the microwave—some mysterious cut of beef, glutinous mashed potatoes, pebbly peas, and cubed carrots. To finish it off, she'd spread Cheez Whiz on top of the vegetables after transferring the meal from the microwavable packaging to our plates, zapping them again until the cheese was bubbly. My mom was an early adopter of the microwave, and the beast of a machine took up a large portion of kitchen-counter real estate. It was her favourite appliance, processed cheese her favourite ingredient, her go-to for adding protein to any meal. She was a Kraft mom: Cheez Whiz on crackers for snacks, cheese sandwiches for our lunches, cheese slices spread across casseroles glued together with creamed soup from a can, Kraft Dinner on Fridays when she was exhausted from her week's work making last meals for residents of what we nicknamed the Hotel California, given its check-out policy.

I'd taken a bite of my cheesy vegetables too soon after they'd emerged from the microwave and burnt the roof of my mouth. The Tang was meant to soothe the pain, but the acid bit at the burn.

I took another mouthful in hopes of a different result. Annalise looked up from cutting her meat and said, "Why weren't you at track practice today?" Some Tang went up my nose as I choked and began to cough. Undeterred, she added, "Come to think of it, I can't remember seeing you at practice for more than a week. You didn't get cut from the team, did you? That would be embarrassing."

I glanced across the table at her. Between us sat the lazy susan filled with condiments. To the left of it was a large bowl of potato chips that served as appetizer, main course vegetable, or (with dip) dessert. In front of my dad and to the right of the spinning wheel of condiments were two bowls of onions, one fried, the other raw.

My dad loved onions, all kinds. He insisted my mom serve fried onions with most meals; they were his go-to garnish. His favourite lunch was a cheese and onion sandwich. His favourite soup, French onion. Against my mother's objections he also insisted that we have a salad available for every meal, preferably one filled with onions—red onions, green onions, even sweet onions in a pinch. A bowl of it sat between me and my dad.

I broke eye contact with my sister and took a bite of mashed potatoes. I didn't have the heart to say that my heart wasn't in track anymore. The truth was I felt bad about dropping track because Mr. Ashby was the one who'd convinced me to take up running. He was the one I was letting down, just as much as myself. He'd said I had the build for distance running, thin but wiry, and talked to me about the zen of the open road, mind and body in unison. He himself had run the Boston Marathon. I swallowed the potatoes and said, "I needed to make my studies the priority. I've got too much to do right now." I looked up at her. She was staring at me, slowly chewing. I shifted my gaze to the painting behind her, a traditional Dutch farmhouse.

Jeff, sitting between Annalise and my dad, looked around the table, then fixed his eyes on me. "That's funny, because Madame Leblanc asked me today about you. Apparently, you've been skipping her class. Not only that, but you haven't turned in your assignments, and you flunked your most recent test. I didn't know what to say. You really put me in an awkward position." My brother turned his eyes from me to our father.

I couldn't make eye contact with my dad but glanced at my mother before saying, "It's just French class. It's not important. I really need to concentrate on math and science, not some stupid language. That's what counts for getting into university, for scholarships."

"Every test, every grade, every class counts if you want to succeed," my father said. "Why are you failing?"

What I heard behind his words was "Why are you failing *us*?"

My chest and throat tightened. I tried to hold back the tears that were coming. Success versus failure—potent, almost sacred words passed down from my Dutch-immigrant parents. Words that shared a kind of magic with "hard work" and "sacrifice" and "family honour."

"He's crying," my sister said simply.

"I'm not," I yelled. "It's the stupid onions in the salad."

"What a milksop," my brother said.

"Jeff, enough!" It was my mother who intervened. She put her hand on my arm, her touch almost worse than the verbal barb I'd received. I couldn't look at her. "Those onions are actually Vidalia, Evan. They're sweet onions."

Why couldn't they all just leave me alone? That's all I wanted, all I believed I'd earned after years of studying hard trying to keep up with my brother, to live up to his reputation as the golden boy. Jeff, a year ahead of me, was a favourite of the teachers—top grades seemingly without a lot of effort and hard study, gracious and polite and funny, heading off to the University of Toronto that fall, enrolled in pre-med. The apple of my dad's eye.

Then a year behind me, Annalise, the school's top distance runner already and only on the junior team, star in cross-country and track. Like Jeff, tall and blonde, with smarts like him to match her height, driven like him. Teachers already talked about how one day she could be a Rhodes scholar. I'd had no idea who or what or where

Rhodes was. I'd had to look it up.

Always with a special friend or a group of teammates, she'd walk by me in the hallways at school, deep in conversation or staring ahead, ignoring my existence. Occasionally acknowledging it by giving me the finger or calling me Runt, the nickname she'd labelled me with now that she was taller than I was. I chose to interpret such gestures as signs of affection.

And there I was, stuck in the middle, nicknamed Milksop by Jeff, who'd found the word in some old book he'd studied in English. He'd toss it at me as he mussed my mop of brown hair, jostling my glasses about so I couldn't see straight. Quiet and studious, but no star in the academic heavens, I sometimes felt like a foundling, so different was I from my brother and sister.

"Time to spill your guts," Jeff said.

Two weeks later, my parents summoned me to the living room. I climbed the stairs from the basement rec room to face them. From his wingback chair, my father directed me to sit on the sofa. My bottom sank into the soft floral cushion as I dropped into the corner furthest from him. My mother sat in the matching chair across from me, knees together, hands folded in her lap. Jeff and Annalise were sitting beyond my mom and dad at the dining room table, pretending to study for exams.

As instructed by my brother, I'd spilled my guts all over

that dining room table at that dinner. In the days that followed, I tried to get my groove back, I really did, whether
motivated by the shame I felt or an urgent need to please
my parents, I'm not sure, maybe both. But it was too late; I
held strong for a day, attending my classes, attempting
homework, but it didn't stick. The day I walked away from
school into the city, I became a dropout.

My father lifted a tumbler filled with ice and whiskey
from the small table beside him, took a serious sip, and
said, "Son, we're deeply disappointed in you." I studied the
plastic film covering the shade of the floor lamp on the
opposite side of his chair.

"What your father means is that we're worried about
you," my mother quickly added.

Dad stared at her and held up his hand before she
could say more. "Don't put words in my mouth." He
turned back to me. "Your mother and I have come to a
decision. Your brother has contacted Mr. and Mrs. Logan.
You will be working on their farm this summer. It's all
arranged." As he explained, I tried to look him in the eye.
That didn't last long. Soon, I was looking past him out the
sliding doors to our small patio. Against the privacy fence,
a row of globe cedars occupied a raised bed made of rail-
way ties. Last month, my mother had planted petunias in a
neat row in front of the cedars, as she did each spring.

So this was Jeff's idea, or at the very least, he'd con-
spired with our dad. The summer before, Jeff had enrolled

in a government program putting city kids on farms for the summer. He'd come back from Logan & Sons Dairy tanned and muscled, even taller if that was possible.

He knew sending me to the farm would appeal to Dad. As my father reminded me now, he'd worked on a farm in Holland when he was a teenager. That was in the years just after the war. Hard work, manual labour, getting his hands dirty—it had made him the man he was today, and it could make a man of me too, if I applied myself. A big if.

I don't know what I expected. I figured summer school was out of the question, a shameful defeat that wouldn't solve the underlying problem—the sloth that had come over me. Possibly being given a fresh start in the fall, redoing courses I'd failed? There was no guarantee that simply a summer away from school would help me get back my missing mojo. Some sort of anti-sloth psychotherapy? For my immigrant parents who'd lived through the war as children, such therapy was a foreign country. Work was therapy.

Dad especially was the ultimate bootstraps man, and he believed that hard work solved all life's problems. Still having trouble? Well, try harder, work longer, press your nose more firmly to life's grindstone! Sacrifice some of your schnozzola to win the Game of Life!

"If you don't shape up by the end of the summer," he said, "you're done with school, even if they do decide to let you back in."

My mother was crying quietly by now, which doubled the weight of my guilt. Then Dad added a bigger stick to the big stick he'd already whacked me with. "Screw this up, and on September 1st, you'll start the night shift at Cameron Confectioneries, minimum wage." The bottom rung on the ladder of the Sweet Treats Industrial Complex. At that time, Dad was a salesman for Cameron's, the largest producer and exporter of Canadian candy and chocolate bars, including the famous Moose, Goose, and Beaver bars. Then came the biggest stick. "Once you start there, I'll give you one month at home. Then you'll have to move out and start paying your own way. It's time you pull yourself up by your bootstraps, one way or the other." He'd make a man of me somehow, the hard way if necessary—through shock therapy. My mother was now weeping, but trying to contain it. My father gave her a dirty look.

From the dining room came Jeff's voice. "Time to face the manure, Milksop."

Chapter 4

So on a Sunday evening late in June, my mom and dad removed me from the townhouse in south suburban London where we lived, drove north out of the city into a countryside I'd never seen, through towns with unfamiliar names like Arva and Lucan and Hensall, and delivered me to the farm of Niall and Constance Logan for my two-month sentence.

Because I'd lost my bootstraps that winter term at WLM-KSS-my-ass, I found myself in the laneway of Logan & Sons Dairy in the green-filtered light of enormous maple trees, standing beside my parents' car, holding a small suitcase while my folks went forward to greet the man who'd emerged from the barn along with a large dog, and the woman who'd come from the house, a boy and a girl following shyly in her wake.

Having introduced himself and my mom and complimented Mr. and Mrs. Logan on the nice place they had, my dad turned and waved me forward impatiently. I stepped into the sunlight, still bright at this hour given the recent summer solstice. I watched the dog, whose eyes never left me. It seemed to be sizing me up, its gaze judging me as falling short. I looked away and shook hands with the Logans, who told me to please call them Niall and Connie. I thanked them politely, masking my nerves, my sadness, and my resentment and desire to please, with shyness—an old ploy of mine.

They were a curious pair, Niall not much taller than I was at the time—which was short—but Connie almost as tall as my dad, Dutch tall. Niall was carrying a bucket—he'd been in the middle of some chore—and wore dark green work pants, steel-toed work boots, and a brightly checked long-sleeved shirt—his daily uniform, I would find out. His shirt was unbuttoned at the collar, unlike mine. He looked to be in his late thirties, with a bit of grey beginning to show in his dark hair. His bearing seemed wary and reserved in the face of my dad's salesman energy. Connie was big-boned with a warm, open face and jet-black hair up in a bun, and she wore a sundress with a print of small lavender flowers on it. Her sandalled feet were large, as were her hands. These hands had swallowed up one of the hands of each of her children. She introduced them as Finn, 7, and Jane, 5. They waved shyly at me. I waved back just as shyly.

"Back in Holland when I was a teenager," my dad was saying, "I worked on a farm near the village where my family lived." Almost word for word, he repeated the story I'd heard before—his theme the good honest work that had made him the man he was. Of course, at the dinner table I'd heard him criticize the milk quota system of Canadian dairy farmers, calling it nothing but socialism in disguise. As part of his bootstraps philosophy, he was an advocate of free-market capitalism. All enterprise must be free, totally unconstrained.

I was afraid he might start debating the quota system with Niall—or worse, make a joke about it—so I looked around for something to count to distract me and calm my nerves. You see, at that time, I loved all things mathematical. It was the only natural gift I had, though it hadn't saved me from flunking. I loved numbers, especially prime ones, numbers running forward and backward from zero, fractions and decimals, tables and graphs and equations. The equal sign was a miracle that ordered the universe. Math made perfect sense. People? Not so much. Very little really, an amount that couldn't be quantified.

From what I could see standing in the Logan laneway, the house was swaddled around its stone foundation with bands of flowers—too many for me to count, an overwhelming display. So I turned to the house itself: five windows in front, two on the main floor and a pair above on the second floor, then a smaller window in a central dormer near the roof. On the side facing the laneway, six. Eighty-eight panes of glass in total. I'd have to add in the windows on the far side and the back later. Then two doors on the front, one opening onto a porch spanning the house, a second on the upper floor opening onto a small balcony without any railings. Two doors on the side, the one Connie had come out and one further back, on what looked like an addition. So at least four exits, three practical, the one on the second floor less so but still doable in a pinch—my emergency exit.

The house seemed to have been added onto a couple of times, the front red brick structure older than any house I'd seen, the upper windows with gothic arches. At some point, a white clapboard section had been built onto the back, more like a story and a half, with a side porch, and then behind that a one-story structure with that second side door. The house's gables, I noticed, weren't green.

The conversation seemed to be winding down, polite niceties having been exhausted, when my mother said, "Can you make sure Evan goes to church? There's a Reformed church in Blyth." Not any church, not the

Logans' church, if they had one, but the "Dutch church." My chest tightened, my face grew hot. I saw Niall's expression turn even more wary. He looked down at the dog, the dog looked up at him. Was he thinking he'd gotten himself saddled for the summer with a Bible-thumping dyke-hopper?

The state of my soul was one of my mother's favourite obsessions and deepest worries, and my educational implosion seemed to have taken her concern to new depths. Every year on my birthday, she told the story of how she'd nearly died when three months pregnant with me, meaning I would have died, along for the ride as I was. She'd been rushed to the hospital for an emergency appendectomy while my dad was on a sales trip. Then she'd tell the story of how in my first year of life I could have died from a combination of scarlet fever and measles. The doctor had scolded her thoroughly when she finally took me to see him. She blamed herself for the heart murmur it left me. Each birthday, she'd offer up this cocktail of near-death experiences, bringing out the album with her favourite baby photo, black-and-white me sitting on the floor with a forlorn, perplexed expression, as if I'd just pooped my diaper. She'd point out my teeth and tell me again I was such a rough breastfeeder I left her nipples cracked and sore, even bleeding sometimes. *Too much information, Mom.* It all left me feeling strangely ashamed of my infant self, guilty for almost dying when she almost died and more guilty for making her feel guilty about my almost infant mortality. I sometimes thought if I'd truly been a good son, I would have spontaneously aborted myself during her appendectomy, or at least been stillborn several months later to spare her years of pain and worry.

Connie said, "Of course we can arrange that for Evan."

"That's such a relief. Evan's been going through such a difficult time," my mom added. "He needs spiritual guidance." *Please, Mom, please don't.*

"Jeff explained everything," Connie said.

Dammit, I thought. *I'm sunk before I even get started.*

"Well, we better be off," Dad said. "Work starts early tomorrow morning."

I offered a silent prayer of thanks to my dad for interrupting. He shook my hand firmly. I interpreted the shake as his final warning to locate my bootstraps in the coming days and start pulling. As I'd been taught, I gripped his hand firmly in return, so much as to say, "I won't let you down."

My mom hugged me, saying, "I'm sure this will be good for you." Wondering, I waited for it—the Bible verse she'd leave me with before abandoning me. She took me by the shoulders and said, "Remember, 'Blessed is the one who perseveres under trial because, having stood the test, that person will receive the crown of life.'" Then she kissed me on both cheeks.

I watched my dad drive down the tunnel of the laneway, turn left onto the gravel road, and accelerate away, my mom offering one last wave as a plume of grey dust lifted high into air before drifting and settling.

I'd been farmed out by my parents.

CHAPTER 5

I turned back to the Logans. "Well," said Connie. "Let's show you around and get you settled in. Finn, take Evan's suitcase in the house for him, will you?"

I passed my bag to Finn and followed Connie and Jane to a low, squat building thirty to forty yards past the house. Niall walked beside me and cleared his throat once but said nothing.

Connie unlatched the door and stooped through the doorway. Short as I was, even I had to duck slightly and turn sideways to make it through. Inside, the space was tight; right away, I felt closed in. "This is the chicken coop," Connie said, "and this room is the hatchery and brooder. These chicks here are three days old."

I fought against the claustrophobia as I studied the chicks. The floor of the pen seemed alive with a swarm of yellow puff balls moving about in an un-choreographed dance, like disco dancers on steroids—too many and too mobile to count. Low-hanging heat lamps cast a reddish glow over the birds, who began cheeping loudly at the sight of Connie. The heat lamps brought to mind fast food joints, the chicks future occupants of a Kentucky Fried Chicken bucket. Though just three days old, the little peepers had already raised a stink.

Until then, I'd had little exposure to animals, certainly not this close up. I was a city kid whose wildlife sightings were confined to squirrels, my exposure to domesticated creatures restricted to dogs on leashes. Dad's nostalgia for farm animals hadn't translated into a love of pets. He didn't allow a dog or cat in the house, and my mom wouldn't have wanted one anyway, given their lack of hygiene.

Jane reached into the pen and gently grabbed a chick. She held it up to me. "Isn't it cute?" Its cheeping rose above the rest of the chorus, and it tried to flap its tiny wings. It soon gave up and settled in Jane's grip. "You can pet it." Its tiny eyes, like black beads, darted about as it tilted its head this way and that. Its clawed feet, oversized for its body, stuck out below Jane's hand. I brought up a forefinger to the chick and touched its soft head, making a slight patting motion. I could feel the skull beneath the down. "Stroke it, like this." I ran my finger down its head and neck until my fingertip met Jane's hand. The chick let out a single loud cheep, whether of joy or fear, I had no idea, but I pulled back my finger. Jane laughed. "Don't be afraid. They don't bite."

"But they do peck," Connie said, smiling.

Milksop, I scolded myself. *This won't do.*

During this, my first close encounter of the fowl kind, Niall took the watering dishes out of the pen, filled them from the bucket he'd been carrying, and placed them carefully back among the chicks, who crowded around. They dipped their beaks into the water, then lifted them up and tilted them back to swallow.

Finn had rejoined us by then. He asked his mom if he could feed the chicks, and when she said yes, he opened a lid on a bin, filled a scoop from within, and brought it to one of the feeders, a long rectangle of metal. He lifted the top off, a kind of lid with two lines of round holes, forty in total. He ran the scoop of feed from one end to the other, filling it smoothly. He shooed the chicks away as he put the top back down. They crowded around the holes, jostling each other, pecking wildly at the feed, scattering much of it around the feeder on the straw bedding that covered the floor, a pale-yellow background for the bright-yellow chicks. Finn smiled up at me for a moment. I considered asking if he wanted help, thinking that might make a good impression on Niall and Connie. I wasn't fast enough. While I carried on a silly internal debate, Finn got back to filling the three remaining feeders. The feeding frenzy was going strong as Connie led us out of the coop. She latched the door behind us and said, "No point putting out a 'free meal' sign for foxes and coyotes."

"Or bears," Finn added.

My alarm must have shown, for Connie said, "Finn, don't tease Evan, at least not the first hour he's here." I assumed she meant there weren't really any bears, but then she finished her thought. "There hasn't been a bear sighting around here for years."

The rest of the tour was all business. Niall and I left Connie and the kids, who went up to the house, and he led me toward the barn, hip-roofed and weathered grey, sitting across the lane from the house. More flowers bordered the side facing that direction, the reds of what I would later learn were poppies, the oranges of tiger lilies—so different from the petunias in the tiny front yard of our townhouse.

When we were halfway to the barn, a girl emerged from it. She was in the long shadow the barn was casting. Given the recent summer solstice, it was still light out, but the sun would soon be resting on the horizon. I said, "Do you have another daughter?"

Niall stopped so abruptly I bumped into him. "How old do you think I am?"

The girl walked out of the barn's shadow into evening sunlight, and I saw she was a young woman, not a girl. She had red hair pulled back in a ponytail, the colour dark red like rust, and she wore a purple tank top and jeans. She had a red bandana around her neck. As she approached, I could see how strong her shoulders were, how muscled her arms. She was tanned, but her face was covered with some blotchy redness, like an unripe strawberry beginning to turn. It was almost as if she was continuously blushing, though I couldn't imagine what she had to blush about.

I'm embarrassed to say I was smitten—instantly. It's not like I heard an angel choir, but she did seem haloed in light. I'm sure it was just a trick of the setting sun. "Hallelujah" did pop into my mind.

"All done, Niall," she said, ignoring me. I straightened up, trying to stand tall. I put my shoulders back and chest out, my puny runner's chest, and hooked my thumbs into my belt. "Call me when you need me," she added. *I need you* was the thought that came to me. I stared at her, hoping she was telepathic.

Niall said, "Probably the end of the week. Maybe the twins too."

She turned to me. "What are you staring at, fuzz face?" My hand went to my chin. She offered me a smile or a smirk, I couldn't tell which, before turning toward a car parked near the barn, an old, red Toyota Corolla. I watched her walk toward it, open the door, and slide in. Moments later, the car disappeared into the tunnel of trees.

"Need a written invitation?" Niall was at the barn door, waiting for me. I jogged over, her face filling my mind, her body too, all of her if I'm totally honest. I tried to dispel the image, knowing I needed to concentrate on Niall and what he was showing me.

We entered the milking parlour, which had two rows of metal stanchions where the cows would be milked, coming out of the pasture through the door at the far end. An area to the right held a large pen for the calves, which had bedded down for the night on straw. They were leggy creatures nestled together and tangled with each other. They had big eyes within comical faces; their large ears twitched against the flies.

Niall showed me the bin filled with grain. "You'll be responsible for feeding this to the cows during each milking." We climbed a ladder through a hatch to the top part of the barn, enormous and high. "You'll throw down hay for the cows from up here," he said simply. We climbed back down, and he took me over to the milking equipment. "This is a surge bucket." It was a large can to which a machine was attached. From the lid ran a black rubber hose. At the end of the hose was a mechanism with four cylinders. "These," he explained, "attach to the cow's teats and draw the milk out of the udder. This little section of plastic here in the lid will show you when the milk's coming and when the udder's empty."

I was disturbed by this talk of cows' teats and udders, as well as the machine that would attach to them. To be honest, between that and the mystery woman I'd met, I think I missed some important details. Plus, I was too shy to ask questions. I'd always been reluctant to ask for help when I didn't understand something, which got me in trouble or led to minor disasters. Besides, I was somewhat overwhelmed by the barn—not just its size and height— and distracted by the smell of manure and urine, as well as the buzzing of flies around my face.

I was relieved when Niall took me out of the milking parlour through a door into the milk house, a bright and clean room. A large refrigerated stainless-steel tank stood in its centre. Niall put sanitizer on my hands, then worked some into his own before opening the lid to display gallons of milk, a milk bath really, slowly stirred by metal paddles.

Startled, I said, "It's not white. Has something spoiled it?" Yes, these were practically my first words to the man who would be my boss for eight weeks, the man I needed to impress so that in the end I could impress my father.

When I looked at him for an explanation, I caught the tail end of a scowl. "This is what milk is supposed to look like, whole milk straight from the cow. Pure, all natural. By the time it gets to the grocery store, it's been pasteurized and processed into all the different, amazing products that come from milk."

He explained about milk and cream, butter and cheese and yogurt, but I was too distracted by the colour of the raw milk, a sickly yellow in the fluorescent light. I thought, *I'll never be able to drink milk again, at least not without seeing these swirling yellow currents.*

By the time we left the milk house, dusk was falling and the mosquitos were rising. Niall walked briskly to the last building on our tour, a large machine shed. I struggled to keep up while swatting my arms and neck. We entered through a large, open doorway. Niall flipped a switch and a dozen machines appeared, many of them enormous, all capable of killing me, I was sure. That evening, he offered no explanation other than to say the next day we'd be taking two tractors out to do some field work.

"Tractors?"

"Yes, I'll be on this one here, and you'll be driving that one there." He proceeded to show me how to start the tractor and operate it. Busy with the controls, he didn't notice my panic. Though I was almost 18, I didn't have my driver's license, not even my beginner's. I hadn't operated anything more complicated than my bike, and preferred to walk, run, or pedal my way around my neighbourhood. If I needed to go further into the city, I'd bus or get a ride from my parents or my brother, who not only got his driver's license as soon as he could, but went on to get his motorcycle license, against our mother's wishes and worries. To my shame, my sister, who would turn 16 later that summer, had already signed up for driver's ed in the fall.

Everything Niall showed me blurred together. "Any questions?" he said. I tried to find my tongue but failed. The tour done, I followed him to the house. I felt doomed.

The back door opened into a mud room with hooks for work clothes, a large tray for boots and shoes, and an open closet for coats and coveralls. There was also a bathroom with a large industrial-style shower. I followed Niall's example and took off my shoes. I excused myself to use the washroom, locked the door, and relieved myself. I wasn't relieved at all. I put down the toilet lid and sat, wondering if I could sit there for eight weeks.

Eventually there was a knock. "Are you alright?" Finn said.

"Be right out."

"My mom made you a sandwich, in case you're hungry."

"Just need to wash my hands." I got up and scrubbed them raw.

Finn had left open the door from the mudroom to the kitchen. As I approached, it framed the family. Jane sat on a high stool beside Connie at a counter where they looked to be beating something. Niall was at a large wooden table reading the paper; the dog lay on the floor beside him. Finn sat beside his dad, colouring. In the background, a radio played country music softly. I hesitated a moment, until Finn looked up. "Here's your sandwich," he said pointing to a plate covered with a cloth napkin.

"Thanks." I stepped into a room smelling of flour and yeast. The dog made a low growling noise.

"Mac, enough," Niall said.

I gave Mac a wide berth. "Don't mind Old Mac," Finn said. "He won't bite you."

"Old Mac?" I said.

"Yeah, like Old MacDonald had a farm," Finn said.

"He thinks he owns the place," Connie said. "It makes him a bit territorial."

I sat across from Niall and removed the napkin. "What kind of sandwich is it?" I said, lifting half and studying it.

"Roast beef and cheese," Connie said. "I hope that's okay. You're not a vegetarian, are you? I can make you something different if need be."

"No, no, this is great. Is this homemade bread?"

"Of course, silly," Jane said, holding up hands covered in flour. "My mom makes the best bread in the world, and I'm her helper."

Connie continued kneading the dough.

"Thanks, but you didn't need to do that for me. Store-bought bread would have been fine." *Safer*, is what I thought.

Connie smiled. "We rarely buy bread."

"That beef's from one of our cows," Finn said, smiling.

I tried to hide my discomfort, both at the bread and the beef. Having been raised on store-bought food—the more highly processed, the better—I found something comforting in all that packaging, ingredients identified and quantified. Store-bought bread was sliced by a machine, each slice the same precise thickness. These homemade slices were irregular, the ingredients unknown by me, untested. I tried not to let it bother me, or the fact that I was eating meat from an animal that had lived in the vicinity. The calves I'd seen came to mind.

I took a bite and looked around the kitchen. I'd never been in a house so old and worn. My dad was a restless soul who believed in renting, not buying, so we moved frequently, usually from one new townhouse or semidetached home to another—all of them cookie cutter modern. This farm kitchen had well-worn linoleum and aged countertops. A large, white rectangular sink with a big window above it facing the barn dominated the kitchen. The upper cupboards had glass doors, revealing neat stacks of dishes in some and a jumble of cooking ingredients in others. On the opposite side of the room was a large walk-in pantry. From where I sat, I could see several shelves covered with mason jars of different sizes containing food I couldn't identify. None of them had recognizable brand labels. On the wall behind Niall was a shelf where the clock radio sat, tuned always, I would learn, to the local radio station to catch the weather, the farm news, and the local gossip. A healthy dose of country, bluegrass, and folk music filled the spaces between. The shelf also held a few books, one the *Farmer's Almanac*, as well as two photos, one each of Finn and Jane when younger. To one side of the shelf hung a painting of a rugged seascape—a craggy, rocky coast, rough water extended to the horizon, and a sky of mixed sunlight and cloud that felt equally windswept. On the other side, photos of cows, a boy holding them by halters decorated with ribbons, were pinned up. Among these a calendar showed a picture of an enormous bull, his "equipment" fully on display. Beyond this wall was a small open room with a west-facing window. The room held an old, stuffed rocking chair, a small, low table and chairs for the kids to work and play at, bins of toys, shelves of books, and a worktable with a sewing machine on it.

"It looks like it's going to be dry this week," Niall said, closing the newspaper. "We'll get started on the cutting tomorrow and try to get the hay in before the rain hits on the weekend." I wasn't sure whether he was talking to me or Connie—or possibly just himself, sharing his thoughts aloud.

"We'll hope for the best," Connie said. "By the way, Evan, how's your brother? Such a nice young man."

"Such a good worker," Niall added before I could reply.

"Jeff?" I said. "He's pretty much the same."

Connie said, "If you're done, Evan, I'll show you to your room. I'm sure you'd like to rest up for tomorrow."

That sounded ominous, if well meant. I got up and brought my plate to the sink, long trained by my mother to do so. "Can I put this in the dishwasher?"

"Dishwasher?" She held up her hands, still covered in flour. "These two hands are my dishwashers, along with the four hands of my two helpers, the dish dryers. These do the job just fine. Follow me."

Chapter 6

onnie led me down a hallway. I caught a glimpse of a dining room and a parlour before we climbed to the second floor, where we passed a bathroom and three bedrooms. There I saw neatly made beds covered in quilts. Was Connie a neat freak like my mom, who, I have to confess, still made my bed for me, in fact all the beds in our house? The journey upstairs was filled with creaks as we climbed the stairs and travelled the wooden floors. In places the boards felt soft and spongy beneath my feet, the finish worn.

I followed Connie up a second flight of stairs, narrower and steeper than the first, into the attic, which had been roughed in at one end but not fully finished. It contained a jumble of stored objects, including a baby buggy. The other end, the front of the house, held the room I would sleep in for the next eight weeks. She showed me in and pointed out a supply of towels and washcloths on top of a dresser, suggesting I use the washroom before there was a line-up for it. She pointed out a laundry hamper as well, saying she did laundry almost every day and was happy to do mine.

I looked at her a moment, feeling I didn't know what —grateful, confused, forlorn—and thanked her.

"You're more than welcome," she said, then paused. I had nothing to fill the space, unsure if there was a customary reply expected among country folk. She turned and left.

I listened to the creak of her steps descending. When they faded, I went and sat at the top landing, listening to the Logans' unfamiliar evening routine—dishes clattering, Jane and Finn running upstairs, stories being read, goodnight kisses, then the murmur of married conversation, eventually the radio going silent.

I turned back to my room and closed the door with a quiet click. The twin bed had a wrought-iron headboard and footboard and was covered with a quilt, though different from the ones downstairs. It was made from old, worn blue-jean material—recycled patches of many shades and sizes from pants and overalls worn by who knows how many present and past occupants of this house, fabric worn and faded from years of working this farm. The bed creaked as I sat on it and took in the rest of my cell.

Beside the bed stood a large, old-style wooden desk with a wooden chair on wheels. On the near side of the desk, within reach of the bed, was an old bronze reading lamp, the kind with a flexible goose neck and a cone to direct the light. I imagined the generations of children, studious on not, who'd sat here doing their homework, Niall included. An old chair, which looked to be the mate of the one I'd seen in the children's room off the kitchen, sat beyond the desk in the corner.

Against the far wall and tucked into the corner behind the door was a large bookcase with five shelves, all filled, that reached the ceiling, and two cupboards in the base. Before my troubles, I'd loved books, trusted them. Maybe not as much as math, but there was something about strings of words on pages, black letters fixed on paper, unlike the slippery words that people said, disappearing into the air. After, even these printed words couldn't be trusted. No matter how the story ended, happy or sad, it felt like lies, all lies.

I turned away from the shelves of books to the darkly stained dresser on the other side of the door, sitting beside the laundry hamper and facing the foot of the bed. The towels and face cloths Connie had provided sat on top, waiting for me. I studied the intricately designed metal handles, considering whether to unpack my suitcase and neatly order my clothes in the drawers by types—underwear and socks, T-shirts and shorts, running clothes, jeans in the bottom, shoes at the foot of the bed. I'd have to ask Connie where I could hang the Sunday suit my mom had insisted I take. I decided to worry about all of it tomorrow.

The only clothes I pulled out were for running—my black short shorts, which should have been illegal given the fashion crime they were committing, my yellow tank top, like the shorts made of polyester, and my yellow Nike marathon shoes. I draped the clothes neatly on the corner chair and positioned the shoes in front of it so that tomorrow, when my work was done, I could slip them on and go running.

I searched my suitcase for my running log—the one Mr. Ashby had us start a year ago when he'd set up a training plan for us over the summer so we'd be in prime shape for cross country that fall. I'd kept accurate records in it religiously through that summer and into the following winter; it's also where I'd recorded Ashbyisms when he'd offered them. I placed the log at the edge of the desk nearest my running outfit.

Satisfied at having accomplished this much, I sat in the desk chair. Above the desk was the dormer and the room's one window, the one I'd seen at the top of the house. I could tell now that the glass was old and wobbly, the bottom pane propped up with a pole to let air in through the screen. With the door closed, air flow was stifled. I peered into the dusk, seeing little but long black snaky shapes twisted together and shifting with the breeze, hearing only rustling and the odd hoot of an owl. Something landed on the screen and clung to it, its wings outspread. I pushed the chair back and leapt up. Just as quickly as it had come, the bat was gone.

I'd had enough of this day, of this place, and my sentence hadn't officially started, not until midnight. I pulled out my Texas Instruments calculator and did the calculations. Yes, I brought my calculator to the farm. I loved numbers but I was no Einstein. I placed it centrally on the desk. 8 weeks = 56 days = 1,344 hours = 80,640 minutes = 4,838,400 seconds.

I got out my alarm clock and set it for 5:15. I'd been told by Niall—warned really—that morning milking started at the ungodly hour of 5:30. For months, I'd found it a slog to drag my body out of bed and pull it to school by 9. Getting up tomorrow seemed impossible. I set the clock as a formality so I could show I'd tried.

I also pulled out of my suitcase an object likely to be as useful on a farm as my calculator—the Janus paperweight Mr. Ashby had given me. Though I had nothing to hold down, I placed it on the desk corner beneath the reading lamp, one face positioned to look at me while I slept, the other angled toward the window. I turned on the lamp, sat on the edge of the bed, and studied it.

"You never get a second chance to make a good first

impression." That was one of my dad's favourite sayings. He applied it regularly in his salesmanship; he reminded his children of it whenever he sent us out into the world. I was reluctant to measure the first impression I'd made on Niall and Connie, setting it beside whatever first and lasting impressions my brother had made on them. My mind drifted instead to that girl, the first impression she's made on me, likely the lack of any impression I'd made on her. I saw her again walking toward me in the evening sunlight, her face, her slipping into her car and driving away.

Eventually, I unbuttoned my shirt and draped it over the footboard. I dropped my jeans to the floor, pulled off my socks, and turned off the overhead light. I bent the gooseneck lamp so it shone on the bookcase. I climbed into bed, cocooning myself in the sheet, blanket, and denim quilt against the night chill quickly replacing the day's dissipating heat. The farm had no sheep to count, and I hadn't yet met and numbered the cows, so I counted the books instead. 173, a prime number. That offered small but cold comfort.

I took off my glasses, placed them beside Janus, and turned off the light. Darkness invaded the room and settled onto me, the heaviest blanket of all. The girl's face, her smile-smirk, came to me again when I closed my eyes. I felt the weight of an unfamiliar, uncontrollable feeling descend on me, a silly schoolboy crush—and below the weight of it, fear.

Chapter 7

The sound was loud, raucous. In the fuzzy territory between sleep and waking, I thought I was in the chicken coop. There was knocking. Was I pounding to be let out of the coop? Had Connie latched the door with me still inside? As the pounding continued, the sound of a bell—not a little tinkling bell but a loud clanging and clunking, like a church bell gone crazy—finally broke through.

I opened my eyes and checked my alarm clock. 5:30. I'd shut it off without waking. Janus stared at me with disapproval. *Dammit*, I thought. I snuggled deeper into my cocoon.

The pounding and clanging continued. "Evan. Milking!" Niall was knocking and ringing a cow bell. "Coboss!" he added.

Coboss? I hadn't a clue what it meant. I threw the blankets off and put my feet on the floor. "I'm up."

The knocking and ringing faded, but cheeping flooded in and seemed to grow louder. I grabbed my socks and pants from the floor and looked out the window. I was in the top of the trees, and they were filled with noisy, ill-mannered birds hidden among the leaves. As I found a T-shirt in my suitcase, I considered that city birds were much more civilized.

Niall had the cows coming out of the pasture by the time I got downstairs, pulled on my sneakers, and dragged myself to the barn. He was yelling "Coboss, coboss!" Old Mac was barking encouragement as he ran among them.

Inside the barn, I hung back and counted the cows as they entered the door at the far end. Most lumbered in, a few trotted, but they all seemed to know which milking station was theirs. Their entry into the barn was orderly and civilized—no stampede. 43 total. Prime number.

Niall began locking the cows' heads in the stanchions. "Good of you to join us." He looked up. "Supertramp."

"What?" He pointed at my T-shirt. "Sorry. I've never gotten up this early." I rubbed one of my eyes for dramatic effect.

"The cows can't wait to be milked until you're ready." He paused in his work and looked at me. "They're waiting now to be fed." Several were mooing loudly into the empty trough in front of them.

"Right." I started scooping feed into the trough, counting as I went along the line of cows on one side of the barn and then the other. I'd never been close to cows. Their heads were massive bulges, and they seemed to chew their feed with an odd sideways motion of their jaws that made a grinding noise. Totally lacking in manners. When I learned later that they had four stomachs, I wondered if head size and chewing style coincided with such a serious digestive system. It didn't take me long to discover that it resulted in a lot of shit coming out the other end into a different trough in the floor.

I climbed the ladder to the hay loft. When I went to lift a bale, I could barely move it. I struggled to drag the bales to the opening and push them through. Tired, sweaty, covered in hay and dust when I got back down, I forced myself to lift and carry the bales into place before cutting the twine. I gave each cow a flake of hay, following the same order as with their grain, which they'd finished by that time.

After, I thought I was done—break time—but Niall called me over. He filled several black buckets with milk from the can he'd been using. "Each calf gets one bucket of milk. Take these over and put them carefully in front of them. They'll knock them over if they get too excited."

From their bawling, it sounded to me as if they were already there. My arms were still tired from the hay, and that made the buckets feel heavier than they probably were. The calves buried their snouts in the buckets, jostling them about as the milk emptied. When one pulled out its snout for a moment, it had more than a milk moustache. It was a full beard.

"You can let them finish for now. Take this milk can and follow me."

I grabbed the two handles of the can and lifted it as he walked ahead to the milk house. If anything, it seemed heavier than a bale of hay. I had to lean it against my leg and walk with a limp. Niall opened the door and closed it quickly behind me. "Never prop this door open," he said. "This room has to be kept sterile and clean." When I reached the tank, I put the can down carefully. My hands and arms ached. He showed me how to detach the lid from the can and where to prop it so it stayed clean. "Now lift the can and pour the milk in. Use one hand on the handle and the other on the bottom."

I grabbed the handle with my left hand and looked inside the can. It was full. Try as I might, I couldn't get it off the floor. The harder I tried, the more the milk sloshed about and began spilling.

Niall sighed. "You've heard the saying, 'There's no point crying over spilled milk.' Well, here, that's a lie. Spilled milk is money down the drain." He passed me a squeegee with a long handle. "After I've emptied the can, clean up the milk by pulling it into that drain." I stood back and watched. Niall lifted the can with one smooth motion and poured the milk into the tank, the paddles mixing it smoothly into what was already there. He reattached the lid and said, "When you're milking, you'll have to fill the can half full and empty it more often. That'll add time, but it's the only way this'll work, unless you can build up some arm strength."

"When I'm milking?"

"Finish the clean-up, then bring me the can."

The empty can I could manage. He was finishing off one cow when I arrived. He stood up and brought me a small pail filled with a reddish liquid. "The first thing you do is sterilize the teats."

"How?"

"What do you mean, how? You get in there, crouch down, and use this cloth in the bucket."

"I have to go in there between the cows?"

"How else are you going to milk them? They don't milk themselves."

I took the pail and moved toward the opening between the two cows, turning sideways to make myself thin. I tried not to touch them. If the cows' heads were enormous, their bodies were gigantic. With their freakishly tall legs, I was dwarfed. Their width and roundness cramped me. And they didn't stay still. Their tails swished against the flies and lifted to release massive poops and large streams of piss. They shifted their weight from side to side, twitched their skin, and occasionally lifted a hoof against the flies. They were heaving masses of hide, flesh, and bone.

I kneeled down to the cow Niall had assigned me. The udder was a huge sack covered with coarse hair through which large veins travelled—rivers in a pulsing geography. The four teats were dark, protruding tubes that felt fleshy but rubbery as I stained them red with the sterilizing fluid. Enormous mammary glands. I thought about what I'd learned in biology class about mammals, humans included. Cow breasts and nipples. What did bulls think of these?

Niall brought the milk can to me. I think he let out another sigh, but I couldn't be sure. "You'll get used to it." Maybe he was trying to convince himself as much as me. "You'll get more confident working with them and will move quicker. Now, attach the cylinders to the nipples one at a time. Suction will do the work, and the machine's action will start the milk flowing. When there's no more milk coming through the glass, then Gertie here is done."

"Gertie?"

"That's her name. All my cows get names once they're ready to milk. Not until. Calves and heifers have to graduate before they get one. One more thing. You do need to watch them. Sometimes, they try to kick the machine."

Milking proceeded. Niall finished the cows down one side, then joined me to do those down the other side. Each time I stepped between the cows I had to push back panic.

Niall told me to run my hands along their backs and talk to them, but beyond sterilizing their teats, I didn't touch them or begin any conversations. I did remember not to overfill the can and had emptied it several times without spilling.

Towards the end, though, I was getting restless and daydreamy while waiting for cows to finish giving their milk, impatient for it all to be done, hungry for breakfast. It seemed unfair the cows got to eat before I did, my one stomach empty while their four stomachs filled.

Absent-minded, I'd now milked too many cows and the can was full. I thought, though, maybe I'd figured out the rhythm of lifting the can and could manage it with a single significant heave, like a weightlifter. I was also reluctant to let Niall know I'd screwed up his instructions.

I began carrying the can toward the milk house door. My arms ached and the handles cut into my fingers, but I was determined. The moment I thought this, I lost my grip. The can hit the cement floor with a bang and fell over with a clatter. The lid popped off and the milk spilled out in a pool that flooded the floor as the can rolled and rolled and rolled.

"Jesus Christ!" Niall rushed over, grabbed the can, and turned it upright. He looked inside at what little was left, then lifted his eyes to me. Daggers.

Forty-five minutes later, I sat at the breakfast table—disheartened and tired but also fuming—exactly at what or whom, I couldn't tell. My brother and my father came to mind. Niall? Those damned cows? Me, myself, and I for my screw-ups, my puny arms, and my self-pity?

I'd had to wash down the spill site with a hose and scrub it with a brush while Niall finished the milking. As he began releasing the cows from their stanchions and they lumbered out of the barn, I felt relieved that morning milking was over. I was wrong. Niall grabbed two shovels and brought one to me as the last cows headed back to the pasture. "Scrape any manure and wet straw into the channel here." He did one side, I did the other. I shovelled soft cow patties and urine-soaked straw, all the while thinking, *My life is shit.*

When we were finished, he pressed a switch on the wall and the channel came to life. The river of manure, urine, and straw rotated around the floor and out a small door in the barn wall. Curious about where it went, I stepped outside. An elevator lifted the manure, then dumped it onto an enormous pile of poop, causing clouds of flies to lift, drift, and settle.

Niall's final act confused me. He went into the milk house, retrieved a pitcher sitting upside down on a shelf, and dipped it into the milk tank. I trailed him up to the house, speculating that maybe he needed the milk for testing. After I'd cleaned up, I was shocked to see the pitcher of milk sitting on the breakfast table. They were going to drink it.

Finn and Jane were sitting at the table. They greeted me brightly with "Good morning!" Though I felt there was nothing good about it, I managed a polite reply and a weak smile. Finn added, "You guys are late for breakfast. What took you so long? I'm starving."

Niall said nothing. I noticed Connie looking at him. She turned to me and said, "Evan, what would you like for breakfast? How about cereal?" I watched Finn and Jane pour Cheerios into their bowls and douse them with milk from the jug.

I thought of those enormous udders, the teats this milk had come out of just an hour before, the yellowish tinge and thickness of it. I felt my gag reflex warming up. "Isn't that raw milk? Shouldn't it be pasteurized to make it safe?"

Niall looked at me, elbows on the table and hands folded. "That's just a regulation for milk that's sold commercially. A precaution." He unfolded his hands, filled his bowl with granola, and poured milk over it. "This milk is perfectly healthy. I've been drinking it since I was a baby." That seemed to settle the point, for he spooned up his cereal, chewed loudly, and said nothing else until breakfast was done.

At home, I typically had a bowl of Corn Flakes drowned in powdered milk—in keeping with my mom's allegiance to processed food—plus several spoons of sugar to combat the cardboard taste. But my stomach churned as I imagined the raw milk entering my mouth and sliding down my esophagus. I chose the lesser of two evils, toast made from homemade bread slices of irregular thickness.

When the toast was ready, Connie brought me two pieces on a plate. I have to confess they smelled wonderful—toasty, as it were—though I'm certain it was that by then I was ravenous. "Pass the butter and jam, please," I said to Jane, who sat beside me, a buffer between me and Niall at the head of the table.

As I spread the butter, Jane said, "That butter's from our cows too."

I stared at the toast. "You make your own butter?"

"My mom churns it."

Was there anything this Agri-Wonder Woman couldn't do? I continued to stare at the butter melting into the bread. Butter churned on-site from raw milk delivered by those cows, not a store-bought rectangular cuboid neatly wrapped in foil. I wasn't sure I could stomach it, but I had to try. Perhaps the jam would cover the taste and hide it from view. I looked at the jar. This wasn't store-bought jam. It was a plain mason jar with no label, no branding, no list of ingredients.

Finn said, "My mom grew the strawberries for that jam. She grows the best strawberries and makes the best jam in the whole world."

"Thank you, Finn," Connie said. "Maybe not the whole world, but at least on this farm."

"You grow your own strawberries? They weren't from

California?" Given my limited experience with grocery shopping, I thought almost all fruit and vegetables came from the Golden State.

The kids laughed, Connie smiled, and Niall sighed. By the time I looked his way, I couldn't tell if he'd grimaced, rolled his eyes, or both.

My face reddened. I didn't need his disapproval on top of the upsetting breakfast offerings. So what if I was an ignorant city kid, a milksop to boot? He was a rural rube! Probably owned a closet full of straw hats and bib overalls worn specially for Saturday night hoedowns. I'd show him. I spooned a large blob of jam on both slices of toast, spread it to the edges, and cut them neatly in half, as close to true half as I could manage without a ruler. I raised a piece to my mouth and took an enormous bite. I showed no hesitation, no weakness. The taste of the jam was fresh and fruity, lacking that synthetic store-bought taste, but I powered through it, taking one enormous bite after another and washing it down with gulps of apple juice.

I had the glass to my mouth when Jane said, "My mom made that apple juice too."

I almost managed not to spit a mouthful back into the glass.

Chapter 8

Niall rose from the table and was instructing me to follow him before I'd finished my toast. In one motion, I stood, stuffed a half slice in my mouth, and downed my glass of homemade apple juice—bursting at the cheeks. My anger had dissolved, and I was once again determined to show him I could get the job done. I reminded myself my future—whatever the hell that was—depended on it.

Niall was outside in the yard, by the tractors he'd shown me the night before. *When had he brought them out? In the middle of the night?* I hadn't noticed them on my way to and from the barn. Guess that happens when it's dawn's early light and you're sleepwalking.

He pointed to the tractor I was to take and told me to follow him. He climbed aboard his tractor and started it. He warmed it a few seconds before engaging some lever and heading down the laneway to the road.

I heaved myself up onto the tractor seat and studied the levers, buttons, and dials, trying to remember Niall's instructions for starting this monster machine. The only thing that made sense to me were the numbers—the speedometer and the RPM gauge.

I turned the key, assuming it was the correct first step. Nothing happened, not a sound beyond a blank, meaningless click. I turned it again. Nothing. I looked up. Niall was barrelling out of the laneway tunnel and heading left down the road, kicking up dust.

I looked at the controls, which were becoming blurry. I moved a lever, said a quick prayer along the lines of "Dammit, start, you bastard!" and turned the key again and again and again.

What came to me in that moment was one of Mr. Ashby's favourite Einstein sayings, one I'd written in my running log: "Insanity is doing the same thing over and over and expecting different results." Apparently I was ready for the funny farm, not the dairy farm. One time when Mr. Ashby said this, I shot back, "Like me expecting a better finish in cross-country?" He'd let a grin spread across his face, while his eyes crinkled up the way they always did when he found something amusing. "Clever boy," he said, another favourite phrase of his. I'd badly wanted Mr. Ashby to think me a clever boy.

As I sat atop the silent tractor, my eyes flooded. Sweat or tears or both leaked onto the insides of my glasses so that everything got even blurrier. Through pools and rivulets of salty water, the tractor was now simply a mass of red and black and silver metal. My brother's favourite taunt, "Milksop," rose in my mind.

I considered my options. One, go inside and shut myself in my room. Two, hide in the hay mow. Three, maybe best of all, run away. I had a general sense of the right direction (away), but just as I was bad at following instructions and asking for clarification, my sense of direction wasn't terribly reliable. Jeff often said, "Sure you're not a woman? You've got a feminine talent for getting lost." Sexist pig.

I was debating these choices and getting more and more worked up about them when Connie came striding out of the house. She explained that I needed to engage the clutch or nothing would happen. She had me push it to the floor, then adjust the throttle and open the choke. I turned the key and the engine came to life. She closed the choke, then explained the accelerator, the brake, and the gears. She put it in low for me and told me to go into medium and high when I felt comfortable.

At first, I pressed gingerly on the accelerator, until the machine was inching forward. When I was comfortable with the tractor's motion, I pushed the accelerator forcefully and began up the laneway like the proverbial tortoise in pursuit of that bastard the hare. By the time I reached the road, Niall was a plume of dust in the middle distance, rushing to the horizon.

I couldn't will myself to gear up, the feel of the machine was so new, starting with the steering wheel, given that I'd never controlled one. The tractor was so open, and I felt high off the ground. It was unlike riding as a passenger inside a car or even pedalling a bike—the machine loud, me vulnerable up there in the seat.

Above the engine, I heard a clatter behind me. I hadn't noticed until then that I was pulling some implement—a rusty attachment that looked like a metal alligator.

I turned to focus on keeping Niall in sight. Ahead on the right, a tractor came out of a laneway, blocking my view. It was a much bigger tractor, bright blue with a roof to protect the driver from sun and rain. It was pulling a yellow implement that looked like it could swallow a whole cow—or two or three people—and spit them out the back.

The road didn't seem wide enough for both tractors. I slowed and veered over as far as I dared. The tractor came up even with me. There she was, in the driver's seat—the same girl, the sight of her crushing me again. I tried to sit tall and wipe the fear off my face as I stared up at her. She smirk-smiled and waved, her hair in a ponytail flowing behind her, that red bandana around her neck. I raised one hand slightly off the steering wheel in a pitiful salute but gripped it again when I felt the tractor's right tires catch the edge of the ditch. As she sped by, I read "New Holland" on the tractor and "Vermeer" on the ravenous-looking implement she was pulling. A cloud of dust obscured my view for some moments, then settled on me.

I used my T-shirt to wipe off my face and glasses, then looked ahead for Niall. Far off, I could see a toy tractor and its tiny dust cloud heading to the left. I was in danger of losing sight of him. Either I needed to turn back and ask Connie for more help—another failure—or grow a set of balls, as my brother would say, and gear up.

Dammit, I thought, *I didn't ask for this shit.* I pulled back onto the road, shifted from low to medium to high, and put my foot to the floor. The tractor sped forward, the big tires blurring and spitting up gravel as I tried to keep it steady down the middle of the road. I could hear the alligator implement bouncing and clanging behind me.

I looked for something to count. On the right where the tractor had emerged was a two-story modern house with a large front—two pillars framing the centred double doors, one large picture window on either side, eight windows in a row on the second floor. I looked ahead. Niall would soon disappear into some woods. I looked for the turn he'd taken. On the left side of the road I could see some farm fencing coming up. Before finding the turn, I'd count the wooden posts. They became the limit of my outer vision as I travelled along the tunnel of the road, seeing little of the fields and woods and farms I passed. I tried to count as I sped past the posts but was disturbed and annoyed by how many weren't vertical, how many had actually fallen over. Horizontal and vertical created order out of chaos, like the axes of a graph. None of it mattered. I found that concentrating on the road and the machine I gripped made counting impossible.

I'd been thrust into an unruly world, an extension of the downward spiral I'd experienced at school—no bootstraps in sight to pull myself up and out to please my dad. No, I was headed further down. The wind and these feelings worked on me, making my eyes water. I tried to hold them back. Unwilling to take a hand off the steering wheel, I felt tiny streams flowing back from the outer corners of my eyes, landing in my ears. I cursed my brother, who'd told me to cheer up; it'd be like summer camp, he said. He'd had a blast working for Niall the summer before. I hated the idea of summer camp as it was, but this felt more like a prisoner-of-war camp.

Barrelling down this gravel road, I longed for nothing more than to be back in my bedroom, safe among my collection of paperweights.

It had started innocently enough. I had an uncle, single at the time, who went to Expo 67 in Montreal and gave us, his nephews and niece, small mementos. Mine was a little glass replica of the biosphere. Tot that I was, I was delighted with its shape, its geometry, and exclaimed so much about it that everyone thought I was fascinated with paperweights. From then on, I kept receiving them as gifts. From Jeff, a collection of animals over the years—a small pig, a sloth, an armadillo. A sugar skull from Annalise. From my mom one of Buckingham Palace commemorating Queen Elizabeth's silver jubilee. A windmill when my parents made a trip back to Holland for my opa's funeral. A globe with a map of the world on it from an aunt who was well travelled. These were a few of the glass, granite, and wooden objects I'd received, all shapes and sizes—but all heavy enough to hold things down, keep things in place against any wind.

Except for the Janus paperweight I'd brought with me, my collection populated my designated space in the bedroom I shared with Jeff. It was a three-bedroom townhouse, and Annalise clearly needed her own room, so Jeff and I had been stuck with each other in this house, but also in all the ones before. We each had a captain's bed with drawers and shelves underneath to maximize storage in the small room, along with a matching dresser and desk. Jeff claimed the larger share of the room based on seniority and his greater height—it required more space. My parents had put cork board on the wall where they pinned his awards and certificates and badges. For me, they put up a shelf for all my paperweights. There they sat now, along with an overflow on my dresser, plus the biosphere on my desk.

By the time I got to the corner where Niall had turned, I had no idea how many fence posts I'd passed. I saw him up ahead. I wasn't gaining on him, but I wasn't losing ground. I kept my foot pressed to the floor. He turned to the right. By the time I'd made the same turn, he'd disappeared.

I kept moving, looking left and right for any opening in the woods he might have taken, any lane that might lead to where he was. It occurred to me as I searched how odd it was that Niall would be working a field so far from home. Perhaps after this morning's fiasco he was trying to lose me, to ditch me in some out-of-the-way forest, a wilderness where I'd end up wandering in circles.

I came to another crossroads. I stopped. I couldn't see him ahead, but he might have turned off the road into some lane or field. I looked left and right. Nothing. Whatever direction I took, I had a 33.33333333 ad infinitum percent chance of being right. I turned left and brought the tractor back up to full speed.

Two minutes in that direction and I was second-guessing myself, looking for a spot to turn around. I felt a jolt when I realized I'd have to back up the alligator implement. I hadn't a clue how to do that. It would be better to find the next crossroads and hope it was large enough that I could perform a loop that took me 180 degrees.

As I was considering whether I could manage that, the woods gave way to a few open fields before closing in on the road again. Relieved, ahead on the right, I saw Niall. He'd stopped at the edge of a field. He was in it, feeling the tall grass. He stood up, feet apart and his hands on his hips, looking back down the road toward me.

I brought the tractor to a stop on the road. I kept my foot on the brake and considered what to do next.

Niall strode over. He shifted the tractor into neutral and throttled down the engine. "You can take your foot off the brake now. So glad you could join me. What took you so damn long?"

I considered telling him I'd been run off the road by that girl driving the New Holland tractor, and she'd had to stop and get some chains to pull me out—a little white lie for my own benefit, a momentary fantasy of rescue. "I've never driven a tractor before."

"Okay, but I showed you last night. Driving a tractor's not much different from driving a car."

I looked away from Niall down where the road crested at a hill, then lowered my eyes to study my shoelaces. "I've never driven a car," I said. "I don't have a license, not even my beginners."

"Jesus Murphy," Niall said. "You're 18 and you don't have your license?"

"I'm still 17," I corrected him.

"Big difference," he said. "So why not? And for God's sake, why didn't you tell me last night? For that matter, why didn't your brother tell me?"

I didn't have an answer to any of his questions, though I could make a guess about Jeff. It was all too complicated, so I just shrugged my shoulders.

I don't know what I expected him to do. I thought maybe we'd head back to his farm, where he'd call my parents to come pick me up. It occurred to me that my eight-week sentence might be shortened by seven weeks and six days. For a moment, I brightened at the thought, but that bit of sunlight clouded over right away with an overwhelming sense of failure—and the likely consequences at home.

After a moment, Niall said, "Well, you're here now. Guess I'll have to make the best of it." He made a curt sound of disgust and spat on the ground.

Chapter 9

"You're going to mow this field," Niall said.

"I am?" I didn't see how. It wasn't like the little patch of grass in front of our townhouse. The field was huge, much larger than the football field at school, and bordered on one side by the road and the other three sides by woods. The grass looked like it hadn't been cut ever—virgin prairie. When Niall didn't respond, I said, "You mean I've got to cut down this tall grass?"

He sighed. It was becoming a regular moment in our

conversations. "First of all, we don't call it grass, though it's made up of different grasses. This is hay—like the hay you fed the cows this morning, remember?" He sounded as if he was explaining things simply, well, to a simpleton—or perhaps a child. "Cutting the hay is the first step, and we can only do that once the dew is off it. That's why we can't do it first thing in the morning. I've checked this field, and it's dry. Once cut, we let it dry for three days—that's called curing." I considered there was no cure for getting cut down but said nothing. "Then we rake it into rows. Finally, we bale it and put it in the barn, hoping to God during all that time it doesn't rain. In other words, the pressure's on once we start mowing, and we've got a helluva lot to do this week and next." He paused to rub his forehead and face. "I've got to get going on cutting another field, but I guess I better teach you how to mow before I head back."

Niall told me to follow him to the back of the tractor. What I thought of as an alligator was, apparently, a sickle bar mower. He released a latch and brought the cutting blades down to the right of the tractor—two rows about ten feet long of triangular teeth one on top of the other. Then he showed me the tractor's PTO shaft, which he said stood for power take-off—the shaft that used the tractor's power to operate implements. "That shaft," said Niall, "is extremely dangerous. Don't go near it when the tractor is running." That was an instruction I could remember. He showed me in the tractor's controls the lever that engaged the PTO shaft. "Now stand well back."

As I retreated, he turned on the PTO. The blades started moving back and forth against each other so fast, they blurred together—making a racket that sounded like thousands of scissors snipping. Niall put the tractor in low gear, then performed a counterclockwise circuit of the field, cutting the outer edge that bordered the woods and the road. The grass fell neatly behind the mower, while the tractor's tires left two tracks in the tall grass, which was waist high.

When he'd completed that circuit, Niall maneuvered the tractor and mower so that it would now go in a clockwise direction—the tractor lined up to ride over the row he'd just cut, the mower positioned to cut the next row.

He turned off the PTO, put the tractor in neutral, and lowered the throttle. He climbed down and said, "Get up and show me how to do it. Just do exactly what I did. Cut the next circuit on the inside." He checked his watch. "I'll stay awhile to make sure you're okay. Keep going until you're done this field. It should take you about three hours in low gear. I should be back by then. If not, just wait for me."

"You're leaving me alone?"

"Is that a problem?" It sounded like a challenge, not a question.

Sure feels like one was my thought, but I said, "Nope. I've got this." Fake it 'til you make it.

He walked to a safe distance. "Let me see you get up on the tractor and start mowing. Engage the PTO before throttling up and putting the tractor in gear." As I climbed up, he added, "One last thing. Watch out for gopher holes and rocks."

Three simple steps I could handle: engage the PTO, throttle up, put the tractor in low gear. I began moving forward, making sure the tractor followed the path Niall had cut. I glanced over to make sure the mower was catching the next path of hay. I was a bit too far to the right so I was missing some. I moved the tractor to the left.

When I came to a corner, I had to go forward and backward a few times to line up the mower correctly. I gripped the wheel so hard for the whole circuit that my fingers ached by the end. During my next circuit, I noticed how wobbly my first one had been compared to Niall's. I completed one more circuit and looked up. Niall was gone.

I kept at it, pushing back against my obsession with mathematical precision. Between the roar of the tractor and the incessant click-clacking of the mower, I couldn't really think anyway.

I looked for something to count, but nature didn't cooperate. The grass blades in the field were innumerable, the trees in the surrounding woods irregularly placed, not in neat rows and columns that would have made a satisfying grid. Plus, they were all different varieties—not helpful at all. All I could do was slowly count my circuits as I worked inward on the field.

Sometimes I stared straight ahead and concentrated on the path I had to follow. Other times, I watched the grass fall behind the blade. If I looked closely, I could see grasshoppers launching ahead of the blade, mice scurrying away. Birds swooped and darted over the field, and sometimes seemed to be dive-bombing me as my mowing disturbed insects. In one circuit, I barely missed running my tires into an enormous hole in the ground—a gopher hole, I was sure. The field felt eerily alive below ground, at ground level, and in the sky. I felt alone with it yet watched by something—I had no clue what.

Cross-country races took place, well, in the country, but those events felt very different from this. Masses of people in short shorts loped through woods and across fields, up and down hills, whatever the weather—which in the fall was generally cold and wet—covering a circuit that landed them back where they started. A mob of rather ridiculous two-legged mammals, when you think about it. Perhaps the creatures we startled as we ran thought of us that way.

I tried to focus on cutting a neat swath of hay, one that would please Niall. The morning was heating up. I'd forgotten my Blue Jays ball cap, and the sun beat down on my head, turning my hair into a hot mop. I started sweating, and I could see the skin on my arms begin to redden. I kept pushing my glasses up on my nose from the sweat and vibration of the tractor. I'd forgotten the elastic I used to keep them in place when running. The elastic and hat were sitting in the suitcase I hadn't bothered to unpack.

I entered a trancelike state as the tractor moved forward and the blades cut. I lost count of my circuits. As I was re-counting from the outer edge inward, three things happened simultaneously. A grasshopper landed on my cheek and clung to it. The tractor's right tires rode over a deep gopher hole. The sickle mower dug into the dirt, made a loud clanging noise, and came to an abrupt stop while the belt that ran it snapped and launched into the air like a kite tossed by a hurricane.

I fumbled for the lever to shut down the PTO, remembering at least this instruction from Niall, then backed up the tractor, put it in neutral, and lowered the throttle. I looked around, whether to see if someone had witnessed my screw-up or to find help, I don't know. Maybe both.

I got down and walked over to the gopher hole. "Bastard!" I yelled as I peered in. I inspected the mower. Some of the alligator teeth had been bent and several were missing. I searched for these and found them near a rock that clearly bore teeth marks. It had fought back and won. I tried to pick up the teeth but they burned my fingertips. I waited for them to cool and searched for the snapped belt, which had flown into the uncut grass. Grasshoppers jumped ahead of me as I parted the sea. I saw the belt ahead, but when I went to grab it, it turned out to be a snake. I fell backward and scrambled away.

I searched slowly now, and when I came across the belt I was more cautious picking it up. I returned to the tractor, grabbed the broken teeth, which were now hot solely from the sun, and debated what to do next. I could wait for Niall, but he could still be several hours—time wasted, and the field left uncut—another strike against me. How many would I get before I was called out and sent back to the dugout? This was life, not baseball. The mower obviously needed to be repaired. Niall would be angry.

There was no help for it. I'd have to get the tractor and the damaged mower back to the farm. If Niall wasn't there, Connie would know what to do. An Ashbyism I'd written in my running log came to me: "A mistake is a mistake twice over if you don't learn from it." I had no clue what lesson the broken mower was teaching me.

I struggled to lift the blades into the vertical position. When I got them as high as I could, I looked for whatever latch or pin Niall had removed when lowering them. My arms began shaking. I lost my grip and jumped back as the blades dropped, nearly catching my legs.

After two more attempts, it became clear I'd have to drive the tractor with the blades down and sticking out to the right. I'd need to be careful not to hit any signs as I hurried back to the farm.

At the road, I looked both ways, understanding at least

that much about driving. I turned left into its centre and brought the tractor into high gear.

In five minutes, I was lost.

I knew I'd made a mistake when I came to a heavily wooded area. In the middle, it had a narrow bridge with no railings, just cement curbs. I would have remembered this bridge. I hugged the left side so the mower would clear the right curb. I tried not to look down into the water, but I was damned thirsty by then. The stream looked sluggish, more a pool than running water. I considered stopping to cool off, maybe get a drink, then remembered it wasn't chlorinated city water. It would be filled with microscopic organisms, those creatures squiggling and wiggling on a slide.

I continued through the woods and emerged into open farmland. By now, the skin on my face, neck, and arms was red and raw. My lips were dry and cracked. My Supertramp T-shirt clung to my back with sweat, and from the waist down I felt moist, swampy. I kept going, getting desperate. I needed to ask for help, but for several miles all I saw were tractors in the distance working fields. All I passed were collapsing barns and decaying farmhouses, some with second-floor doors that opened onto vacant air.

Finally, I saw a pickup coming my way. I pulled over and waved as the driver approached. As he passed, he raised his right forefinger off the steering wheel. What the hell? Maybe I hadn't properly signalled for help. This happened twice more, the same signal from the driver. Was that some universal farmer greeting? What happened to stopping and chatting about the weather?

I was determined to stop the next pickup, whether heading toward me or coming up from behind. I'd take the middle of the road and hold my ground, forcing the driver to pull over. With this lame idea it became clear the heat was cooking my brain.

Before I could enact my plan, I came to a paved road busy with traffic. Civilization at last! Cars and pickups and even transport trucks flowed in both directions. They had to be travelling from one town to another, maybe even to what might be called a city. I reflected that I didn't know the population numbers that defined villages, towns, and cities. I'd have to look into it later. It was important to learn such mathematical distinctions and keep them straight.

My joy lasted only a moment, a product of the blazing sun, for it came to me how truly lost I was, and I realized there was no way I could travel the highway before me on this tractor, for I didn't have a driver's license. That, and the traffic simply roared by.

I looked across the highway into the distance. An Ashby proverb about solving math problems came to me: "Getting lost is a necessary precondition for being found, disorientation for discovery." Such a guru. I pictured him sitting cross-legged atop a mountain dispensing his wisdom with a finger in the air.

Far ahead, I thought I saw water. *Thank God! Could that be Lake Huron? Have I gone that far?* It was hard to know, for it could be just heat waves wobbling the horizon, along with my heat-baked brain. I looked up at the sun, which was now ahead of me, and I understood the error of my ways. In my wanderings, I'd headed west from the hay field rather than east back to the farm. It was now past noon, and I'd been travelling farther and farther away from where I needed to be—taking responsibility for my mistakes.

But why not just do a runner? If I could get across this damned highway, I might follow the gravel road to the lake. There, I'd abandon the tractor and take a swim to cool off. Then, in the immortal words of Rick and Roger, I'd take the long way home—or to anywhere but here. If I followed the coast south, I was bound to reach a town eventually. And if it were a port town, I could stow away on a laker. Gordon Lightfoot's "Wreck of the Edmund Fitzgerald" came to mind and gave me pause.

It might be better, then, to shut down the tractor right where I was, walk across the highway, and stick out my thumb in a southerly direction. I'd never hitchhiked, though, and I was reminded of all my mother's stories of young people who'd disappeared, abducted or murdered or sold into slavery. It would also mean sitting in a car with a stranger, explaining who I was and what I was doing. I'd never been a good liar. Worse, I'd have to make small talk.

These, of course, were the foolish thoughts of my seventeen-nearly-eighteen-year-old self, influenced by the heat operating on my brain, my parched throat, and my empty stomach—together acted on by my growing fear of facing Niall, if I could find him.

I really had only one option. Turn back east, then hope for a familiar landmark or a friendly face that might set me on the right path. But how to turn around? The gravel road was too narrow to do a 180 turn on it. I didn't know how to perform a three-point turn, and I'm not sure how it would have worked pulling a mower. That also made backing up the tractor to the nearest crossroad impossible. There was nothing for it. I'd have to wait for a break in the traffic, swing wide onto the highway, and loop around back onto the gravel road.

Back and forth my head pivoted on my neck, sending a jerky "no" to the universe. Minutes passed. I got a crick and massaged it with my sweaty hands. Finally, I judged I had enough time, with one vehicle heading north toward me but just appearing at the crest of a hill. I swung out and performed a sweeping loop in what felt like slow motion. Either I really wasn't moving fast enough or I'd misjudged the car's distance, for the driver honked loud and long. I glanced up to see her giving me the finger, and it wasn't the friendly farmer salute. I smashed my foot down on the accelerator, cleared the asphalt, and roared down the gravel road, counting to ten before stopping.

I needed to calm my heart, which was performing a tattoo in my chest. I took off my glasses and wiped my face with my sweat-soaked T-shirt, then used it to clean my glasses—which only succeeded in smearing the lenses. I looked around at the blurry world. A bronze blob was approaching me. Even through my streaked glasses I could see that the blob was a Ford F-150 pickup, and Niall was at the wheel.

Chapter 10

Sitting atop the tractor, I was between the proverbial rock and a hard place—the highway behind me, Niall before me.

He put on his hazards, climbed out of the truck, and walked over. Not once did his glare falter. I was the first to break eye contact, looking down at my shoelaces covered in dirt, with a fine layer of road dust on top. His hand reached in and shut down the tractor.

"I've been looking for you," he said. "If one of my neighbours hadn't stopped to tell me he'd seen some strange kid riding around on one of my tractors, pulling a mower still in the operating position, I wouldn't have had a clue where to find you." *Could neighbours,* I wondered, *recognize each other's tractors?* They looked pretty much the same to me—both the neighbours and the machines. "So just what the hell are you doing?"

Good question. I'm sure my dad asked the same one using slightly different words. As I explained what happened in the field and how I'd gotten lost, he rubbed his forehead, then his face with both hands. He went to inspect the mower before I'd even finished. When he stood up, I thought he was going to kick the tire of the tractor. Instead, he stared at the mower a few moments with his hands on his hips, then in one smooth and angry motion put the blades in the vertical position and locked them in place.

He walked back to the truck. I waited for some sort of instruction, but he was busy searching the bed. He pulled out a gas can, walked back over, and began filling the tank. "You wouldn't have gotten much farther. You're running on fumes." When he was done, he said, "Start it up and follow me. Think you can manage that without screwing up?"

I did that one thing right; he went much slower on the journey back to the farm than he had leaving it. It was a long, meandering trip, but eventually certain landmarks looked familiar, including the fence posts I'd failed to count hours before. We were nearing the farm when the New Holland tractor and Vermeer implement I'd seen that morning came roaring back down the road. The girl in the driver's seat waved a greeting to Niall and offered me a quizzical look as I trailed him. Her bearing—sitting up straight and high in that seat, her ponytail flowing back in the wind, her red bandana still roguishly tied around her neck—suggested to me she'd had a highly productive morning. I looked away from her.

Once we were in the laneway, Niall signalled for me to pull the mower around to the machine shed. He wanted me to back it in, but when I tried I only managed to jackknife it. I pulled forward to make another attempt, but Niall waved me to get down and took over. He deftly maneuvered the mower straight back to a work bench.

He shut down the tractor. "I need you to pass me tools as I fix this mess, that's all. Can you do that?"

I offered a meek yes, without telling him that I knew about as much about tools as I did about tractors. I could tell a hammer from a saw, a pair of pliers from a screwdriver, but not much else. I struggled to hand him exactly what he needed as he took apart the mower blades, asking for this size wrench and that type of screwdriver, then a ball peen hammer as he heated and pounded the bent blades.

He'd been working at it for about a half hour as I stood by. Tired, hungry, and thirsty, I wanted to sit down but didn't dare do so, thinking it would add insult to injury—Niall pounding away and sweating trying to fix my mistake.

Connie appeared in the doorway of the machine shop. She was carrying a jug of water, two glasses, and a sandwich on a plate. She yelled to be heard over the pounding, "Ni, take a break!" He paused and gave the blades one more blow before standing up and wiping his forehead with a hanky he drew from his pocket. She looked at him steadily, then turned to me. "Here, Evan, grab these glasses from me." She put the plate down on the work bench and filled the glasses. I passed one to Niall, who took it without comment. I thanked Connie and drained the glass. Connie smiled and said, "Thirsty?" as she refilled my glass.

I nodded and murmured "Yes," then downed the second glass.

"I'm sure you're hungry too after your morning's work."

"Work?" Niall said, looking into his empty glass.

Connie turned to him and poured him another glass. "It's his first day, and it's been a tough one. He's been out in the heat and the sun for hours, no food, no water. You're the one who left him there on his own. It's not his fault the mower broke."

Please, Connie, please no, I thought. *This isn't helping.* Standing there listening to her chastise Niall, I wished I was invisible. I thought of my mother, defending me to my father, and how useless that was.

Niall took a sip of water. "Be that as it may, we're now way behind, and the longer we stand here gabbing, the further behind we get."

Connie gave him one last look before putting down the nearly empty jug of water on the workbench beside the sandwich. "Evan," she said, "Here's a sandwich for you and some more water if you need it." With that, she turned and left the machine shed. Niall set his glass down without finishing it and went back to his repair job.

I stood by the workbench and ate my sandwich. Bites stuck in my throat a few times. I had to pause and drink some water.

Niall finished his pounding about the same time I took my last bite. He told me to stand by the door and look out and not turn around. I wondered if it was some kind of test, like in the Bible with Lot and his wife, she who disobeyed and looked back.

From where I stood, I could see the cows in their pasture, grazing contentedly. A few lay in a tree's shade to escape the afternoon heat, though they were still chewing—what I eventually learned was chewing their cud, food they'd brought up from the first of their four stomachs for further chewing. Ruminants, like me.

A laneway ran back from the machine shed to more fields and some woods in the distance. It felt peaceful. Flies and bees buzzed, of course, but the air was filled with bird song, songs I didn't recognize. Along the pasture fence were more flowers, whether wild or planted I couldn't tell. Purples and yellows and whites.

Behind me, a loud buzzing and snapping began, and the machine shed filled with light in a kind of strobe effect. I resisted turning around to see what Niall was doing, in case I turned into a pillar of salt.

After, he showed me how he'd welded the broken teeth back in place, saying, "That should hold for now."

By the time he'd reattached the blades and replaced the belt, it was far into the afternoon. "Wash up," he said. "Time for afternoon milking."

"The cows need milking twice a day?"

He was using a de-greaser on his hands. He let out his now signature sigh. "They prefer that we do."

I worked hard to do things right this time. Niall was silent throughout, and I sensed he didn't want any talk. He had enough on his mind already, much of it piled there by me.

When we were nearly done, Niall told me to go ahead and have a shower before supper. I said, "I can finish," but he insisted.

Supper was ready by the time I'd showered and put on clean clothes. Jane laughed as I sat. "You look like a straw-berry!" She was right. I'd felt the burn on my face, neck, and arms stinging in the shower. My skin still tingled and was growing itchy.

"After supper, I'll give you some cream for that," Connie said.

Connie and Niall ate silently, and so did I. Jane and Finn were chatty, telling me how the feathers were starting to come in on the chicks, just at the wing tips. Finn imitated the chicks flapping their tiny wings. Jane said she and Finn had helped their mom in the garden and had a surprise for dessert. Connie told them to stop talking my ear off and eat up, or there would be no dessert.

"Can I please get it?" Jane said when she was done.

Finn got up and said, "I'll help."

They went to the fridge and fussed about who would carry what. Once they'd sorted that out, they came back to the table, each carrying a bowl.

"Strawberries!" Jane said. "Strawberries for a strawberry," she added, looking up at me. "We picked them." I looked in the bowl. It was filled with strawberries cut in half sitting in a thick liquid.

"And whipped cream," Finn said, holding up the bowl for me to look at.

"From your cows?" I said.

"Of course, silly!"

I don't know why, but I felt myself tearing up—over strawberries, of all things, the red of them, the sweet scent of them, a gift. A milksop, once again. I struggled to hold it in.

Niall got up abruptly from the table. "I'll have mine

later," he said. "I'm going to finish that field."

I stood up. "Can I help?"

"You sit." He was heading to the mudroom for his work boots. "I'll take care of it."

"But I need to learn how to do it right."

"Niall," Connie said.

"I don't have time to teach you." He paused and turned before heading through the door. "Not tonight. Anyway, you've done enough today. Just try not to break anything else while I'm gone." He closed the door behind him.

I stood a moment, feeling myself redden beneath my sunburn. Painful tingling erupted as I sat again. Connie spooned some strawberries in a bowl for me. I thought about where the whipped cream came from and said, "None for me." I picked up the spoon and stared at the berries. When I'd regained my composure, I ate them silently, so sweet and tangy but a bitter end to the day.

After dessert, I felt at loose ends. I was exhausted and sore, both my skin and my muscles, but I wasn't ready for sleep. It was too early, too light, my mind too agitated. Finn and Jane weren't even heading to bed. I was in a house where I couldn't just wander from room to room or plop down on a sofa to watch a baseball game. If I went outside, I'd be confronted with Niall's world and reminders every-where of how I didn't fit in it.

"Can I help with the dishes?" I asked Connie.

"No need," she said as she stood and started clearing

the table. "Finn and Jane will help. You're welcome to get some rest. You're going to need it in the coming days."

"Finn and Jane could have a break." I stood and started taking dishes to the counter before she could argue.

"Can we, Mom, please?" Jane and Finn said together.

Connie paused at the sink. "Alright, just this once. But don't think Evan's going to do your chores all the time now. Bring your own dishes, and then you can play for an hour before bed."

They rushed their dishes over to the counter and ran out the door into the yard. Their laughter and chatter came in through the open window above the sink as I cleared the table. Connie began to fill the sink with hot, soapy water.

We worked quietly for several minutes. She washed and rinsed while I dried and stacked. Eventually, I needed to ask where dishes went, and she pointed out cupboards and drawers.

Outside the window, Jane and Finn were playing with paper airplanes they'd made. They tossed them and watched them float and dip and dive, then chased them and sent them up again.

"It'll still be many years before they're old enough to help their dad," Connie said as she scrubbed a pot.

"Jane too?" I said.

Connie smiled. "Yes, Jane too. It's 1979, Evan, not 1950."

"But I mean she wants to help? I didn't think girls…"

"There's tradition, and then there's possibilities. Dreams. What we're meant to do, maybe born to do." I couldn't fathom it. She rinsed the pot and put it in the dish tray. "Take Niall. Born to be a dairy farmer. In spite of all the hardships."

I picked up the pot and dried the inside. "Were you born to be a farmer's wife?"

She pulled the plug in the sink. While the water emptied, she looked out the window. "I'm not sure I like the phrase. I think of us more as partners in the farm. But yes, I took a roundabout way to get here, but it's where I belong. When I look at Jane and Finn, that's all the proof I need." She rinsed the suds out of the sink while I finished drying the pot. I was about to ask where it went when she took it from me and said, "Don't mind Niall. He's got a lot on his plate right now. He'll come around."

I thought of him out in that faraway field finishing the mowing. "Is there something I can do right now to help him?"

She paused to put away the pot. "I don't think so," she said, "but we can check the barn. He rushed through the afternoon milking."

I put my shoes back on and followed Connie outside. Finn and Jane tagged along. In the milking parlour, Niall hadn't taken time to clean up the manure. Connie said, "If you've got some energy left, you could shovel out the milking stations and put fresh straw down for the morning. I think that would help."

My heart sank at the sight of all the manure, but I said, "Sure." After all, I'd been foolish enough to ask. "So straw is different from hay?"

"Straw's what's left over after wheat and other grains are harvested. Finn, show Evan where it is and help him throw down eight bales."

For the next hour, I shovelled soiled straw into the channel, sent it out to the manure mountain, and put down fresh bedding. When I was done, I looked over my job one last time, turned off the lights, and headed to the house. There was still no sign of Niall, and darkness was falling fast, along with a chill.

"All done?" Connie said when I was inside. The house was quiet; Finn and Jane had gone to bed.

"Yup. And so am I, I think."

"Have a good night, then."

I hesitated. I considered staying up until Niall got back. It felt as if my day wasn't finished unless I did.

"Don't worry," Connie said, passing me a bottle of cream for my sunburn. "There's no need to wait up for him."

I climbed the stairs to my attic room, my legs heavy pendulums by the time I reached the top, where I sat listening for a while to Connie moving about in the kitchen before I got up and headed to my room.

I stood for a moment in the doorway after turning on the light. My running log sat closed on the desk, accusing me. My running clothes lay neatly on the chair, looking ridiculous. I turned out the light.

I undressed in the dark, dropping my clothes on the floor. I turned on the desk lamp, put lotion on my burns, and slid into bed. From there, I counted the books on the shelf but was still unable to sleep. On the desk, Janus looked at me with one of his faces, turned away with the other. A bastard twice over. I'd been startled at first when Mr. Ashby put Janus in my hand. Did he think I was two-faced? I'd discovered that quality in myself around that time, that I could show one face to some people and a different face to others, that there was the face I showed the world and the face I kept inside, hidden. At the time, I thought I was the only one.

But I was wrong about Mr. Ashby. As I'd studied the paperweight in my hand, he said Janus was a Roman god who had those two faces looking in opposite directions because he was all about life's doorways and gates, passages and transitions, beginnings and endings. Doubleness. Time. Mr. Ashby had said that while all stages of life have their doorways, the big ones happened around my age, and he hoped Janus might help me through them. Some helper.

I got out of bed and searched the desk for paper and a pen. Finding them, I sat in the chair and looked at the blank page beneath the cone of light. *Dear Mr. Ashby,* I began. I needed to tell someone. Who better?

When I was done, I climbed back in bed, turned out the desk lamp, and listened to the night sounds. I saw again with embarrassment that girl passing me on the New Holland tractor, twice in one day. Eventually, I heard a tractor in the distance. The noise grew louder until it poured through my window, blocking every other sound.

One day done, fifty-five to go. The number 4,752,000 lit up my Texas Instruments calculator sitting beside Janus, and beside my calculator, my alarm clock set to 5:15 a.m.

CHAPTER 11

"Evan, this is Mar. Mar, Evan." That was all the introduction Niall offered to the New Holland tractor girl.

We were standing at the edge of a large hay field, enormous rows of raked hay ready to be baled. The baler —a Massey Ferguson square baler that more accurately produced cuboids strapped tight with two strands of twine —was hitched to the tractor I'd used my first day, and a large wagon was hitched to the baler.

"Mar?"

"Don't ask," she said.

I was curious, but her tone and crossed arms told me not to mess with her. Seeing her this close in full sunlight, I guessed she was a couple of years older than I was. She was wearing a bandana around her forehead, her ponytail sticking out the back. Another bandana was tied loosely around her neck, and the belt holding up her jeans was made of colourful bandanas sewn together. She was wearing a tank top again.

It was the Friday afternoon of my first week. Patches of skin were peeling off my arms and neck, but at least the itching and burning were gone. Cuts on my hands had mostly healed, blisters had broken and turned into calluses.

I'd woken up my second day feeling soreness in muscles I didn't know I had, an ache in my skin as if it had been stretched tight while I slept. That day had been long and full with finishing the mowing. The Wednesday involved a tense lull as the hay cured. The hay cut on Monday couldn't be raked until Thursday, the Tuesday cutting just this Friday morning. Each day, I'd watched Niall peering into the sky off and on. He was hoping showers didn't materialize; I was hoping they would. The forecast had changed, giving a 50-50 chance of rain. If showers meant a delay on hard labour, maybe a cancellation, I was all for it.

"Evan, you'll pull the baler while I build the load. When a load's done, Mar, you can take it to the barn and get Reuben and Simeon to help unload it. Any questions?"

I had a million, but I wanted to ask them when Mar was out of earshot, not wanting to confirm her suspicion I was a green city kid.

On the Wednesday, Niall had given me the job of cleaning out the mow to ready it for the new hay. It was hot, dirty work.

First, I had to move the old bales from the far end of the barn close to the trap door where I threw down the hay for feeding. He wanted the bales handy for use before any of the new hay was touched. I counted the pile after stacking them—113. I estimated that each bale weighed about sixty pounds, so I moved approximately 6,789 pounds of the stuff—3.39 tons. And the stuff itched. By the time I was done, my forearms were covered with scratches that burned with sweat. My hands were raw and blistered from the baler twine. I thought of asking for gloves, but figured I'd be told they were for sissies.

After moving those bales, I mopped my face with my T-shirt and looked at what was left—a ton of loose hay and broken bales. I needed to use the pitchfork to pile all this hay to one side and then sweep anything left on the floor into it.

Clouds of dust filled the air and settled on me as I worked, turning to mud when mixed with my sweat, settling in my hair and working its way inside my shirt, my pants, my socks, my shoes. The dust covered my glasses so that the barn seemed in a fog. At least I'd remembered the elastic band so they didn't continually slide down my nose. Without it—an adjustable strap I used when running—I'm sure my glasses would have just fallen off as I bent over with the pitchfork to lift and toss the hay, becoming a needle in the haystack, impossible to locate given my nearsightedness.

Sneezes came in series of three, giving me brief breaks from forking and sweeping. I'd inherited my big nose from my dad, and it was capable of explosions.

From within the fog, between sneezing fits I brooded over the injustice of my life. *How the hell am I supposed to locate bootstraps in all this dust?* I asked myself. What happened at school was not my fault. It was out of my control. But it had landed me here on this farm, spilling milk, breaking machines, going nowhere.

I forked the last of the hay into the now enormous pile and swept the barn floor clean, thinking of that long walk into the city and misguided bus ride weeks ago as the first leg of my journey here. And here, I was more lost, if anything.

Mar and I stood eyeing each other while Niall schooled me. A farming simpleton, I obviously needed his teaching, but I felt a fool getting them in front of Mar, who was obviously older, wiser, more seasoned in the mysteries of husbandry. Not to mention much stronger and more beautiful.

As I listened to Niall and studied her cheeks with their red patches, her rust-coloured hair, and her green eyes, I wished it was Mar teaching me the art of husbandry.

"The hay feeds into the baler, which compresses it, ties it with twine, and sends it out the back chute. I'll be standing on the wagon, where I'll grab the bales and build the load."

"Isn't that dangerous?" I said. I imagined Niall falling off because of my driving skills, tumbling to the side or, worse, falling between the baler and the wagon and getting run over. I'd gotten a bit better at driving from finishing the mowing and learning to do the raking, the rake being powered by its own wheels and not the loud, dangerous PTO. But the baler was a much bigger machine than either the mower or the rake, bulky and complicated, a bit like a rhinoceros or triceratops—and on top of that, I would be pulling a wagon attached to this beast, a flat wagon with no sides or front, just a back made of wooden boards in a crisscross pattern of the game Xs and Os. It seemed like a recipe for disaster, this combo of tractor, baler, and wagon, going from two machines to three, increasing the probability of my screwing up by 33.33333 ad infinitum percent.

Mar answered before Niall could. "It's not dangerous if you're careful. Make sure you avoid gopher holes with the wagon. And look out for rocks too." She turned to Niall. "Are you sure you don't want me on the baler?"

"Maybe later, but Evan hasn't got the arm strength to do all the throwing that's needed. Plus, he doesn't know how to fill the mow, like you and your brothers. There's a lot of baling to get done today and tomorrow, and with the rain coming, I don't have time to teach him."

"Fair enough," Mar said. She turned away and strode over to the tractor she'd be operating, fetching the wagons from us as we completed a load, hauling them to the barn where she'd unload them onto the elevator that carried them up to the hay door at the peak of the barn. Inside, her brothers would pile the bales in the mow I'd cleaned out two days earlier.

I turned toward the tractor, which Niall had lined up to move with the baler and wagon directly into the field, and felt a tightness in my chest and stomach. "How the hell am I supposed to learn if he won't teach me?" I muttered.

"What was that?" Niall said, pausing as he walked to the wagon.

"Just wondering what gear I should be in," I called.

"Low to start with," he said. "We'll see how you do and how the baler handles it. This first cut is thick." He climbed up onto the wagon and stood near the front with his feet well apart for balance and his hands on his hips.

I started the tractor and engaged the PTO. The baler clanged to life, the metal tines that picked up the hay began to turn. I increased the RPMs almost to 2000, put the tractor in low gear, and tried to get it moving gently. Niall had to step back with one foot as the slack went out of the connection between the baler and the wagon.

I concentrated on keeping the baler's mouth aligned with the row of hay, often glancing back behind the machine to check for gopher holes and rocks that might have been hidden below the row, and watching as the machine fed bales to Niall. He grabbed them and, with one smooth motion, pivoted and carried them to the back of the wagon, where he placed them snugly against the vertical frame. He built the load in a crisscross pattern that would make it solid and stable. I was both amazed and alarmed at how high he went, how easily he could toss a bale above his head.

To help concentrate and hold back my fear of injuring Niall or breaking machinery, I counted the bales as they came out.

I'd counted 196 when Niall had finished building the first load, with barely standing space left for himself at the front of the wagon. He signalled me to stop and shut down the baler. He hopped down, waved to Mar, and walked forward.

"That's 196 bales." *That should impress him,* I thought.

He looked at the baler. "You can read the counter from there?"

"What counter?"

"The machine takes care of that. You concentrate on driving."

Disappointed, I felt a familiar knot in my chest, telling myself some people just didn't appreciate numbers the way I did.

Mar brought an empty wagon into the field and un-hitched it while Niall did the same with the full wagon. I pulled the baler forward so Mar could hitch to the full wagon. Niall motioned me to pull the baler around to the empty one. I made an arc, bringing the tractor and baler in line with the empty wagon, but when I tried to back up the baler to the wagon, I couldn't do it. The baler twisted to the left. I kept going backward and forward, getting nowhere near the wagon and risking jackknifing the baler, all this while Mar smoothly backed to the full wagon and Niall dropped the pin into the hitch.

He walked over as Mar began pulling the load out of the field. I looked up, defeated. She waved and smiled her inscrutable smile.

Niall explained how to back up turning the steering wheel in the opposite direction to where you want the im-plement to go. "Get as close as you can, and I'll do the rest." I moved the baler slowly as Niall signalled which di-rection to steer it. After I'd made three attempts and burned precious time, Niall ran out of patience or decided it was as close as I would get. I thought he was going to get me off the tractor so that he could do it himself. Instead, he picked up the wagon's tongue and pulled it up to the baler, aligned the hitch, and dropped in the pin. Then he was back on the wagon, signalling me to get moving.

The second load was half built when Niall starting waving both arms in the air. He pointed to the baler. Hay was climbing out the shoot loose without twine tying it in bales. I shut down the PTO and throttled down the tractor. Niall strode to the baler and unlatched a door to get into the machine's guts. "Dammit" was all he said. He began pulling out tangles of twine. Eventually, he took a pocket knife and began cutting away at the tangle, a Gorgon's knot.

By then, Mar was back with the empty wagon. She walked over and asked if she could help. I walked over, as well, looking into the complicated inside of the machine, studying it as if I might discover something helpful. Niall said, "I've got some tools in the bin on the back of the tractor. Can you fetch them for me?" Mar and I moved at the same time. She located the bin first and brought Niall some wrenches and pliers. "She's a temperamental, finicky beast," he said as he worked on it.

"He's got you pegged," I said to Mar, hoping my smart-aleck joke might impress her.

She shot back, "He's talking about you, Milksop."

"Milksop?" I said.

"Yeah, isn't that what your brother calls you?"

"You know my brother?"

"Of course. I worked with him last summer."

Dammit, dammit, dammit! Why did Jeff have to tell her? I

turned away, hiding my face and looking for something to do with my hands.

Niall said, "While I get this sorted, you two pull the loose hay out of the back and spread it out on one of the rows." I couldn't get away from her.

A half hour later, Niall had the knotter working to his satisfaction. To make up time, he told me to put the baler into middle gear, but when the bales started coming out twisted, the twine loose, he made me go back into low gear. There was no help for it.

Niall had built another half load. I blame what happened next on my disturbed state of mind—my anger at Jeff, my embarrassment at Mar knowing I was a milksop. I missed the large rock. The front right wagon wheel climbed it, lifted the wagon's corner in the air, and caused Niall to stumble. Then the tire came down off the rock directly into a gopher hole.

I still see it as if in slow motion—bales bouncing and tumbling off the side of the wagon, Niall falling backward on his butt, more bales landing around him, one a direct hit on his head.

Niall pushed off and kicked away the bales that had tumbled around him, then leapt to his feet with what looked to me like murder in his eyes. He jumped off the wagon and rushed up to me, saying, "Get off that goddamn tractor." His hand shot up and his thumb pointed behind him. "Start throwing those bales back onto the wagon." He climbed back up and started rebuilding the load while I lifted and pushed the fallen bales onto the bed as fast as I could.

I was sweating, my arms were aching, and I was out of breath when Mar came back into the field with an empty wagon. She climbed down to help. "More problems?"

"One big problem," Niall said.

I felt myself redden. "A gopher hole. I didn't see it."

"One problem after another," Niall added.

"Some days, life's like that," Mar said. She was holding the last bale and looking at me, smiling. I ducked my eyes as she tossed it on the wagon.

We'd finished three more loads. By then I'd recovered from hitting the gopher hole. It was getting to mid afternoon, the hot and thirsty part of the day. I'd brought a loaded wagon to the edge of the field and unhitched it for Mar, who hadn't returned from the last load. Nothing more had gone wrong. *I'm getting the hang of this*, I thought. Niall was resting on the next empty wagon, his legs dangling off the side.

I drove smoothly, feeling confident, and brought the tractor and baler alongside the wagon. I swung the tractor over to line up with the wagon's tongue. I heard a loud scraping noise and braked. Looking back, I saw Niall with his knees tucked up to his chin. I'd taken the corner around the wagon too tight and had scraped its side with the baler. If Niall hadn't lifted his legs in time, I could have taken them off at the knee.

"Jesus Murphy, Evan!"

I backed up the baler slowly so that it swung away from the wagon. The fender that guided the hay into the baler was bent outward. "Sorry" was all I could manage. It always seemed to be that way with me. When I'd built up a little confidence with some task, some skill, gotten the least bit cocky, the universe would give me a gut punch to put me back in my place.

"I think I like it better when you're careful, no matter how god-awful slow that is." Niall inspected the fender. He started using his arm strength and body weight to bend the fender back. "Give me a hand," he said.

By then, Mar had returned. She drove over to drop off the empty wagon near where we were pushing and pulling at the fender. She got down and said, "More trouble?"

"Just about lost my legs thanks to Evan," Niall said.

"You'd have a tough time building a load from a wheelchair," Mar said, then turned to me. "Very inconsiderate."

I thought about the harm I might have done and didn't see what was funny about the situation.

"Mar, switch with Evan." That's all he said to banish me from the field. I walked slowly to the tractor Mar had been driving, unhitched the wagon, and watched from a distance as she and Niall finished the load.

Chapter 12

When I first saw Reuben and Simeon, two things struck me. First, they were identical twins. Second, they were throwing Frisbees around the pasture.

These observations distracted me from the image I had of Niall with his knees up to his chin, balled up—worse, a vision I had of him with his legs cut off, blood pouring out of two stumps. I'd tried unsuccessfully to distract myself from this nightmare by cursing my brother, then reciting a string of curses against gophers—evil creatures put on this planet to wreak havoc with hay fields and my sanity—and finally feeling sorry for myself, crushed by my crush on Mar. None of it had worked.

So, as I pulled the load of hay Niall and Mar had finished up to the barn, I had evil in my heart, as the Bible says somewhere—a strong cocktail intoxicating me with anger and shame directed toward Niall and all members of the gopher clan—and embarrassment and envy surrounding Mar. Why I felt this about two people I barely knew and who should have meant nothing to me I couldn't fathom, and my confusion intensified these feelings.

I approached the barn while Mar's brothers continued tossing around their Frisbees. But the discs I could now see were brown and definitely not plastic. The boys paused when they saw I wasn't Mar. They said something to each other, then waved. I lifted a hand briefly in greeting. Then together, they each launched a Frisbee in my direction. One landed on the hood of the tractor and bounced off. The other hit the load of hay behind me.

It became clear to me what they were throwing. Discs of dried cow manure, cow patties. Cow pies. I realized that what I'd seen as I'd approached the barn was Reuben and Simeon trying to hit each other with them. Now that I'd appeared, I apparently made a more attractive target. They continued tossing patties in my direction. Twice before I made it to the barn I had to duck or I would have taken one in the head.

I'd pulled the wagon up to the elevator and shut down the tractor by the time they came up to me. They could have been anywhere between 14 and 16, shoulder-length blond hair and laughing grey eyes.

"You must be the city slicker Mar told us about," one of them said. The other added, "Evelyn, right?"

"It's Evan." We were off to a good start.

"Close enough." They put their arms around each other's shoulders. The one on the left said, "I'm Reuben, and this is my brother Simeon."

"No, you're Simeon," said the other. "I'm Reuben."

"Don't listen to him. He's a born liar."

"Since we're twins, that makes you a liar too. It's in your genes."

"But which pocket of my jeans? That's the question."

"Lame."

I thought about the clowns confronting me and how I might manage them. "How about I just call you both 'Reubeon.'"

"That's a good one, Evy."

I explained I was switching with Mar. Reluctantly, I told them I hadn't done this job before and asked what to do. They told me they'd take care of the hard work, unloading the wagon and getting the bales on the elevator. My job would be to take the bales as they fell off the elevator into the mow and stack them. "Put them any which way you want to. It doesn't matter once it's in the barn."

I knew this advice was dubious. As I went into the barn, I tried to remember how the hay had been stacked when I'd cleaned it out earlier.

What I saw on the barn floor offered no help. It was clear that Reubeon had been stacking the hay. Mar would never have left this mess. The bales were placed haphazardly, without any pattern, except that in one spot they'd attempted to build an igloo with them.

I was considering what I could do to bring some order to this mess when bales started coming through the hay door. When I say coming, I mean one after the other with no daylight between them. Reubeon were working like a machine. I started grabbing bales, carrying them over, and adding them as neatly as I could to the stack of hay, but I couldn't work fast enough.

Bales tumbled on top of the bales I was grabbing, weighing them down, wedging them so that no matter how hard I pulled I couldn't get them out. I'd abandon one bale to grab at a loose one that had tumbled down and knocked me about.

My arms were soon covered with cuts and hay and dust and sweat that burned in the cuts as I tried to move close to 200 sixty-pound bales of hay.

About halfway through, some daylight began to appear between the bales. At first, I was grateful, until I realized that Reubeon were adding a cow patty to the top of each bale, patties that rained down on me. Then suddenly there were bales with just one string or no strings, bales that exploded when they landed.

The bales stopped coming. I worked away at the mountain of bales, slower now. *Why don't the bastards come help me?* I thought. I considered going out and asking for it, but I was pretty sure the kind of help they'd offer would make my life more miserable.

I was bending over to lift one of the few bales left when something wet and smelly started raining down on me. Fresh cow pies landed on my back, my shoulders, my mop of sweaty hair. One of the twins must have been watching my progress. They'd waited and timed it perfectly, loading the elevator with a long line of fresh manure.

I'd had it. When I stood up, they were in the doorway laughing, their arms around each other's shoulders. I grabbed a handful of fresh manure and made a cow pie to smash in their faces. I ran and they turned. When I reached the door, I stepped out and flung the pie in their direction.

I missed them and hit Mar instead—directly in the chest.

Niall and Mar had come up to the barn with the next load of hay, wondering what was taking so long. I must have looked a sight, facing them both.

"That was meant for your asshole brothers," I said to Mar by way of apology, then turned back into the barn, walked over to the remaining manure-covered bales, and started carrying them over to the growing stack, which was, if anything, messier than when I'd started. I heard her calling angrily after her brothers.

"What a goddam mess," Niall said, seeming to read my mind. "All I wanted you to do was unload the damn wagon. Mar's brothers were supposed to stack it, not you."

Mar had returned to the barn. "They've run off, the cowards. I don't think they're coming back."

"Great," Niall said. "This has to be fixed and now we're down two workers, with more hay to get in and a helluva lot more to bale. We don't have time for this damned goofing off."

I carried the last bale over, stopped, and dropped it. "They're the ones who told me to stack. And for your information, I didn't make this goddam mess, they did. All I was trying to do was fix it. How the hell am I supposed to know how to stack? Did those two jackasses show me? No. Did you teach me how or explain it before you sent me up here? No! And what thanks do I get for trying? I get covered in cow shit."

I didn't wait for a response. I rushed out of the barn. Once outside, though, I didn't know where to go, where I might hide. I first went below into the milking parlour, but the feed bin seemed to chastise me; the calves began bawling, thinking I was there to feed them. Covered in shit, I didn't dare enter the milk house, that holy of holies. I tried the machine shed, but the mower and rake mocked me. I looked out across the pasture to the woods in the distance. I'd find no refuge there. In a roundabout way, I found myself in the chicken coop, where the chicks, their feathers still coming in, set up a cacophony of cheeping, they too thinking I was there to feed them.

I needed to get away, to get away from people, from this place, but no place felt safe, secluded enough that I wouldn't be found, found out. I burst out of the coop and strode toward the house. I felt myself breaking into a run.

Finn and Jane were in the yard playing with a small bow-and-arrow set. Not a cheap plastic toy, but not adult-sized. They were shooting at a paper target attached to some bales of straw. A couple of arrows were in the outer ring, a few more in the straw.

"You forgot to close the door," Finn said. I stopped, the urge to go forward fighting against my sense that I had to go back. *Why bother?* I thought. *They're not my concern.* I considered telling Finn he could do it, or the foxes could eat the little fluff balls for all I cared. But I didn't. I went back and secured the latch.

I turned back to the house and rushed through the kitchen door. Connie was doing some task I couldn't see. My vision was getting blurry as I strode past her. "Evan, your shoes. Please take them off in the house." She must have looked up; her nose must have caught the scent. "Evan!"

I took the stairs two at a time and slammed my door. If

there'd been a lock on it, I would have secured it. Without one, a good slam was the best I could do.

I sat on the edge of the bed and counted the books on the shelves. I stared at my running shorts and shirt still lying untouched on the corner chair, my shoes still waiting for my feet, my journal still shut on the desk. I looked at my suitcase lying open, the jumble of clothes. I hadn't bothered to unpack. I considered throwing everything in it and leaving, just walking down the laneway and turning left. Eventually, I'd find the highway and a way home.

Why didn't I? Despite feeling there was no spot on the farm where I could be alone, I felt some safety within its orbit. I was afraid to be unfettered, at loose ends in the wide world.

For that matter, why had I obeyed my father, allowing myself to be transported here in the first place? Why hadn't I refused, thrown a tantrum, stood my ground? Because I didn't have any ground to stand on? Filial obedience. Fear and love, a fearful love. "Honour thy father and thy mother, so that thou may live long in the land the Lord thy God is giving thee." I'd heard it every Sunday for as long as I could remember, the heaviest of commandments for childhood. Was it behind my wish to please my parents, my attempt to prove myself to my father? Did it explain my people-pleasing efforts everywhere I went? Given the results so far, a long life in some unspecified land wasn't looking likely.

From the desk, I picked up my calculator and studied its functions, its numbers and signs and symbols. It couldn't calculate the weight I felt inside. I put it down and picked up Janus. No matter which way I turned him, he offered no exit.

I couldn't sustain my anger for long. I felt it ebbing, replaced by shame at having lost my temper. My behaviour had been contrary to my family's unwritten code, its standard operating procedure. Keep all such ill feelings under control. If necessary, launch a word sharp as an arrow, an insult passed off as a joke. Pair the evil eye with the silent treatment. My specialty—passive aggressive behaviour.

I saw Mar's face again, shocked at getting smacked in the chest by a cow pie. I'd never have a chance with her now, not that I ever had much of one. How could I even face her?

There was a quiet knock at the door. "Evan, can I come in?"

My first impulse was to tell Connie to go away, to leave me alone. Such a mature response, given that it was her house. Instead, I said simply, "Yes."

She swung the door open but remained in the doorway. "I've talked to Niall and Mar. I'm sorry about the twins. They're a couple of real buggers." When I didn't say anything, she went on. "I'm also sorry to tell you that it's almost milking time, and Niall needs you. I'm sure it's the last thing you want to do right now, but the cows can't wait. This is what it's like on a dairy farm. No matter what's going on, the cows have to be milked. It's seriously painful for them if they're not." I was in self-pity mode now and wanted to say, *What about my pain?* while thinking at the same time it didn't exactly compare to the discomfort of a cow's full udder. Connie finished by saying, "I've put out a towel for you to have a quick shower in the downstairs bathroom." She closed the door as quietly as she'd opened it.

What would happen if I just stayed in this room? Niall could hardly come drag me out and *force* me to feed and milk the cows. Pure, perfect disobedience might get me sent home.

But what then? What was waiting for me at home except my father's anger, my mother's disappointment and worry, my siblings' mocking words and, worse, their accusatory lives? In the end, some form of banishment.

I turned Janus around and around in my hands. I stopped and studied one face. Obeying an impulse, I slammed him on the desktop, grabbed some clean clothes, and headed downstairs.

Chapter 13

Sometimes silence is golden, other times lead. The wordless afternoon milking was fraught with the leaden kind. When I'd gone up to the mow to throw down some bales of hay, I'd found Mar still there, re-stacking. We glanced at each other briefly but said nothing. I know I was too embarrassed. I could see the stain on her chest, a brown bruise on her purple tank top.

After the milking, Niall climbed up to the mow instead of going in for supper. Though hungry, I followed. I half expected him to dismiss me, telling me to go in for supper, but he didn't. Instead, he said, "You can help Mar by bringing bales over. I'll stack them." The three of us worked silently until the job was done.

After the next morning's milking and breakfast, Niall fidgeted with the equipment, waiting for the dew to rise off the remaining hay. The home field needed to be finished, and then the far field. I'd learned it was a field Niall leased so that he'd have enough hay for the year, and that this was common for farmers. Their farms were often a patchwork of fields owned and leased to make enough income to get them through the year, often paying off last year's loans with the yield from this year's crops.

I was surprised to see Reuben and Simeon with Mar when she arrived around 10 a.m. "I'll keep them in line," she said. They looked sheepish for a moment, but not sheepish enough. "Good morning, dork," one of them offered. "Look," the other half of Reubeon said, "He's giving us the hairy eyeball!"

I turned my hairy eyeballs to Niall. "Where do you want me?"

"Back on the tractor pulling the baler."

We were done the field around noon. I pulled the baler and last wagon load, about half full, out of the field and toward the barn. Mar and her brothers had finished unloading the previous wagon. Seeing us coming, Mar pulled it out of the way.

Meanwhile, Reubeon were up to more tricks. They

were out in the pasture with the cows, but this time they weren't playing Frisbee with cow patties. No, they were bracing themselves against a cow's side, trying to push it over. The cow was having none of it and just kept walking away from them.

Above the tractor, I could hear Niall saying, "What a couple of idiots." He didn't seem particularly upset.

But Mar was. She ran over and tore into them. They laughed, one of them yelling, "Take a chill pill, sis," as they came to help unload the last wagon.

"What? What's the problem?" one of them said. "Never heard of cow tipping? We were just testing if it worked. You know we're just a couple of curious country boys." The other half added, "Result of our science experiment: it's just an urban legend cooked up by city slickers like Evelyn here."

"Try that again," Mar said, "and I'll tip the two of you into the manure pit."

Connie had made us boxed lunches so we could save time getting to the distant field. Niall ate as he drove the tractor pulling the baler and one of the wagons. Mar followed pulling two wagons; she'd have time to eat when we got there. Reubeon got to stay behind and practically have a picnic since they had plenty of time before Mar would come back with the first wagonload.

Me? I was sitting in the middle of the wagon Niall was

pulling behind the baler, eating a fair amount of dust along with my sandwich. I'm pretty sure I got my lifetime's peck of dirt in that one trip. I could only hope the bouncing was helping, not hindering my digestion of Connie's home-made bread, the butter she'd churned herself, and the roast beef that had once lived in this vicinity.

By the time we reached the field, the day was heating up much more than it had the days before. The air felt heavy. Niall looked up, concerned.

"Feels like rain," Mar said.

"Let's hope it holds off 'til we're done," Niall said.

Personally, I was hoping for a rain delay. "Would it hurt to wait?"

"It would. Once cut hay gets wet, it loses some of its nutrition and value," Niall said as he jumped on the wag-on. "Let's get moving."

Mar added, "You can't put wet hay in the barn. Like green hay, it can catch fire. Spontaneous combustion—not so good for the hay or the barn." She went to unhitch the two wagons from her tractor.

I climbed aboard the tractor, engaged the PTO, and imagined the barn on fire, the billowing smoke, barn cats trapped, the calves in their pen below. If it happened dur-ing milking, Niall would be working fast to save the cows, to release them all from their stanchions and drive them out to the pasture with the help of Old Mac. The fire might leap to the machine shed, the chicken coop, even the house—there was so much old wood on the place, so much fuel that could catch fire.

I pulled my attention back to the baling and kept my eyes on the ground, looking especially for the gopher hole that had beat me my first day. I looked up once when we'd made a circuit of the field to see Mar sitting on the tractor, enjoying her lunch. She smiled with her red cheeks full. I sat up straighter and attempted a roguish wave. At that moment, the front left wheel of the tractor hit a rock, jostling me in my seat. I had to grip the steering wheel and course correct to avoid the wagon wheels hitting the same rock. When I looked up once again, Mar was laughing while coughing, having choked on a mouthful of sandwich.

I didn't relax and look up again until Niall was finished the first load. He had me pull the wagon over to Mar, where he unhitched. After he hitched it to Mar's tractor, we picked up the next empty wagon while she headed back to the farm.

During this exchange, I noticed dark clouds in the west beginning to build off the lake. I pulled the baler and wagon over to where we'd left off and saw Niall studying the sky, feet apart and hands on hips. Was he praying the rain would hold off a bit longer, maybe blow over? Or was he daring it to fall on him and his hay?

We'd almost finished another full load when the first drops hit. An ominous darkness had swallowed the sun. Niall signalled me to stop and shut down the baler. He rushed to unhitch the wagon from the baler, then told me to get down. He jumped onto the tractor, pulled the baler out of the way, disconnected it from the PTO, and un-hitched it. Then he brought the tractor around to the wag-on, expertly backed the tractor to the hitch, and connected the two with the pin.

"Jump up," he said. "We'll try to make it home ahead of the storm."

He barrelled out of the field in high gear. From where I sat at the front edge of the wagon with my feet dangling, I could see first the field and then the road flowing back-wards below me. I bounced with the motion of the wagon and could sense the bales behind me swaying and lurching.

About halfway to the farm, the sky opened its faucet and doused us. There's no other way to describe it. I couldn't see through my glasses. I was drenched in a way I'd never been drenched before, in parts of my body it's possible I'd never reached even in the shower. And this was no cleansing shower, for the tractor's back tires began spit-ting up muddy gravel, pelting me with it. The floor of the wagon where I sat became a puddle, my bottom parked in it.

A few times, I'd run a cross-country race in the rain. Then, I'd been moving, legs and arms and heart pumping, and the moving had made it feel like a test, a trial, even an adventure or a quest to reach the finish line—where I was tired and cold, but victorious by simply having finished, no matter how far back from the winner. There, Mr. Ashby would be waiting for me and my teammates with our sweats and a blanket to wrap around ourselves.

But this, sitting on a wagon of soaked hay, me as soaked as the hay, barrelling down a nowhere gravel road by a driven, for all I knew angry-at-the-heavens dairy farmer—I was a drowning field mouse exposed to an immense, angry sky, a rat on a sinking ship at sea, no shore in sight. I thought of the gopher in its hole, the little devil that started the chain reaction that led to this moment—and the rodent that my brother was for shipping me off to this hellhole in the first place—and I cursed them both, hoping they'd both drown in this storm.

As if in response to my cursing, lightning split the sky, piercing some point of land in the distance. Moments later, thunder rolled across the landscape like a giant bowling ball. I felt like a pin it was spinning toward.

That evening, I sat at the desk in my attic room and pulled from the drawers paper, a pen, and an envelope. Rummaging, I found binders and files, notebooks and journals. I didn't bother with these.

When we'd pulled into the farmyard, we found Mar and her brothers standing within the large upper doors of the barn, looking out at the rain. They'd managed to get the wagon unloaded before the storm hit, but the load we brought would have to dry out for days. More than half the far-off field of cut hay lay soaked and losing its value. It would take days of clear, sunny weather before it would be dry enough to bale, and the forecast was for more rain next week.

Mistakes, accidents, broken machinery, goofing off, practical jokes—all of it had eaten up so much time as to make what was left too scarce to finish the job. Now Niall was the one fasting for it.

The storm had been carried by a cold front so that I was chilled through. I wanted to get changed, get warm, but that couldn't happen until the afternoon milking was done. Only then were we finished for the day.

I felt a failure. I'd failed Niall; I'd disgraced my parents; I'd hit Mar in the chest with a cow pie.

I started writing, the words spilling onto the page.

Brother dearest,
You rat! You putz! You've really dumped me in it – in shit, to be exact. My life is manure because of you. In fact, I've had manure rain down on my head. On top of that, I've done nothing but screw up. You said this would be like summer camp. Well, you lied. This is a Siberian labour camp.
I want to come home, and you're the one who needs to help me get there. I don't care what you tell Mom and Dad. Tell Mom I'm

sick, I'm at death's door, whatever it takes, but come get me, you Jerkasaurus!
Your loving but righteously angry brother,
Evan

PS Did you have to tell everyone here the nickname you've given me? Thanks a bunch! I feel like I'm walking around with "Milksop" plastered to my forehead.

I folded the letter, placed it inside the envelope, and sealed it. The glue tasted horrible, and I got a tiny paper cut on my tongue. That made me feel better, as if I'd done the right thing in writing Jeff such a scathing letter.

I went to ask Connie for a stamp, planning to say I'd written home to tell my family what an adventure my first week had been. At the top of the attic stairs, though, I was stopped by voices. The sound of Niall and Connie talking came from the parlour, their voices low. I sat to listen.

"It's not working out," Niall said.

"It's only been a week. You need to give it more time."

"But he's no Jeff. He's too slow, and barely strong enough to do the work."

"Of course, he's not Jeff. What did you expect? He'd be a carbon copy?"

"It wouldn't be so bad if he didn't screw up so often."

"And whose fault is that?"

Niall made an odd gravelly sound with his throat. "He practically cut my legs off. I don't have time to teach him the basics. Doesn't even have a goddam driver's license."

"Ni, language please. We knew going in there were some problems. He's not here just to provide some cheap labour."

"Dammit, but I'm not even getting that. Maybe if I was getting my money's worth."

"Keep your voice down. You've got to be the teacher now. Be patient. Explain things clearly. Show him."

"Good God! You know I've never been patient. And I'm pretty sure he won't take kindly to being treated like a simpleton, needing everything spelled out. We're bound to have another blow-up."

"I'll say it again. Whose fault was that?"

"What do you mean? That was the twins."

"You're the one who sent him into their clutches. He was practically a sacrificial lamb."

"He needs to toughen up, learn to take a joke."

"It was a shitty joke."

"Very funny."

"That's all beside the point. I'm serious. Give him more time."

"I'll give him another week. If it's as bad as this one, that'll be it."

He's no Jeff. Listening, I'd felt an equal measure of shame and anger. I got up, walked quietly back to my room, and slowly closed the door until the latch clicked. I'd ask Connie for a stamp tomorrow.

My backup plan took shape. I'd tried and failed. Until then, my mistakes had been due to inexperience and incompetence. Now in the coming days I'd add deliberate screw-ups, the more the merrier. If I was going to be a failure, I might as well go all in and become an epic failure. Niall would have to be a man of his word and send me home. There, I'd confess to my father my inability to locate my bootstraps and accept the consequences.

CHAPTER 14

"Far out! It's Donny Osmond!" Reuben and Simeon started singing "Puppy Love" as I approached the car, a red Toyota Corolla. They were sitting in the back with the windows open, and Mar was in the driver's seat.

I'd hoped Niall and Connie were unconcerned about the state of my soul. No such luck. After breakfast, Connie let me know my ride for church would pick me up at 9:30. I'd gone up to the attic and stared at my suit, which was hanging in the dim light at the far end from a hook screwed into a beam. Each morning, it greeted me as I opened the door to begin the day, a ghost or a hanged man.

"Groovy threads," one of the twins said. "Out of sight," said the other. They placed their hands over their hearts and started into "Puppy Love" again.

My mom had bought the suit. She said it was "powder blue," but I felt like a neon sign in it. The jacket lapels were wide, the pants flared at the bottom—a hangover from the days when everyone was drunk on bell bottoms. To give me a bit more height, Mom had bought platform shoes, two-tone blue and white. She said the style was called "spectator." Wearing them, I felt more spectacle than spectator. To finish the effect, she'd bought a pale red shirt (I insisted it was red, not pink). The shirt's large collar could fold over the collar of the jacket, or I could complement the shirt and jacket with a blood-red clip-on tie. Given that my mom was a world away that morning at church in the city, I chose to ditch the tie—a small-potatoes rebellion.

"You're my ride?" I said to Mar.

"It wasn't my idea." She stared out the front window, possibly to avoid the solar flare of my suit.

I went to the front passenger door, but the seat was occupied by a girl, maybe early teens. She glanced at me. Her look said, "Don't expect me to give up my seat for you." One of the twins opened the back door and stepped out. "Hop in."

Squished between Reubeon in the back, I could see Mar studying me in the rearview mirror. "Your big head is in the way. You should get a haircut." This morning her hair wasn't in a pony tail. It was in a bun held by clips and pins, with strands of loose hair escaping the containments. She wore gold hoop earrings. Her neck and shoulders were bisected by the straps of a blue sundress—not powder blue like my suit, more of a royal blue, deeper, with a print of small white flowers on it.

"Where are the seatbelts?" I said.

"Seatbelts? Who needs seatbelts?"

I looked closely and saw that no one was strapped in.

"We're going to be late," Mar said as she pressed on the accelerator.

She sped down the gravel road, kicking up dust. Stones pinged the underside of the car and shot out behind as the car swayed. Each bump and pothole, Reubeon elbowed me in the ribs. They were wearing identical dark grey suits with white shirts, black ties, and black Oxford shoes.

Eventually, we came to the paved highway I'd found in my wanderings the previous Monday. Mar joined a line of cars heading north toward a small town in the distance.

The church sat at the edge of town. It was a modern and plain building made of beige brick, the roof covered with light brown shingles and topped with a large metal cross at the front peak. Tall, narrow windows lined the sides, set high up. The glass was opaque, coloured with yellow and blue and red rectangles.

When Mar stepped out of the car, I was taken aback. She was wearing make-up that covered the blotchy redness of her cheeks. "You look different," I said.

"What do you mean?"

"Just different." I paused, then added, "Like a woman."

"What did you think I was? A gremlin?"

I reddened as she turned and walked toward the church with her sister. Reubeon stayed behind some moments to admire the full effect of my suit—sampling the fabric and turning up my shirt and jacket collars—before rushing ahead, pushing and shoving at each other.

I fixed my collars and dawdled, admiring Mar from behind—her sandalled feet, her calf muscles, the shape of her bottom and back beneath the dress, her bare neck—before she disappeared inside. I felt as if I finally understood the word "attraction." She was a magnet pulling me forward. Unsettled by the pull, I tried to resist it.

I climbed the stairs to the sanctuary. At the door, I was given a bulletin and left to find a seat. Reubeon had squeezed into the middle back row among a long line of teenagers, leaving no space. Smirking, they were drawing their friends' attention to my suit. I looked for Mar. She was in a middle pew near the front among a long line of children. I counted six to her left and six to her right. If these were her siblings, that was fifteen, her and Reubeon included. Maybe she was a Sunday School teacher and these were her charges. Then I remembered it was summer and unlikely Sunday School was in session. The front pew was empty—to be avoided at all costs. I looked to my right at the side pews. In the back one, about half a seat was available. The rest of the pew was taken up by a young couple with a toddler and a baby. With some luck, I might be able to turn it into a full seat. I said, "Excuse me" and began squeezing into the space. Given little choice, the woman signalled to her husband to move over.

I felt relieved to have pulled that off—the perfect seat for a quick getaway, a pull of the ejection lever, in case it was needed.

The organist started playing her before-service mood music. I looked around at the mass of humanity gathered for worship. A few hats on the women, but mostly conservative dresses in dark colours. A sea of suits, also dark—a few light greys for summer but mostly dark greys or blacks, a few daring souls with pinstripes. I couldn't see many shirts and ties from my vantage point, but if the man in the pew beside me was typical, it was likely white shirts with black ties all around. Uniforms slightly less conspicuous than the Amish, though I could see that some men, including the fellow sharing the pew, had Amish beards. On these men, of course, it would be a Dutch beard. The missing moustache, I knew, was a sign of theological *gravitas*.

My lack of facial hair—and my inability to grow anything substantial—signalled I was a theological featherweight. I grew up among people who sometimes lightheartedly called themselves the Frozen Chosen. At the time, I thought myself simply a Chilly Silly. It's possible I'm still of that denomination.

A door at the front left of the sanctuary opened. The minister strode to the pulpit, followed by eight men who filed through and sat in the front pew—the elders of the Frozen Chosen, faces set as in some group portrait by one of the Dutch masters. I checked the bulletin. I knew what that procession meant. Today was one of the four Sundays a year for communion. This was going to be one long service.

The organ stopped. The minister welcomed us to worship, repeated some of the announcements printed in the bulletin, and called us to rise for the opening hymn. The pews creaked as the congregation stood and began singing in unison, "A mighty fortress is our God, a bulwark never failing…"

I wished I could believe it. I hadn't felt it for months. I couldn't sing the words. I couldn't even open my mouth to lip sync them. It was a hymn I'd heard and learned to sing from childhood. From the moment of my baptism, which I'm sure my mother would have done while I was still in the womb if it could be arranged, the minister using the amniotic fluid to bless and protect me, my life had been cradled within the church, and not just in its worship. After all, it offered cradle-to-grave programming, beginning with Nursery for baptized tykes, then Sunday School, with its stories of Bible heroes, its pictures to colour, its verses to memorize. Boys Club vs Girls Club followed, with their male vs female gender-appropriate badges and their segregated camping trips. Later, hormone-charged teens were then thrown back together in Youth Group, which had a number of purposes, chief of which was matchmaking, unofficially church-sanctioned, of course. My mom was pinning her hopes on my finding a nice Dutch girl there, and I'm sure she wasn't the only parent with similar aspirations. (*Would Mar do?* I wondered for a moment, then startled by the idea, banished it.) The other side of the Youth-Group precious coin, the royal face that declared the coin's value, was Catechism class, designed to lead youth to profess their faith in front of the entire congregation, forever and ever, amen. Jeff, of course, had passed this test as he did all tests with honours this past spring. My programming was having trouble sticking. To me, catechism felt like a freight train barrelling down tracks through the mountains; ahead was a collapsed bridge over a ravine, possibly a landslide or avalanche, maybe just a dark tunnel. These were the programs of loving, caring indoctrination I was so far familiar with—yet to come, adult clubs and sacred duties, plus end-of-life care.

"A mighty fortress is our God" reaffirmed by the

congregation, the minister proceeded with the service of confession, beginning with a listing in correct order of the Ten Commandments. I did a mental calculation, thinking it likely I'd broken most of them this past week. I thought it possible I hadn't committed adultery, then remembered how I'd looked at Mar's body when she was walking into church. How sad. I couldn't even manage a pure thought one minute before entering this sacred dwelling. Mind you, I hadn't murdered anyone this week—and then remembered I'd badly wanted to kill Reubeon. At least I hadn't made any idols and worshipped them. Dammit, my Janus paperweight—a Roman god. Was I keeping the Sabbath holy at the moment? Given my state of mind, not a chance. But at least I hadn't stolen anything. I'd broken stuff, spilled stuff, made a mess of stuff, but not that. Then I remembered the paper and envelope I'd pilfered from the desk.

I decided to let the minister's prayer of confession and pardon cover it for me. It was all too tangled to sort out with God, whom I'd kind of ignored all week anyway. Another commandment broken, as it meant I'd had other gods keeping me busy ahead of Him.

That spring, I'd tried to ignore Him pretty thoroughly. Things at my family's church in the city were going about as well for me as they were in school. Trouble in one place fed trouble at the other, a closed loop.

As a family, we always scrambled to get to church on

time. Each week, I got ready early in hopes that my parents and siblings would be more prompt. It never happened. The result? We almost always had to sit in the front pew.

That spring, I couldn't take being front and centre anymore, filing in at the last minute feeling all those eyes upon me in my neon suit. I used the privilege of being a teenager to tell my parents I was going to sit at the back with friends. Which friends, I didn't specify. Soon it became the balcony, where the really late, the slackers, the hangers-on, the divorced, the single parents, and other assorted sinners, along with the theologically unorthodox or undecided, sat looking upon the saints.

I'd loved that balcony when I was a child. It wrapped around the sanctuary in a large U. After services, while our parents drank coffee and chatted downstairs in the fellowship hall, while others went outside for a post-service, meditative smoke, we'd fold bulletins into paper airplanes and fly them from the balcony. We didn't think of the extra work we were making for the custodians, that's how innocent and selfish we were—but I doubt that would have stopped us, given the fun of watching the planes transect the sanctuary, landing near the pulpit or on the communion table. The Holy Grail was to land a plane in the baptismal font, which might be left uncovered if there'd been a christening that morning.

I had a church friend (always different from school

friends), David, a Native boy who'd been adopted by a couple in the church. He taught me to fold a completely different kind of plane. Unlike the long and sharp ones that looked like the French Concorde, his plane was almost like a piece of origami. It was short in the body with wide wings that ended in a flap that turned up. With a heavier nose, his plane flew gracefully, performing curves and loops before landing gently.

The balcony had a black handrail held up by intricately designed metal balusters. One Sunday, David walked the entire length of the railing, balancing with his hands out, each one holding a paper airplane.

There came a time that spring when even the balcony wasn't far enough away from the pulpit. For some weeks, I'd made it part of my running routine to change after the service in the basement washroom, put my suit in the car, and run the five miles home. Now, I didn't bother to stick around. Once my family was in the front pew, I hid in the basement washroom until the service began, slipped out the back door, and started running—running and counting, counting and running as I headed south. To avoid stoplights and heavy traffic, I took a route through the residential streets of Old South London into the outer subdivisions, one of which was ours.

Remembering this now, I felt again the urge to run. I'd missed the scripture reading and much of the sermon. The minister was announcing his third and final point. That was good. He might wrap up in a half hour or so.

I turned my attention from the minister to Mar, the magnet that was keeping me in the pew. She was passing something to her siblings on the right and the left. These had to be peppermints—hard white candies, likely Queen Wilhelmina brand—or *droppies*—tough, black, salty Dutch liquorice.

When done, Mar turned her attention back to the front. Though surrounded, she seemed alone, self-contained as she looked straight ahead. I couldn't tell what she was focusing on, but it wasn't the minister. Of course, it might have been her manner of listening intently, of mulling things over. During the week, she'd been all motion and activity, muscles exerted in service to every task; here, she was pure stillness.

The sermon concluded, the congregation sang a triumphant hymn. While the minister was busy with various petitions in the congregational prayer, I prayed for deliverance—that my letter to Jeff would shorten my sentence, that my mistakes during the coming week, both accidental and willed, would be blessed, that these fearful feelings for Mar might vanish. I wished Jesus had offered a beatitude for those whose life had become a mess, something along the lines of "Blessed are life's screw-ups for they shall eventually find their lives unscrewed." Maybe as a milksop, I was covered by "Blessed are the meek," though I couldn't imagine inheriting anything on this earth.

I sensed a commotion beside me. The baby was fussing. I opened my eyes, having offered my petitions, to see the young mother cover her left shoulder with a flannel blanket. She reached beneath it. It became clear to me what she was doing—releasing one of her breasts to feed her child.

My gaze felt invasive. I turned forward and stared ahead—at the back of all those bowed heads. I listened as the baby's fussing turned to sucking and crooning as it latched to her breast. I could sense the mother swaying slightly from side to side. She whispered beneath the minister's voice, "There, there, my darling." *Why*, I thought, *hadn't she gone down to the nursery? That's where this should be happening.*

I fought the urge to leave. The young mother might take it as an insult. Then again, she might be happy to have me gone.

The baby had finished feeding on her left breast. I glanced over at the child, its mouth and cheeks covered in milk, its eyes and lips still searching. The mother adjusted the blanket after returning her left breast to her nursing bra. For a moment as she took out her right breast, before the baby latched, I caught a glimpse—the breast white and veined and swollen with milk, ending at the dark areola and the rough nipple.

At that moment, the minister said "Amen" and began the service of the Lord's Supper. All I remember of it was the charge not to partake of it in a state of sin or I'd risk eating and drinking judgement unto myself. Since I wasn't a professing member, this wasn't a problem, as I was barred from the table.

When the elders brought the bread and wine around, I passed them to the couple beside me. The baby being done, it was the mother's turn to feed.

The service over, I was the first to exit the sanctuary and head outside—then regretted I hadn't dawdled. If I'd been smart, I would have hidden in a washroom cubicle.

Instead, as the congregation flooded out the doors, I found myself washed by their wave to the perimeter, standing on a shore before a sea of strangers. I'm not sure what I feared more—that no one would talk to me or someone would strike up a conversation, interrogating me for my life story and my credentials for stepping inside their church. The first is what happened.

That spring, before my parents knew what was happening, I'd told them I didn't feel like going to a Youth Group overnight retreat. Jeff and Annalise were going, so I had to. No choice. For me, the retreat was no treat—bonding games, personal faith talk, sloppy agape Christian pop sing-along to guitars. I checked out early, finding my sleeping bag in the common room of the lodge where we were staying and cocooning myself in it.

Some hours later, the others came to bed. Their arrival

in the room unsettled me, brought me out of sleep for a moment. "There he is," someone said. "Sleepy from the Seven Dwarfs." The others laughed. "One of the foolish bridesmaids who fell asleep waiting for the bridegroom." There was little laughter, the joker having pushed it too far by saying something lame. But in Rick and Roger's words, I'd become the joke of the neighbourhood. "Let him be," someone else said. It might have been my little sister. Whoever it was, that I needed to be defended this way seemed more painful than the joke. I drifted back to sleep, feeling the laughter a needle lodged in my chest. Some days, all these years later, I feel it there still.

I watched the milling congregation and considered that my suit might be keeping people away. People chatted in groups of three or four. Outdoors, the noise and laughter contrasted the solemnity of the service. Perhaps they were opposite sides of the same coin, worship and fellowship, a coin that I seemed to have lost or misplaced, like that widow in the parable.

The largest group huddled together were the young people, Reubeon and Mar among a dozen or so clustered against the adults. Many of the guys had loosened their ties and undone one or two buttons of their shirts, a few had even removed their jackets and held them over their shoulders by the crook of a finger. Some guys and one girl were smoking, though they looked underage. The smoking seemed openly tolerated, as many of the men had also lighted up. Like the pattern of the service, like communion, the smoking too seemed part of a worship ritual.

Mar was standing beside a girl with dark hair in a pixie cut; they were talking with their heads close together. They must have shared a joke because they started laughing, and Mar linked her arm with the girl's, their shoulders touching. I had never been as jealous of an arm as I was of that girl's.

A tall fellow with dark hair that stood up like a brush moved close to Mar. He took a drag on his cigarette and offered it to her. She shook her head. Undaunted, he put his arm around her shoulder and whispered something into her ear. She stood very still. When he slid his hand down to her waist, she unlinked her arm from the girl beside her, opened her purse, and pulled something out. She must have called out to her brothers, for they turned towards her. She gently removed the hand from her waist and turned in my direction. She was holding her car keys. The look on her face was what I had imagined watching her in church—set and firm, inwardly focused. What I didn't expect was the heightened redness of her cheeks, makeup unable to mask the blotchiness.

So that she didn't catch me staring at her, I turned around and headed to the car, happy to leave behind the fellowship of the saints.

Chapter 15

The next morning, I squinted at Janus for a few minutes before planting my feet on the floor. I needed courage to be two-faced, for I was determined to activate my getaway plan. My letter to Jeff was stamped, thanks to Connie, who was oblivious to the betraying contents it contained. The envelope was sitting in the mailbox at the road, the red flag up to let the postal carrier know it was waiting to wing its way home and enact my salvation. As a back-up, today and in the coming days, I'd see what mistakes I could make to convince Niall to send me home.

I chickened out during the morning milking. It came to me to mess up the cows' feed, neglect sterilizing their teats, poorly attach the milking machine so their udders weren't drained fully, even spill some more milk, maybe gallons of the stuff. What did I care? I found the liquid offensive in the first place.

But I couldn't do it. I couldn't punish the cows just so I might get away from them, from Niall, from Mar and Reubeon and church. What had these bovines with their big beautiful brown eyes ever done to me? And those calves, just starting their cowy lives, how could I deny them their life's milk?

I thought of the young mother in church nourishing her baby from her breasts. What I was considering seemed monstrous, against Nature.

I couldn't keep a commandment to save my life, but apparently I was also lousy at perpetuating any practical, self-interested evil. What had become of my total depravity? I felt abandoned. When I needed him, where was my twin, Evil Evan? Damned moral compass. Nothing here but Even Evan. Perhaps my religious programming had stuck more than I was willing to admit. I couldn't will myself to mess up. How sad was that?

I needed to get a grip. I'd have to mess up in some other area of farm life, maybe drop some bales of hay on Niall if he walked under the trap door, possibly break some expensive machinery, say a prayer aloud at the table for more rain to fully ruin the hay left in that far field.

At the breakfast table, I watched Finn and Jane pour milk over their cereal, Cheerios this morning. They chatted about their plans for the day, while Connie and Niall sat quietly drinking their coffee. Jane was excited to help her mom bake bread after breakfast, plus she had a secret about lunch today—then spilled it. Her mom was making biscuits, the best in the world, she said. Finn was excited because the raspberries were ready and they were going to start picking some. You had to wear long sleeves, he said, because the canes were prickly. They didn't want you to pick their berries, but he'd do it because they tasted so good.

I watched Jane and Finn eat their milk-soaked cereal and decided to stick with toast. The week before, I'd tried to eat my cereal various ways, without much success since Connie didn't have a supply of powdered milk. I tried dry cornflakes—the taste of cardboard. Cornflakes with water and sugar—sweet, soggy cardboard. Cornflakes with apple juice and sugar—MacIntosh-flavoured cardboard. Corn-flakes with orange juice—wet cardboard from Florida. Cornflakes doused in tomato juice—bloody cardboard.

I sat at this family table, a family of not-quite strangers anymore, and chewed my toast while chewing over my plan. If I managed to get rescued from the farm by Jeff or kicked off it by Niall, what was there really at home for me? I'd have to carry my failure in my small suitcase and unpack it in front of my disappointed father and my worried mother, after which my father would enact his ultimatums. I was sure he was not to be moved. But would a night shift at the candy factory really be so bad, me left alone during the day to sleep?

When my dad started at Cameron Confectionaries, he gave us a tour of the factory. The smell of chocolate and sugar was overwhelming. The building was a maze of machinery—huge cauldrons in which a child might drown, stainless steel pipelines like arteries running through the plant, assembly lines with belts on which thousands of chocolate bars in perfect rows and columns marched forward, like phalanxes of Roman soldiers or an alien robot army in a sci fi earth-invasion movie. A stark contrast to all the chocolate, the glaring synthetic colours of candies swirled in vats as they got funnelled into packages, some of them hard or soft circles and squares, others beans, still others animal shapes—psychedelic ducks and bears and worms.

Maybe finding my own job, moving out, and fending for myself would be the kick in the backside I needed. Surely I had a bit of survival instinct somewhere inside me. But where?

I felt my resolve ebbing. This was my way, especially the past few months. Determination quickly defeated by second-guessing and over-thinking. Like the Saturday storm, the lightning and thunder and rain within me seemed to move on, leaving a few broken branches strewn about, ditches running high and fast, then empty once again.

Didn't I have a right to my own life? I could march home—or run or take the long way home, in the immortal words of Rick and Roger—and stand up to my father, give him hell. Hadn't he done that by leaving his parents in Holland, sailing across the ocean from that tiny nation to this vast country, more than half a continent really, settling into the life he'd made himself?

Settled was not the word, though, for my father, when I thought about the job changes, the moves from one rental house to another, his pursuit of the American dream in Canada. Yes, he'd actually wanted to go to the US but had to settle for the other America. Regardless, it all made him seem a giant of a man to me, someone who'd strode across an ocean at my age.

Maybe he was actually waiting for me to stand up to him, to show some backbone proving I wasn't the milksop I seemed to be.

I mentioned at the beginning of this tale those big, bigger, and biggest sticks he wielded over me as he shipped me off to the farm. What I didn't say is that he'd offered a carrot too. If I proved my worth on the farm, and if I couldn't or didn't want to return to school, he'd take me under his wing, make me a junior salesman at Cameron Confectioneries. I saw myself in the role, wearing my blue suit, red tie, and spectator shoes, visiting corner stores and groceries, spinning out my sales spiel, laying it on thick to persuade owners and managers to stock Cameron's candies and chocolate bars. I'd be pushing indulgences, selling sugary sweet salvation. Then again, maybe they sold themselves. My dad didn't realize it, but to me the carrot he'd put on my plate tasted somewhat mushy and rotten. Maybe the night shift was more appetizing.

Jane's laughter interrupted my ruminations. "You look like a cow."

I stopped chewing. "I do?"

"Yeah, the way you were chewing."

I realized then I'd had the same bite in my mouth for a few minutes, reduced to mush. I swallowed, took a big bite, and started chewing fast and loud. With my mouth full, I said, "Better?"

She smiled. "Much better."

I swallowed, then shoved the rest of the slice in my mouth.

Finn said, "Now you look like a baked potato." I paused in my chewing. "Your face is round now and it's all brown from the sun."

"And you have two eyes," Jane added. "Potato eyes."

Finn said, "Before, you looked like a peeled potato."

I crossed my eyes at them.

The baling of the far field had to wait until the end of the week. Reuben and Simeon either weren't available or Niall had decided they weren't needed, for Friday midmorning Mar showed up alone.

Niall judged there were about three loads in the field. We'd get it all baled, then bring it back and unload it. Niall would work the elevator while Mar and I stacked the bales in the mow.

It took an hour to first unload the wagon that had sat in the yard since the previous Saturday's storm. It should have taken less time, but Niall first came into the mow and explained to me how to build the mow properly in rows and columns. He sent the bales up slowly so I'd get the hang of it and Mar would have time to direct me, as needed. I can't lie. His patience with me was unnerving.

When we were done, Mar hitched a wagon to her tractor and Niall coached me in connecting to a second wagon, the third one still out in the field with the baler. "Slow and steady," he said. "You'll get the hang of it soon. Before you know it, you'll be a pro like Mar."

I assumed he'd drive the tractor out to the far field, but he climbed onto the wagon and, sitting on the front edge, gave me the signal to head out. I drove in middle gear, that being the highest speed that felt comfortable. If he was impatient, he didn't show it. But I felt bad, knowing he and Mar could easily barrel down the road. I wondered if she was itching to pass me. I wouldn't put it past her to try.

At the field, Niall unhitched the wagon from the tractor and connected me to the baler we'd left there. He guided me through backing the baler to the wagon, teaching me how to turn the steering wheel to avoid jackknifing the baler, to correct the direction when it was moving out of line.

Before we started baling, he checked the hay. "It's dry, alright, but there's little freshness left in it. Nothing we can do about it now."

By then, Mar had left the tractor and wagon at the edge of the field and walked over. She climbed aboard the wagon as Niall did. "Many hands make light work," she said. "It doesn't feel right sitting on my ass while you do all the heavy lifting."

Niall said, "There'll be plenty to go around later, but suit yourself."

On the way to the field, I'd concocted a plan to jerk the baler into motion roughly, throwing Niall off-balance on the wagon, but it was my plan that got thrown off-balance by his patience with me.

I started looking for gopher holes—not to avoid them but to aim for them, to see the wagon's front wheel dive into them and the load of bales leap up and fall off. As I came upon them, though, at first I thought, *well, the load's not big enough yet, and I need a really big screw-up now, since it's been an epic fail at screwing up all week.* The load grew and grew as Niall and Mar took turns grabbing the bales coming out the chute. Ahead I saw a monster hole. I tried to bring to mind Niall's anger and impatience the previous week, my confused feelings for Mar, and her brothers' treatment of me. What I was about to do seemed suddenly so juvenile. At the last second I navigated the wheels wide of the hole. It disappeared beneath the wagon.

Between them, Niall and Mar pulled the full wagons back to the barn. "You've had some practice pulling an empty wagon down the road," Niall said to me, "but a full load carries a lot of weight. We'll give you a chance another time. Climb aboard for the ride home."

I said nothing about my fear of heights and scrambled to the top of the load. I considered lying flat on my stomach with my arms and legs spread for stability, but thought Mar would find this hilarious. I imagined her sharing this picture of me with her brothers or the other young people in their huddle at church, looking over her shoulder and laughing at me waiting by her car.

Instead, I sat cross-legged with my hands bracing me in what I'd calculated to be the middle of the load. I'd counted the number of bales across and front to back. It was past noon by then and hot. My stomach was empty, and I felt myself baking atop the sun-soaked, itchy hay, relieved only slightly by a warm breeze tainted by tractor exhaust, as Niall barrelled down the gravel road. When my fear lulled, I looked around at the vast landscape and felt for just that moment above my ordinary life. I turned my head back to check on Mar. She smiled her inscrutable smile and waved up at me, then snapped an imaginary whip in my direction.

I looked forward and down, fear flooding back in.

After lunch, we unloaded the wagons. Niall tossed the hay onto the elevator once again, while Mar and I stacked the bales in the mow.

It was the hottest part of the day, and the mow was stifling. A big lunch had filled the hole inside but left me bloated. Within minutes I was sweating, my T-shirt soaked, sticking to my back. Sweat ran into my eyes, stinging, and dripped onto the inside of my glasses. Breathing hard, I struggled to keep pace with Mar, who was working steadily. I didn't want her doing more than her fair share of the work, one bale for her then one bale for me, but there were times when she outpaced me, grabbing two in the time it took me to get one stacked. I'm sure she was unimpressed.

The bales stopped coming, the elevator shut down. Mar had outpaced me by twelve bales. One wagon done, two to go.

I parked my bottom on a bale and hung my head. I tried to breathe normally. My arms were covered in flakes of hay and had a new set of scratches, stinging with sweat. Mar came to me, pulled a bandana out of her back pocket, and began folding it. "Here," she said, holding it out. "I can't stand watching you wiping the sweat out of your eyes all the time. You're slowing us down."

I looked up at her outstretched hand. Her arms were also scratched. They were glistening with sweat, her shirt was soaked. "Thanks, I think." I took the bandana from her and shook it open, then removed my glasses and wiped my face.

"No," she said, taking it from me. "It's for around your forehead." I put my glasses back on and watched her refold the bandana. She passed it back. "Tie it behind your head." I fumbled to do it. "Never mind." She took it and motioned for me to turn sideways on the bale. She kneeled on it and tied the bandana snuggly around my forehead. I felt the heat from her body, sensed her hands so close to touching me. Done, she sat on a bale nearby.

"Thanks," I said. "Feels good." I looked at her bandana belt, a rainbow of colours. She had another around her neck and one tied as a kerchief over her head. "So what's with the bandanas?"

She played with the one at her neck. "Isn't it obvious? They're practical as hell for farm work, especially in heat like this."

"But as a belt?" I pointed at her waist. "That doesn't seem especially practical. I mean, what if you have to go to the bathroom really bad. That knot must be a pain. Wouldn't a big leather belt with one of those giant cowboy buckles be more practical? More your style?"

She snorted. "What do you know about style? I've seen your style." After a moment, she added, "I just like a little bit of colour."

The elevator started up again, and after a few moments bales started tumbling into the mow. We got back to work, trying to keep out of each other's way. Occasionally, I failed. I'd offer a "Sorry" as I moved aside.

When the second load was finished, there was another pause. We sat again, drinking water Connie and Niall had insisted we bring into the mow.

The water felt as if it was filling my whole chest cavity and abdomen, though I knew it was simply filling my stomach. It was a curious feeling I couldn't make sense of, but so satisfying.

After a few moments, I said, "You've got a really big family. Were those all your brothers and sisters sitting with you in church, or are you the church's designated babysitter?"

She looked flushed, more than normal. I couldn't tell if it was simply the heat. "Lame. Yeah, they're my brothers and sisters. What of it?" After a moment, she added, "Guess my mom hasn't been able to say 'no' to my dad. He wants what he wants."

"I didn't see them."

She took another drink of water. "My dad's an elder. He was at the front. My mom was playing the organ."

Pillars of the church. "They must be busy people. Bet you have to mind your brothers and sisters a lot. Are you the oldest?"

She took another sip. "What's with the third degree?

Yes, I'm the oldest. And yes, when I'm home from school, I do have to help out—except when I'm here, working for Niall." She paused. "That's what the oldest girl has to do, doesn't she?" She spun the empty glass between her hands, back and forth, looking into it.

"School?"

She looked at me. "Yeah, school. I just finished my first year at Western. I'm in the nursing program."

"You're hoping to be a nurse?"

"Duh, that's usually what happens when you take the nursing program."

"Sounds rewarding. Important."

"I'll let you know."

I hesitated. "Noble even."

"Noble?" She laughed. "You're a strange one, aren't you?"

More than you know, I thought. *More than I know.* After some moments of awkward silence, I said, "So what is it?"

"What's what?"

"Your name. Mar. It must be short for something. Martha?"

She poured another glass of water and ignored me.

"Mary? Marilyn? Marietta?"

She turned to me, the red deepening on her cheeks. Her green eyes sharpened and stared me down. "I told you before 'don't ask.'"

"Just curious." I'd been moved by the Spirit. I felt that

magnetic attraction pulling me closer. "Marcy? Marni? Margaret?"

"So this is how city kids win friends and influence people?"

"Marcella? Marisol? Marlie?"

"Listen, Evelyn, bite your tongue or be prepared to get a bloody lip."

I believed she'd do it. I deserved to be called Evelyn, but I wasn't going to give her the last word, especially when I seemed to have struck a nerve. "Margarine?"

"Sad one, Milksop." Strangely, my nickname on her lips sounded like a term of endearment. She added, "You don't give up, do you?"

I thought a moment. "Actually, I do—a lot of the time." I waited to see if she would offer up her full name. I'm not sure why I wanted it. She didn't budge. At last, I said, "I've got it. It's Marionette, isn't it?"

I'd meant it as a lame joke, but her face clouded. "I'm nobody's puppet."

The elevator started up one last time, and the bales began raining down through the hay door.

When we were finished, we emerged from the dimness of the mow. The sunlight was blinding. As my eyes adjusted, I heard laughter. It was Finn and Jane, playing nearby in the yard. Pointing at me, Jane said, "Now you look like a mushroom."

I looked at Mar for an explanation. "It's your hair. The

bandana's pushing it up into a mushroom cap. That, and you're covered in dust." I pulled the bandana off my head and held it out to her. "Keep it," she said and turned towards her car. Partway there, she waved her hand in the air. "Catch you on the flip side, Sunshine."

Sunshine? I'd been a little storm cloud for months.

Later that evening, I sat at the desk with another piece of paper in the cone of light. *Dear Mr. Ashby,* I wrote. *There's this girl, I'm afraid.* I couldn't keep my feelings inside. He was always a good listener.

Chapter 16

I sat at the top of the attic steps and strained to overhear a conversation that would commute my sentence. It was Saturday night, Niall's deadline for deciding whether to give me the boot. An hour passed. Nothing. Eventually, Niall and Connie climbed the stairs to their bedroom. I sat in the silence for some time before retreating to my room.

There, I turned on the light, closed the door, and looked around at what was left of my life. A jumble of clothes in an open suitcase, an unmade bed, an accusing paperweight, a calculator that figured out very little for me, an untouched fitness diary, running clothes smooth and flat in the chair, shelves filled with someone else's books. I flipped the switch and undressed in the dark.

The next day I went to my second church service. Again, I studied Mar driving, watched her walk into church with her sister. I went up the steps, sore from another ride filled with Reubeon ribbing, and hung about the foyer. After a brief struggle over entering the sanctuary, over having to sit there listening and not singing and watching Mar for an hour, I retreated to a cubicle in the basement washroom until the service started. In the stall, I found no helpful graffiti. When I heard the congregation begin singing the opening hymn, I went to sit on the front steps, looking at my spectator shoes while music and singing and the minister's voice seeped out the front doors, kept open for air flow, as had the rectangular windows, propped up with hymn books and Bibles.

During the sermon, rain began to fall lightly out of a dull, overcast sky. I got up and stood within the doorway, looking out upon the landscape. The Old Testament reading had been Psalm 19. I wished I could believe the landscape before me, the blue sky hidden by clouds and the earth overspread with fields and woods, was speaking with that voice, but it seemed more silence than sound, and what sound there was—the wind, the buzzing of flies, the rain, the odd car passing—didn't offer something sensible.

I retreated to the basement until the service was over, shut up in an empty Sunday School room.

There, I prayed again for some decisive outcome, one that would prove to my dad his plan had been totally misguided—and that he needed to repent of his harsh treatment of me, his second-born son. He'd have to admit it was physically impossible to pick yourself up by your bootstraps—Newton's laws proved that decisively.

That evening, I waited for Niall and Connie to take me aside after supper, once Finn and Jane were in bed, and tell me it wasn't working out, I could go pack my bag because my parents would be picking me up in fifteen minutes or so. Niall would give me an envelope with my meagre earnings, which I'd tell him to keep because I'd been such a screw-up. Connie would send me on my way with a loaf of homemade bread, a jar of her strawberry jam, and a quart of whole milk. No such luck.

Old Mac was barking at me from the tree limb outside my window. I thought, *How'd you manage the climb, old buddy?* I opened an eye. Predawn light offered a dim white glow at the window. I checked my alarm clock. 4:45. I put the pillow over my head to steal back the half hour of sleep I was entitled to.

I tried to remember what day it was. Yes, the Monday of my third week.

Niall's voice was added now to Mac's barking. "Get up,

Evan! The cows are loose."

Had I dreamed his voice? No. He opened my door.

"Come on. Get up!"

Niall hadn't come in my room before. This was serious. Once I was vertical, he headed downstairs. As I pulled on my pants, I heard the screen door slam behind him. Then his voice came, alternately yelling "Mac. Come on, Mac. Get them home," and "Coboss, coboss, coboss." Strangely, he too sounded as if he was in the tree outside my window. I looked out into a fog. Below, I could make out Niall's dim shape floating down the tunnel of the laneway.

I followed at a run down the stairs, pausing only to slip on my sneakers. The laneway trees guided me to the road, where I hesitated, listening. I could hear Niall and Mac in the field across the way, along with the lumbering movements of the cows. Water droplets covered my glasses and clung to me. Hearing no vehicles, I hurried across the road and through the ditch. My feet were now soaked as I entered the wheat field. Within the fog, the large, dim shapes of cows appeared, every sound amplified and brought close. Legless in the mist, they looked like barges jammed tight on an eerie canal, possibly the Styx.

It came to me. Last evening I must not have properly latched the gate to the pasture after filling the water trough for the cows. Would Niall figure it out? Might this be the mistake that got me sent home?

I skirted the cows, calling out to Niall. From somewhere to my right his voice replied, "Get around behind them. We'll herd them to the laneway."

Get behind them? How? I thought. I couldn't tell where behind them was. They were milling about, eating the wheat and trampling it down. I feared getting trampled into the crop circle they were creating and briefly imagined the headline that would result. MILKSOP SPILLS GUTS IN WHEAT FIELD.

"I don't know which way to go," I said.

"Follow my voice. Keep walking toward the sound."

As he called to me, I trampled a path of my own in the wheat as I skirted the masses in the fog. Niall emerged, looking as soaked as I was, Old Mac beside him, looking up for direction. "Walk slowly toward them," Niall said. "You may have to slap some of them on the rump to get them moving."

"Won't they kick?"

"Not often and not behind. They're more likely to get you at the front with a head butt. So be careful if they turn on you. It could mean they're a mite bit annoyed." Niall started up with his "Coboss" call again. I joined him, the word sounding foreign in my mouth. Mac ran off, barking from one side and then from the other as he herded strays.

Either the cows had gotten the idea or they realized it was almost milking time, for they started flowing out of the field and across the road to the laneway. "Run ahead,"

Niall said. "Don't startle them, but get the barn door open, the one into the yard."

Run ahead? When I could barely see my foot touching the ground in front of me? When my glasses seemed to have melded with the fog?

I made for the laneway at a trot, holding one hand out in front of me. Keeping the lumbering masses of the cows to my right, I used the laneway trees as guideposts to find the barn. I got to the door just as the lead cows arrived. It was heavy and hadn't been opened for a while. Grass was growing up into it. I unlatched it and pulled, my feet slipping. It didn't budge. The cows began crowding me at the door. One nuzzled my arm. The wet tail of another swatted me on the back of my head. If I didn't get the door open, I might get pinned against it, squashed into an Evan pancake. And if I wasn't careful when I got the door open, I might just get that trampling I feared.

Maybe it was that fear, a rush of adrenaline, but I gave the door a yank that released it from the grass and dirt. I travelled with the door as I pulled it wide. It reached its full width with a bang, and a wheel popped out of its runner at the top.

Once all the cows were through, Niall began pulling the door to close it, but it resisted. He saw that the wheel had come out. "Give me a hand lifting it back in." After the door was secured, he said, "I'll start milking in a minute. First, I need to do a quick check they're all here, then look at the fence to see how they got out. There might be a break to repair. Just give them some hay this morning. They've had their fill of grain already."

I went up to the loft, listening to the animals grunting and mooing below, the calves beginning to bawl for their milk. The new hay smelled sweet, but my feelings were bitter as I threw down some of the older bales, flakes of hay clinging to my clothes and skin. I needed to prepare myself for Niall's tongue lashing, which I'd endure if it meant going home. Then again, if I gave him back what he dished out to me, that might be the tipping point. Bosses, like parents and teachers, didn't appreciate back talk.

I was spreading out the hay when he returned. He was smiling. "You forgot to latch the gate last night, didn't you?"

I was confused. Where was his anger? Was he smiling because he now had all the ammunition he needed to get rid of me? "I thought I did," I said, "but to be honest, I can't remember. I don't suppose cows can figure out how to unlatch a gate?"

"Not unless they grow hands." I kept spreading hay while he retrieved the milking machines from the milk house. Maybe he'd hit me with it when he came back. "Simple mistake," he said as he came in with the machines and brought one over to me. "No harm done, except to that field. After milking, we'll have to go to Van Dijck's farm and explain what happened. He ain't going to be happy."

"Van Dijck?"

He went to milk his first cow. "Yeah, Jacob Van Dijck. That's his wheat field got trampled." He kneeled, sanitized the teats of the first cow, and attached the machine. He stood and looked at me. "Mar's father."

By the time we pulled into the Van Dijck Farms laneway, the fog had lifted and the world was once again its plain self. I surveyed the face of that large house I'd passed my first day—one central double door with two pillars framing it, one large bay window on either side of the door, the second floor with eight identical windows evenly spaced. All very orderly and balanced, on a large scale.

Niall drove into the yard, put his pickup in neutral, and engaged the parking brake. He left it running as we got out. Ahead, a man was driving that New Holland tractor toward us. On the front, pierced on a fork fit for a giant, was the largest bale of hay I'd ever seen—a round bale. As it got closer, I recognized the driver as one of the elders from church. Jacob, Mar's dad—and the father of all those other children, including the Reubeon twins.

When he saw us walking over, he throttled down the tractor but didn't get down. "You've come to talk about my offer?" he said.

"Afraid not. There's another matter we've got to discuss."

"Give me one minute. I'll get this in the barn first. You

know the ladies don't like to be kept waiting." He throttled up and headed into a long rectangular building. *That's a barn?* I thought. It looked nothing like Niall's. It was much larger, with red siding, a large door through which the tractor could fit easily, and a grey tin roof.

I wanted to ask "What offer?" but felt it was business that was none of my business. Until Jacob returned, I stood looking about. A hip-roof barn stood near the house, freshly painted red with white trim. Several other buildings were equally large. I could see through the door of one stacks and stacks of round bales. The building beside it contained more tractors, even larger than the New Holland, plus enormous implements—the Vermeer machine I'd already seen, which I understood now made those round bales, along with tilling and seeding equipment, a mower larger than Niall's and of a different design, along with a rather fancy red rake with a series of yellow, elaborate wheels looking like an ancient civilization's images of the sun. But what dominated the shed was an enormous green combine. It had a yellow, stylized deer on it, and was pristine, as if it had just been through a car wash.

Jacob parked the tractor outside the barn, left it running, and walked over. "So, Niall, what is this business?"

Until then, Jacob hadn't looked at me. He did when Niall introduced me and explained what had happened in the wheat field. I felt pinned by his gaze. "Sorry about the damage."

"So you're the city kid." He turned to Niall. "Well, let's go have a look."

Niall drove back and parked his truck in his yard, and we walked to where Jacob had parked at the side of the road. Like the combine, his truck—a black, late-model Dodge Ram—was clean, though the outing to the field had stirred up some dust on the bottom panels of the doors and truck bed.

He walked into the field a small distance to study the damage, the large extent of it clear now. I stood at the edge while Niall followed. Jacob kneeled, studied the ground, and picked up some stalks of trampled grain. He stood and held them.

"Well?" Niall said.

"That's deep," Jacob replied.

"What's deep? The damage?"

"No," Jacob said, smiling at Niall. "A well—it's deep, a very deep hole."

"What would you need as fair compensation?"

"This is not too much," Jacob said, sweeping his arm in a gesture that took in the trampled area. "A small area in a large field, and I have another large field. Let's say we forget this if you tell me you are considering my offer."

Niall leaned over and swept up a stalk of wheat. "You know I've already done that."

Jacob looked at me but spoke again to Niall. "So maybe you want the city kid here to pay from his wages, to learn a lesson about the business of farming?"

"Just give me the number," Niall replied.

"It's not necessary, but suit yourself. I will do the calculation and let you know."

Niall held out his hand and Jacob took it.

Niall changed the milking routine that afternoon. I'd gotten used to it, but he decided the cows needed silage, and it would be my job to give it to them.

"Silage?" I'd said. "What's that?"

"There's different kinds of silage, but this silage is corn that's been harvested green and put in the silo." It was all the explanation I would get. "Take that wheelbarrow and place it under that chute. You'll need the fork to give it to the cows." When I had the wheelbarrow in place, he showed me the switch for turning on the blower that sent the silage into the chute. I was about to ask him how much silage each cow got, but he'd already turned to go back to the milking. It would have to wait until the wheelbarrow was full.

I hit the switch, and a noise like the sound of a mighty wind began. Silage started raining down on the wheelbarrow, but mostly on me. I'd pushed the wheelbarrow in too far, misjudging where the silage would land. To get the barrow into the right position, I leaned into the stream to grab the handles but was knocked to the ground by a shower of moist, brown bits and chunks of corn stalks and leaves and ears all chopped up.

I struggled up and grabbed the handles. When I pulled them, they proved too slippery. I lost my grip and my balance, landing on my ass. I was in danger of being buried under the silage as the pile atop me grew.

The stream stopped as the machine's cyclone sound wound down. "Thought you were Reformed, not Baptist," Niall said, standing by the off switch.

"What do you mean?" I said, pushing the pile off me.

He came over and held out his hand. "Well, most folks are happy with just a few sprinkles when they get baptized, but you went in for the full dunking."

I grabbed his hand. "Thought I wasn't gonna come up for a second." I started brushing the silage out of my hair and off my clothes. I removed the bandana Mar had given me and shook it out.

"You smell like a brewery." I put my shirt to my nose, tested my armpit, and smelled the bandana. Fermented corn was invading my backside and sliding into my crotch, making my groin swampy, but a shower would have to wait until milking was done.

When we'd finished, Niall said, "Every day now, I want you to check the gates before coming in for the night. Make sure. We wouldn't want Jacob losing any more of his wheat. I don't need his brand of grief."

I marched off to do as I was told.

After showering, I asked Connie whether there'd been any mail for me.

"Not today," she said. "You're expecting some?"

"Not especially," I said, forking some green beans on my plate.

She paused. "Homesick?"

"Something like that."

Niall glanced up at me a moment as he cut his meat. I chewed my beans meditatively.

Jane laughed and said, "Evan, you're chewing like a cow again."

"Maybe I am a cow," I replied, "in disguise." I mooed.

Chapter 17

Each day that week was the same. I checked if there was a letter for me. Connie would apologize that no, there wasn't. Uncle Albert's definition of insanity—I was living proof of it. Perhaps I was also insane expecting Jeff would bother writing back at all, let alone come and fetch me home.

Friday. The mail truck had come and gone. Nearing the end of the third week, whatever hope I had of my sentence being commuted was stillborn. The afternoon work Niall had planned for us was interrupted by what seemed to me a crisis, what to him I assumed was an ordinary event.

One of his cows was calving. To be precise, one of his dry cows was giving birth to her calf, after which her milk would come in and she would join the wet cows in the milking parlour, while her calf would go into the calf pen with the other youngsters. A female calf, a heifer, would grow up to be bred and join the milking cows. A bull calf would likely grow only old enough to be slaughtered for meat. In the bovine world, it was definitely better to be born a heifer.

It was a sign of how little I knew that I simply thought cows were nonstop milk-producing machines—the production units that led to jugs and cartons of milk sitting in grocery store refrigerators, to the powdered milk my mom reconstituted with water from the tap. I'd learned about mammals in biology, so I had no excuse. I knew what it was to be mammalian, but I would only come to understand from this cow giving birth what it took—and what it cost—to get the milk flowing. I'd sat beside the nursing mother in church, and it hadn't clicked. I'd endured my mother's stories about the pain she'd endured nursing me, and—foolish me—I'd never connected the dots.

Suzie was the cow's name. Soon into her labour, Niall could tell something was wrong. He called in the vet.

A tall, grey-haired man wearing blue coveralls and green boots, the vet entered the pen where Niall held Suzie by a halter. The vet examined her vital signs, then used a stethoscope to check the calf. "There's no heartbeat," he said. Niall continued to hold the halter he'd put on Suzie and to rub her neck, making soothing noises and calling her a good girl. The vet dropped his stethoscope in his bag, pushed the short sleeve of his coverall up, and washed his right arm with a strong-smelling liquid. He held Suzie's tail out of the way with his left hand and slid his right hand into her. After some moments, he said, "The calf's in breech position."

Niall looked grim but continued to rub Suzie's neck. "Dead for sure?"

The vet pushed his arm in up to the shoulder. "Afraid so." After some time, he said, "I can't get it turned." He pulled his arm out. It was covered in slimy liquid—amniotic fluid. He grabbed a towel, wiped his arm off, and looked around. "Can you bring her out and tie her to that post? I need to get some gear from my truck."

Until then, I'd been standing outside the pen. Niall asked me to retrieve a lead rope from a hook on the wall and to open the gate. By the time he'd brought Suzie out and tied her to the post, the vet was back with a rope and pulley.

I stood off to the side, watching and waiting for any instructions. The vet tied the rope to a post behind Suzie, then brought the loose end running through the large pulley forward and laid it near her rear hoofs. The pulley had a large chain with a hook attached to its end.

The vet sanitized his arm again, then slid it in up to the elbow. I could tell from the flexing of his muscles and the bracing of his feet, he was pulling. Niall held Suzie's halter and braced his feet in the opposite direction even though she was tied securely to the post. Suzie was looking backwards, her eyes wide, the whites bright and shining.

The vet was sweating. I considered asking if he needed help, but the words wouldn't come. Perhaps I sensed in that moment there were no words to offer.

Slowly, the vet's arm emerged. In his hand, he gripped two small hoofs. When he had them out far enough, he called to me. "Pass me up the chain."

I hurried over and lifted it to him. With his free hand, he looped the chain a couple of times around the calf's legs, just above the hooves, and latched the hook securely into one of the links. "Now pass me up the loose end of the rope." Once he'd gripped it in his left hand, he pulled on it until there was no slack left. Only then did he release the calf's hooves.

He held the rope with both hands. I thought he might yank or pull hard, but he didn't. He kept up the pressure, slow and steady, almost gentle. The calf began inching out. When the hind legs were out, he said. "Come hold the rope for me."

I came over and said, "I'm not very strong."

"That's okay. You don't need to pull. Just lean back."

I gripped the rope with both hands, wrapped a loop around each, and braced my feet the way I'd seen Niall and the vet do it. The vet went forward. "It's coming now. I'm just going to help it along." I couldn't see what he was doing, only the pulley twisting and turning. "Okay, stop pulling."

Before I could register what he'd said and relax my grip, I fell backwards as the calf came sliding out onto the barn floor. When I sat up, the dead calf was lying at my feet.

The vet examined Suzie then, making sure the after-birth had come out, ensuring that she hadn't been injured during the delivery, that there was no internal bleeding, her vital signs good. He talked to Niall as he performed the exam. Eventually, he said, "Sorry about the calf, Niall. A good-looking heifer too. Suzie's going to be okay."

While the vet worked on Suzie, I stared at the calf. Its fur was soaked, its hind legs stretched out, its front legs curled up, its neck and head bent unnaturally up and back. I stared at its black and white markings, wondering how likely any other cow had ever had markings identical to these. Were they as unique as people's fingerprints?

It was dead and slimy and beautiful. The diagrams in the biology textbooks I'd studied were colourful, clean and flat with lines and labels and scientific terms making sense of all the systems in the body, the human body, a mammal body like all the mammal bodies here in the barn, this one stillborn.

I realized then what a difficult business it was to be a female mammal, what a messy business it was to be born, how filled with risk. I'd been born this way myself, and the imprint of the event was undoubtedly somewhere in my brain, but certainly not as a memory. I had my mother's stories surrounding my birth, as well as those about Jeff and Annalise, stories I'd tried to ignore or dismiss or push aside as embarrassing or too intimately about my mother for me to want to know. Here, looking at the calf, I couldn't escape my beginning, couldn't pretend I was some foundling.

The vet finished examining Suzie and began packing up his gear, his instruments and the gear and tackle. Niall untied Suzie and removed the halter. She turned to her calf. She began licking with her enormous tongue, nuzzling and licking, licking and nuzzling. I couldn't bear it. I turned away from it all—the vet, Niall, Suzie and her calf, myself—holding back tears, and looked for something to do, anything to busy myself, to not see what I'd seen.

Niall was more quiet than usual during the afternoon milking. He'd moved the dead calf to a corner of the barn and had busied himself with Suzie, making sure her milk was flowing, her udder healthy, and that she got some rest.

I'd given the cows their grain and was in the middle of getting them hay. "Move over, Gertie." Niall had milked two cows and was on the third. He'd warned me that

Gertie could be troublesome, sometimes kicking at the cylinders on her teats or moving around so much she knocked the can over. "Move over," he said again, louder, and braced himself against her with his shoulder and shoved. She leaned back against him, squishing him against the next cow over, Alice.

He squeezed out of the vice she'd put him in, yelling, "You goddam stubborn cow."

For the second time that day, I watched, mesmerized and helpless. Niall grabbed a feed shovel and whacked Gertie with it on her flank, yelling, "Get over!" When she didn't budge, he hit her again. She mooed and looked at him over her shoulder but didn't move. She went back to eating her hay.

Niall threw down the shovel with a clatter and grabbed the pitchfork leaning against the wall where I'd left it. I stood paralyzed as he thrust the pitchfork at her flank and yelled, "Get the hell over, you bitch!" She let out a high-pitched moan but moved, at last. Niall quickly threw down the pitchfork, sanitized Gertie's teats, and attached the machine.

When he stood up, his face was sweaty, his chest and abdomen and armpits damp. He caught me staring. Our eyes locked a moment. My gaze felt invasive, but before I turned away embarrassed, afraid my face disclosed my horror and judgement, I saw on his face frustration and anger and shame I'd rarely seen in a grown-up man's.

"Goddam cows," he said, and strode from the barn. As he left, I could see the back of his shirt soaked with sweat as well.

For some moments, I stood still, listening to the swish-swish suction of the milking machine and the grinding of the cows chewing. I felt at a loss. I thought about the look I'd seen on Niall's face, the second face he'd shown me, and strangely my father's face came to me. I'd never seen my father that angry, lose it that badly, but there was something familiar in it. From below the frustration and shame, what had surfaced was sorrow, possibly a deep, abiding sorrow. That's the only word that came to me.

Perhaps I was only imagining this, linking Niall and my father this way, excusing their hardness, a toughness I'd tried to emulate. I walked over to Gertie.

All I could do was continue with my chores, with the necessary actions of my hands, which felt alien, detached from the rest of my body. Given what had happened, and Gertie's nature, I was reluctant to do so. She had four pinpricks of blood where Niall had pierced her, but the damage didn't look serious. Such tough hide. I thought again of female mammals, of mothers and daughters and what they endured for the sake of their lives, of life.

At that moment, the door to the milk house opened. *Thank goodness,* I thought. *He's come back.*

It was Connie, dressed in overalls. She came over, glanced at me a moment, then studied the four dots of blood. "I'm going to finish this milking for Ni." She checked the machine to see if Gertie had given all her milk. It was still flowing, so Connie retrieved from the milk house a cloth and antiseptic solution. I watched as she cleaned the wound.

We got back to work, saying little beyond the occasional instruction. At the end, she walked over to the dead calf. "Such a loss," she said. "Years of lost potential." The thought came to me that this was a hell of a way to make a living.

When we went in for supper, Niall was gone, where, I have no idea. It was a quiet affair all around, not even an update from Finn and Jane on how big the chickens were getting and what comical behaviour the birds were up to. After checking to make sure the gates were all latched, I went up to my room and sat at the desk fiddling with my calculator, turning Janus around and around, dwelling on all the pain, on this painful day.

I took out a sheet of paper. *Dear Mr. Ashby,* I wrote. *Something happened today...* If I could, I had to explain it to someone. He, of all people, would understand.

Before climbing into bed, I heard Niall's truck return. Shortly after, a tractor engine started up.

In the morning, the dead calf was gone.

CHAPTER 18

I glanced up from my bowl and looked sideways at Jacob Van Dijck as he took a spoonful of pea soup into his mouth, chewed momentarily, then plucked out a bit of ham gristle and placed it at the edge of his plate. As he swallowed, he looked down the table at his wife. He'd removed his suit jacket but still wore his tie. To protect it, he'd tucked a large linen napkin into his collar at the neck. He spooned up another bite. Without looking up, he said, "Rebecca, T."

A tiny voice piped up, "Total depravity!"

Jacob was sitting at the head of the longest dining room table I'd ever seen, more like a table you'd find in a boardroom. His wife, the church organist, sat at the foot, her face in shadow because it was backlit by sunlight from the windows behind her. From the ceiling between them hung two chandeliers. On the floor lay thick, beige wall-to-wall carpet. Their fifteen children were arranged eight on one side, seven on the other, with me on the odd side stuck between Reuben and Simeon. Jacob was clearly a man who'd taken to heart the command to go forth and multiply and subdue the earth. A large, leather-bound Bible sat on the table to his right.

Mar sat across from me with her youngest siblings on either side, one still in a highchair, another in a booster seat. A plastic runner beneath them protected the carpet.

Her mother looked down the table. "Jacob, really, is this necessary? We have company."

When Connie told me the day before that I'd been invited to lunch at the Van Dijcks after church, I'd said without thinking, "Why?"

"Punishment for your sins," Niall said as he read the paper at the table. It was Saturday afternoon, almost exactly twenty-four hours since the death of the calf.

"Ni!" Connie gave him a look—ineffective since he didn't look up from the paper.

"What?" he said. "He's responsible for Jacob's trampled wheat." He looked up at me. "Let me know if he's got a dollar amount for the damage." He turned back to the paper.

"Can't I turn it down?" I'd planned to get out of church my third Sunday by pulling the stunt I'd performed at home—changing into my running clothes in the basement washroom and making a run for it as the service started. I hadn't decided whether I'd just ask Mar to leave her car unlocked so I could stow my suit there, carry it awkwardly while running, or just ditch it.

My plan was foiled by this invitation to Sunday dinner at the Van Dijcks. If my read on Elder Jacob was right, dinner would likely involve a lengthy interrogation. He'd want to check my understanding of the sermon, as well as my agreement with it—all to test my orthodoxy. I'd actually have to go into the sanctuary and pay attention.

Connie thought about my question for some moments. "I don't think that would be wise. I'm sure Mar and her brothers have told their parents about you and they just want to be hospitable to a young man, also Dutch, far from home."

"But I'm not Dutch."

"Close enough," Niall said. "Plus, you can be my spy. Report back to me what good old Jacob is up to these days."

"Ni!" Connie gave him another look.

During the service, I'd taken mental notes and a few written ones, when I wasn't distracted watching Mar. I was as ready as I could be for whatever questions Jacob shot at me, but I wasn't prepared at all for a meal that might turn into a catechism class.

Jacob spooned up another mouthful of soup. I watched him carefully in case he shot the next letter at me. He pointed his spoon to his left. "Benjamin, U."

A second tiny voice piped up, "Undeniable Selection."

"Close," Jacob said, "but no." He pointed his spoon vaguely in my direction. I felt my heart jump. "Levi, U. Correct answer?"

"Unconditional election."

"Correct."

"How many points do I get?"

"None. Just the blessing of your earthly and heavenly fathers, which should be more than enough for you."

I glanced at Levi. It didn't look like enough.

When I went to take another spoonful of soup, I discovered the tip of my tie sitting in my bowl. I looked to my right and my left. Reubeon busied themselves with slurping their soup. Their mother glared at them from the foot of the table. "Reuben. Simeon. Manners."

I glanced at Mar. She looked away when our eyes met, busying herself with helping her siblings manage their spoons, but she couldn't disguise the reddening of her cheeks. I cleaned my tie with my napkin as best I could, staining the white linen and spreading the green over my red tie, making things worse.

I went to take another bite, but an elbow from either side jostled me so the spoonful spilled back into the bowl. This elbowing continued throughout the meal. As it progressed, it did occur to me that the more my suit got stained, the better my excuse would be for skipping church for the rest of the summer—and for ditching this suit once and for all. They were doing me a favour. I soon gave up trying to prevent Reubeon's brand of hospitality. Instead, I gave them openings for their elbows. By the end I had plenty of pork chop, gravy, green beans, and carrots spilled into my lap. The whole time, I did struggle to keep these spills from travelling onto the carpet, which was in pristine condition; there was no plastic runner beneath *my* chair. Thanks to Reubeon, the food stains were dampened by splashes of water. There were several jugs of it on the table—no milk, which I found odd, given there were supposedly gallons of the stuff out in the milk house. I noticed Jacob was drinking red wine, not water.

He pointed down the table again. "Sarah, L." The girl sitting to the right of Mar's mother said in a bored voice, "Limited atonement." It was the sister who'd ridden in the front seat of Mar's car each Sunday.

"Correct. Zeb, I."

A voice near Mar piped up. "Eerie grace, Papa!"

"Wrong." Jacob sighed. "Irresistible, Zeb. Repeat after me. Irresistible. Irresistible." He sounded it out slowly. Zeb tried his best, but it was too big a mouthful for the little tyke. Mar glanced at me, her look annoyed. Had I been smirking?

Jacob scraped his bowl of the remnants of his soup, then looked up at me and smiled. "Perhaps, Evan, as our guest you could tell us the last letter and what it means?"

My first test. "Perseverance of the Saints, Mr. Van Dijck. As in, once a believer, always a believer. Mind you," I added, "some people say 'preservation.'" I preferred it; I wasn't much good at persevering.

Jacob's smile was unchanged, though his eyes registered some disappointment before he looked around the table. "TULIP, children, TULIP. Correct doctrine to keep you on the straight and narrow path. Don't be led astray into the wide highway by heretical nonsense." With his final words his gaze returned to me.

I considered that Jacob likely wouldn't appreciate the theological nonsense I'd come up with during moments I'd been bored with my catechism homework. GOUDA: God's Orderly Universe Delightfully Amazing. That's what I'd thought a year ago. More recently I'd felt compelled to change it. Now it was God's Overwhelming Universe Damned Awful. In Jacob's eyes, I'm sure I'd be a candidate for excommunication.

As a couple of children got up to remove the soup bowls, I took in the room—large with a bank of windows behind Jacob's wife (we hadn't been introduced) and wrapping around the corner to give a full view of the farm buildings. On the walls were reproductions from Dutch masters, all Bible scenes, along with a pair of wooden shoes. A china cabinet held behind glass numerous pieces of Delft pottery, and a large sideboard in a modern design dominated the opposite wall. The furniture, the whole house—all of it seemed new. If there had been an old farmhouse on site, all traces had vanished.

The main course was served, and with it the true interrogation began. "So, Evan. Mulder, I don't know any Mulders. Tell me about your family." I described my parents, remembering to explain where they were from in Holland (places I knew only by name), when they'd come over, what my father did for a living—my credentials, as it were.

Jacob said simply, "So you're all city people." I considered telling him my father once worked on a farm. Before I could, he'd speared a piece of pork chop with his fork and pointed it in my direction. "Do you know Hennie and Peter VanderStelt? We come from the same village." I should have seen it coming. Dutch bingo. It would have helped if I'd had my church directory with me. Jacob pelted me with names like tulip bulbs: the Meyers, the Van Eeks, the Koks, the Krygsmans, the Vosses, the Van Niejenhuises. On and on. I searched my memory bank for connections and associations. Though I had an enormous number of aunts, uncles, and cousins on both my mom's and dad's sides, apparently they were unknown to Jacob, he unknown to them. He smiled and swept his fork slightly up and to the side, a gesture that seemed to release me from the search for mutual connections. I'd failed Dutch bingo, epically.

As we ate and I continued to spill food in my lap, he did eventually turn his attention to weightier matters, starting with the sermon. To be honest, I couldn't follow the nuances of his theological hairsplitting, so when he turned to me for some reply, I stuffed mashed potatoes in my mouth and murmured noncommittally.

Given my own tepid response, I expected Jacob to quiz me further, perhaps test me on the Heidelberg Catechism, beginning with the question of what my only comfort in life and death was. Instead, he went right for the jugular. "What's your opinion about women?" he said.

I looked at Mar. "Women?" She paused in her chewing. I felt myself redden.

"Yes," he said. I turned back to him. "Women." He pointed his fork at his oldest daughter. "Mar believes that women should be deacons. She's even foolish enough to think that women can be elders and ministers also. Do you agree with her?"

I took another bite of mashed potato and chewed slowly. I felt thirty-four eyes on me, along with Reubeon's two elbows. "To be honest," I said when my mouth was empty, "I haven't thought about it much."

"You must," he said. He pointed his fork alternately at me and Mar. "It's wrong on two counts. One, it's against the Bible, and, two, it's against nature."

"Case closed, then," Mar said.

"It must be accepted. It is true."

Mar's mother intervened, "Please, Jacob. Don't start. Not with company."

"But it's good to discuss things. Iron sharpens iron."

I felt an iron blade at my throat, two iron elbows in my ribs. Whatever iron I had in my own constitution had rusted through long ago.

Undaunted, he turned to politics. "This is all the fault of Trudeau. He's ruined the country's morals, and he almost destroyed the economy." It was a theme that I'd heard my dad pick up at the dinner table too. Jacob continued, "It was a good thing that God saw fit to have Joe Clark and the Conservatives beat Trudeau. They will fix things—so much red tape, taxes so high. The Liberals tried to destroy the individual's initiative, to handcuff business. The Conservatives will restore free enterprise and liberate the small businessman, like me."

The phrase *fuddle duddle* came to mind; I constrained it from popping out my mouth.

My father's theme exactly: Conservatives are the party supporting all people who could recognize a bootstrap and pull themselves up by it. I did imagine getting Jacob together with my dad so they could debate the dairy farmers' quota system, a sacred cow if ever there was one. I wasn't sure who would win, but it would be fun to watch them duke it out.

"The Progressive Conservatives," Jacob continued. "It's right there in their name. They are the champions of progress in this great Dominion of Canada." He paused to chew a mouthful of beans. "That is why I came to this country. There were few opportunities left in Holland, little land to get started and to grow. Here, there was land, good land for sale, as the older generations, the pioneers, gave up farming, many of them simply failing because they wouldn't move forward, they wouldn't embrace progress." He paused to take another bite. "Take Niall," he said. "His people have been here more than one hundred years. They did a great service clearing away the forest, creating fields, but now those ways, the old ways, have passed, and Niall refuses to understand that." I saw again Niall in the milking parlour, that look of shame and sorrow on his face. I felt my heart rising in anger against Jacob. "He clings to the past—milking in an old, inefficient barn using outdated equipment; making little square bales when I've offered him to borrow my round baler." A desire to defend Niall and all those bales of hay came to me. It was futile; no words came. Jacob took another bite and chewed meditatively, then looked at me and said, "Mar will show you after dinner the new methods I use—efficient, highly productive. Dutch farmers have always been clever. After all, we stole land from the sea and made it some of the most productive in the world. Dutch know-how married to modern methods—that is the way forward." He turned from his beans to finish his pork chop. As he cut whatever was left off the bone, he said with something like a chuckle, "Well, that Niall. I admire him. He's a stubborn Scotsman. But I'm afraid that will not help him."

Jacob's wife said, "And you, my dear, are one stubborn Dutchman."

"Yes, dearest, but I am stubborn for progress and success, for the future, not for the past." He swept his knife through the air. "My stubbornness has made all of this possible." I wasn't sure whether he was referring to the farm, the house, or his children—possibly all three. "To God be all the glory," he added.

Earthly success credited to heaven. *What*, I thought, *did that say about earthly failure? Of Niall's struggles, of my father's own Dutch stubbornness and what it had made possible—a rented townhouse, me and my siblings?*

Dessert was a piping hot apple crumble. I was served mine after Jacob received his. He dug in right away, but I paused and looked around. "Go ahead," Jacob's wife said to me, "If you wait 'til everyone else is served it will be cold." My thought had actually been that ice cream might be coming. I picked up my spoon and brought a steaming bite to my mouth to blow on it, but Reubeon's elbows dropped it onto my crotch. I could feel the heat through my pants and underwear. I grabbed it quickly with my fingers, burning their tips.

While I was sucking my fingers, Jacob picked up the

topic he'd dropped as the main course finished. "I've made Niall a very fair offer to buy him out. Perhaps he told you, maybe not. Both his milk quota and his land. I have the capacity to absorb it. He would do well out of the bargain, keeping the house and a couple of acres, living off what I would pay. Either he will sell to me and come out the better for it, or soon enough the bank will take what little is left of his family farm."

"But what about his cows?" I said.

"He can keep them," Jacob waved his spoon in the air. "They're no good to me. My herd—they're all purebred Holsteins. The best producers in the world. Niall's, not one purebred among them. I can't have them mixing with my herd." He took another bite. "Niall can sell them for slaughter, make some use of them that way."

Jacob pointed his spoon at me. "It is simple. Someone needs to make him see sense. The good Lord knows I've tried." He turned his attention from me to Mar. The glance was short but stern before he began spooning in the rest of his apple crumble.

When he was done, he picked up the Bible to bookend the meal with scripture and prayer. All the spoons went down until he was finished.

Had Jacob directed Mar to give me a tour of the farm so she could persuade me to become his agent at Niall and Connie's, her father's mole?

We went outside after Mar had helped clean up her younger siblings and clear the dishes with her sisters. The boys were exempt from helping. Reuben and Simeon tousled my hair as they got up from the table, saying, "See ya later, Evelyn."

As they rushed out, Jacob said, "Reuben! Simeon! Remember, afternoon milking. Don't be late again."

I went to clear my own dishes, but Mar's mom stopped me and told Mar to take them instead. When I objected, the red in Mar's face deepened. She hesitated a moment, then made the journey around the table to take my plate and dessert bowl. My utensils fell to the carpet. We both kneeled down for them. "Let me," she said.

After she'd changed into farm clothes, she led me out-side—me still in my stained suit—to the milking barn. It was so unlike Niall's hip-roof barn. Jacob's was large, made from modern framing rather than massive beams, with a spacious central aisle that opened at either end for tractors to drive through. On either side of the aisle stood a long line of bunks for grain and feeders where the large round bales could be deposited. The cows—too many for me to count—occupied pens on either side, each cow with a numbered tag in her ear. An aisle ran around the outside, one that seemed sunken. When Mar showed me, I under-stood why. The many milking stations were set up so that the milker could stand with the cow above, the udder at chest level, no crouching required. All the milk went direct-ly into a pipeline that sent it to the large tank in the milk house—no carrying heavy milk cans back and forth. It did all seem ingenious and efficient, milking on a large scale with less labour. Maybe Jacob wanted me to praise all this to Niall, make Niall feel like a dairy-farming dinosaur.

We came to the far end of the barn. "My dad made it so that he can keep adding sections onto the back as he gets more cows and more quota. He's already set plans in motion to build this fall. He's certain Niall will give in." She looked at me. "He expects me to talk to Niall and Connie, thinks I have some sway with them. He's like a dog with a bone when he wants something. He doesn't let up gnawing at it."

I looked around. "Where's the pasture?"

"When the cows are wet, they stay in the barn 24/7. It offers better control of their feed and leads to higher production. There's another barn and a paddock for cows that are dry, along with the heifers." She pointed off to the right. "In front of that barn, there, that's where calves are kept." I counted twenty-five small white hutches, each like a little igloo with a small fenced-off area. Mar led me over. We spent some time silently scratching their ears and letting them suck our fingers.

We skipped the large machine shed and headed for the old barn, its red walls and fresh white trim bright in the afternoon sun. "Why did your dad keep it?" I said. "Seems to me it doesn't fit with his picture of the future."

"You'll see." She opened a door, and we stepped from the bright sun into shadow. Even before she found the light switch, I could hear the nickering of horses, their hooves shifting around the straw in their stalls. "These are my dad's Friesians. Purebred." Four massive horses occupied the stalls to the right. To me, the stall walls didn't seem strong enough to contain them. I'd gotten used to working with Holsteins, large as they were, but these heavy horses at their shoulders were taller than I was. "He takes them to fairs. They're trained as a team to pull the wagon over there." She pointed to an elaborate wooden wagon that might seat a dozen or more people. "He loves to show them off and give people rides. He actually has a smaller buggy and does weddings with that one."

Mar went into a tack room and retrieved some treats for the horses. She filled my hand. "Hold the treat in your hand out flat, and they'll scoop it right off. Don't make a fist or you'll get your hand bitten." The horses nickered at the sight and smell of the treats. I watched their mouths snuffle up the food off Mar's hand. That gave me a good look at their enormous teeth. She scratched the horses' necks and talked softly to them, calling them by name.

I looked at the food in my hand. I looked at my hand, studying the lines that transected it. I liked my hands, including all my fingers, which I preferred still attached. I judged it best to use my left hand, since I was right-handed. I approached the first beast, placed a treat in my palm, and stretched it out flat. The mouth reached for it and snuffled it up with its lips, which were surprisingly soft and supple. The horse quickly ground up and swallowed the treat, and looked for more.

While I continued offering treats, Mar opened a door at the far end of the barn. She came back, opened the nearest stall door, and stepped inside. I backed away. "You need some fresh air, don't you?" she said, taking off the horse's halter. She patted it on the rump and it lumbered out.

When she had all the horses out, I went to look. In a small paddock, two stood drinking from a water trough. Mar walked among them on her way to a gate. She opened it, and they trotted through it into a pasture. One stopped and knelt in the grass, lay on its side, then rolled back and forth, its legs in the air.

Mar watched them awhile. She seemed to have forgotten I was there. I was about to call out when she turned back to the barn, lost in thought, and her face wearing sadness openly, until she saw me standing in the door. A mask seemed to settle over her—disdainful one moment, bemused the next.

She closed the bottom half of the barn door, walked by, and grabbed two manure forks. When she held one out to me, I said, "What? In my suit?"

She looked me up and down before settling her eyes on my crotch, stained with a smorgasbord. "That's a suit? Look like barn clothes to me." She glanced at my spectator shoes, covered in dirt. "Those shoes, though, they're way too fancy for mucking stalls." She found me a pair of rubber boots.

As she brought them over, I said, "It's Sunday, my day of rest."

"No rest for the wicked."

"I thought it was 'No rest for the weary.'"

"Weary, wicked. Not sure it makes any difference."

I removed my jacket and hung it on a hook. I unlaced my shoes and said, "You're not planning on flinging horse shit at me, are you?" I slipped on the boots, which were big and loose.

"That's my brothers' trick, not mine. I have others up my sleeve." She picked up a bucket and walked into the first stall.

"I think your brothers are full of shit." What prompted me to be bold enough to say it, I don't know, but she stopped and looked at me. I entered the stall, the boots flopping on my feet. I waited to see if she would defend her brothers. She took her fork and began picking up the clumps of horse manure, piles of small globes, ovoids really, shaking the fork up and down to separate the manure from the straw, before dropping it in the bucket. I started mucking, imitating her technique as best I could, working more slowly and much messier.

We worked quietly for some time. Occasionally, our forks banged together as we both tried to empty a load into the bucket. I was conscious of her body near mine, her skin beginning to glisten, her breathing to deepen. This close to her, I felt awkward within my skin, the magnetic pull toward her reorienting all the molecules in my body. I was alarmed to find myself having impure thoughts about her. They zipped back and forth between my brain and my groin like an alternating electrical current. I was afraid she'd notice.

When we were done the first stall, we each grabbed a handle of the bucket and dumped the manure in a wheelbarrow she'd brought into the aisle. I leaned on my fork while she wheeled it out to a manure pile.

As we started the second stall, she said, "So why don't you fight back?"

I dropped a load of poop off the fork and scrambled to pick it up. Good question. "Two against one, I don't like those odds. Besides, I tried that, remember? Look how well that turned out—for me and for you."

"Nothing will change if you don't stand up to them."

I felt my face flush. "So you really think I'm a milksop too?"

She dumped a forkful of manure in the bucket before answering. "I didn't say that. To be honest, I took everything your brother told me with a grain of salt. I make my own judgements."

I felt emboldened. "I appreciate that. I can tell you have a mind of your own." *Plus a beautiful body to go with it*, I wanted to say—but I wasn't that bold. "Like your brothers, Jeff can be a pest. Sometimes it's best just to put up with it." I thought of play-fighting with my brother when we were kids, games that sometimes turned to real scrapping, usually ending with me in a headlock, Jeff rubbing my hair with his knuckles to make my scalp burn, or pinning me to the floor, his knees on my arms while he let drool slowly stream toward me before sucking it back up. Sometimes he didn't do it in time. I thought, too, of a grade-school fight I'd been in where a classmate, Roddie, for reasons that still mystify me, picked a fight at recess. We tussled and rolled around on the ground while our classmates surrounded us, egging us on. It ended in a draw when a teacher separated us, but I came out the loser, the two of us sitting outside the principal's office until she was ready to discipline us, me crying, not from any punches, but from getting in trouble, Roddie unrepentant.

"There's good-natured teasing and then there's plain meanness. It's a fine line between them," she said.

I straightened up and leaned on my fork. Possibly I *was* just a sucker for punishment. "How am I supposed to tell the difference? For all I know, this is how country boys treat each other. I can take some teasing. Here, I'm a guest, whether it's in your parents' home or your car or this stall. It's not my place to make a scene or raise a fuss. Guess I'm just trying to figure out and follow country manners."

Mar had paused to listen as I said this, possibly the longest string of words I'd offered her. "But they're doing it *because* you're from the city."

"Nothing I can do about that."

We went back to cleaning the stall. Eventually, she said, "And those two are the ones my dad wants to take over the farm."

"'Cause they're the oldest boys?"

"Reuben was born first, five minutes ahead of Simeon, so technically he's the oldest. My dad would like them to run the place together. That's one of the reasons he wants to get bigger, so the farm will be large enough to support two families."

"But what about you? You're the oldest."

She dumped manure into the bucket, banging the fork hard against its edge. "You really *don't* understand country manners, do you? My brothers have what I don't have, what's hanging between their legs. In my dad's mind, that rules me out." She bent to pick up another forkful of manure. "Not that I want to take over the farm."

I tossed more globes into the bucket, thinking about the dinner conversation. "You and your dad don't see eye to eye on a lot of things, do you?"

"We haven't pretty much from the time I was born," she said. "I learned early that he'd wanted his first-born to be a son. When Reuben and Simeon came along, it was almost as if I didn't exist anymore—except as an ongoing disappointment."

I watched the swiftness, strength, and efficiency of her movements—which I'd seen plenty of during haying. I saw her at the table taking care of her youngest siblings while Reubeon tormented me. "How's that possible?" I said. "You're in university, going to nursing school, and he's disappointed in you?" As I considered my own slump in school, I found it hard to believe. And if Mar couldn't please her father, what hope did I have of pleasing mine—except, of course, for the bits dangling between my legs.

"It's not what he expects of me."

"What does he expect?" I waited, but Mar didn't reply. Instead, she stepped up the pace.

By the time we were finished, my body felt swampy. I was generating enough heat to cook the leftovers staining my clothes. My shirt and pants clung to me as Mar wheeled the last load of manure to a pile outside the barn.

To get some air, I went and stood in the far doorway looking at the Friesians. They'd paused in their grazing and were standing in pairs, oddly it seemed to me. The first pair were head to rump, their tails swishing each other's faces to keep the flies off. The other pair looked like they were fighting. Facing each other, their necks were entwined and they were nipping each other. Worried, I yelled out to Mar.

She came running. I made room for her in the doorway. Looking out, she laughed, then turned her face to me, her arm leaning on the door. "They're not fighting, Evan. They're grooming each other."

"Oh" was all I could say, looking back at her smiling face just inches from mine. The electric current from my brain to my groin went haywire. Thankfully, she left to finish emptying the wheelbarrow. I turned back to the horses.

Such was horse friendship, mutually beneficial. When

I'd fallen and tumbled down the school slope that spring, what few friends I had were left behind perched atop the academic hill. These were the nerdy kids of my grade, the ones who got called dorks—excessively brainy and awkward turtles oblivious to their social outcast status or perhaps so confident in the protection of their intelligence that it didn't matter. These were the kids on the Reach for the Top team —enormous memories for trivia, along with knowledge about subjects other students didn't care to know. Their only weakness was sports trivia, which they disdained.

I'd attached myself to the nerds, hoping some of their genius would rub off on me or perhaps be absorbed by osmosis. I loved math and was good at it, but not great. At one point, I'd dreamed of becoming a math genius, of solving unsolvable puzzles, finding the answer to a problem that filled an entire blackboard. I found out soon enough that I was at best above average, horror of horrors, perhaps simply normal.

Outside of school, we played games. Risk was a favourite, with its theme of global domination. Really, we would play any game that required smarts to win, where the stakes involved some form of supremacy or sovereignty. At school, they were all members of the Chess Club, a game that made me anxious. Yahtzee proved to be much more my speed. Perhaps they'd all sensed this about me; from what I could tell, my disappearance made hardly a ripple in their pond.

Something hit me in the back. When I turned, I got smacked in the chest. Mar was pelting me with balls of dried horse manure from a bucket at her feet. "That's for hitting me with a cow pie." She seemed to have armed herself with an unlimited supply of ammunition. "Gonna fight back?" she said.

I picked some up and whipped them harder than I should have. She dodged most but not all of them, laughing. After a minute more, she yelled, "Truce!" and joined me at the door. "They're beautiful, aren't they?"

The word struck me as odd, whether coming from her or applied to these horses, I wasn't sure. "Yes, beautiful and very, very big." She laughed. I added, "Your dad has a thing about purebreds, doesn't he?"

Her smile faded. "He's got a thing about purity in general."

When we emerged from the barn, a muscle car had appeared beside Mar's Corolla. Leaning on it with her arms crossed was the girl with the black hair in a pixie cut, the girl I'd seen Mar with arm-in-arm at church. She was watching Reuben and Simeon tossing a football around with the guy whose dark hair stood up like a brush. That morning, I'd watched him approach the pew where Mar sat, leaning over to say something to her and tousling the hair of her sister sitting nearest the aisle.

I glanced at Mar. In the full sunlight, I could see her

face's blotchiness turn vibrant. "I'll get my keys and drive you home," she said.

"Go long, boys," he shouted.

Reuben and Simeon took off, yelling, "Here, Gerrit! Here!"

Gerrit cocked his elbow and released a perfect spiral. He watched its long arc as it ascended and then descended to the twins, who—pushing at each other—fumbled the catch. "Nice try," he said and turned toward Mar. The girl, too, now noticed us. She smiled and waved, then pushed away from the car and walked toward us.

I noticed Mar blushing. She seemed determined to ignore Gerrit as he walked toward her. She'd already waved back at the girl and now said simply, "Lily!"

Before Lily and Gerrit were close enough to hear, I said, "I think I'll walk. You've got company."

Chapter 20

Connie was shocked at the state of my suit. "What kind of dinner was it? I don't think I'll be able to get those stains out. Your only hope may be the dry cleaner in town."

I held open my jacket to offer the full effect. "I kind of like it better this way."

"What will your mother say?"

I considered. She might be rendered speechless. I'd say to her within earshot of my father (and hopefully Jeff and Annalise as well), "See what you put me through this summer? I'll be scarred for life. You should be ashamed."

Sitting at the kitchen table with a coffee, Niall seemed amused. "Is that what passes for Dutch hospitality?"

"Reuben and Simeon's hospitality, with one or two gifts from Mar, as well."

Connie said, "Mar? Really? Those twins I can believe, but not Mar."

"She had me cleaning horse stalls. Things got messy."

Niall said, "So you met Jacob's prize Friesians, did you? Cares more about those horses than his kids."

"Ni!" Connie said. "You know that's not true."

"I know no such thing." He turned to me. "So did you get the royal tour? What did you think of his operation?"

I said as little as I could. I didn't want to be stuck between Jacob and Niall. It wasn't my battle, and I hadn't a clue why they thought my opinion mattered or carried any weight. In this game—and the game of life for that matter—I was nothing but a pawn.

"Did he mention his offer?"

"Once or twice."

"In other words, he gave you an earful on the subject."

"Pretty much."

"Figured that's what he was up to." He glanced at Connie, then twirled a spoon with his fingers like a baton, studying it. He put it down, then rose to his feet, his hands pressing the table, and headed outside. Connie busied herself at the sink filling the kettle. Watching Niall from the window, she overfilled it before she could get it on the stove. She said to me, "See if he needs some help."

"I'll just change first," I said, and headed up to my room.

That evening, I hung my soiled suit—now a dirty, headless ghost—on the attic hook beyond the baby buggy. I'd decide what to do with it tomorrow. If Jeff wasn't going to rescue me—and chances weren't looking good—the suit could now at least get me out of church for the rest of the summer.

I retreated to my room. Perched on the desk, Janus seemed to be laughing at me out of both faces. I mocked him in return—a paperweight sitting there inert, holding down not a single sheet of paper. I picked up my Texas Instruments calculator and sat in the corner chair on top of my running clothes. I ignored my running log and punched the numbers in. I'd endured three weeks: 21 days = 504 hours = 30,240 minutes = 1,814,400 seconds of hell. Mostly, but not entirely. Then I calculated what was left: five weeks = 35 days = 840 hours = 50,400 minutes = 3,024,000 seconds. At least I'd be asleep for a good portion of it.

I climbed into bed and performed a mental inventory of the day. Eventually my mind dwelled on purity—Jacob's passion for purebreds, Mar's comment about his obsession with it. The thought had a magnetic pull. I worried it might apply to me. Unable to accept life's impurities, had I just said, "To hell with it"? Was that what made me a coward?

I saw myself again in Jacob's horse barn speaking boldly to Mar. Soon, I was alarmed to find impure thoughts about Mar zipping once more between my brain and my groin.

We were in the barn's hayloft, and she was taking off my soiled suit.

She was wearing nothing but a bandana around her neck.

Each day that week, the fourth week of my sentence, followed the same pattern. The true heat of summer had arrived. Dawn was an oven door opening, a wave of heat rolling in from the eastern horizon and crashing onto the last day's wave—one that was barely receding by the time the sky began to lighten, a wave still holding me in the grip of its undertow. At the top of the house, my attic room collected and retained the day's heat, bearing down on me lying in bed, half covered and tangled in damp sheets.

The morning air was languid, breezeless. In the house, the window curtains hung still. In the barn, the only motion was the swish of the cows' tails against the congregating flies. The sky was bleached out, a dull white blanket of haze.

By early afternoon, the land was a furnace. In the pasture, the cows lay down in the shade of the lone tree. Then the sky became a bellows stirring up the hot air. Dark thunderclouds built in the west over the lake. They piled high, blotted out the sun, and billowed towards the east.

A moment would come when large drops began pelting the dusty laneway and the limp leaves of the trees. Then the clouds poured out the water they'd picked up streaming across the lake. This waterfall was lashed about by a wind that shook the trees as if to strip their leaves and snap their branches, along with lightning that threatened to split them, thunder an afterthought, a warning it would be back again tomorrow.

Once the storm passed, the sky cleared but the heat remained. During the afternoon milking, steam rose from the cows' wet hides.

At night, I would lie half covered on my bed, Mar visiting me, deep sleep evading me, a sliver of my mind waiting for the next wave of heat to roll in with the dawn.

Midweek, a letter from home arrived. Niall and I had come inside to get changed, soaked from getting caught in a downpour. I took the letter from Connie and headed upstairs, leaving a trail of drips.

I ripped open the envelope before undressing. It wasn't from Jeff. It was from my mother, a letter tucked inside a birthday card.

I dropped into the desk chair.

As expected, the card was religious in theme. The cover showed a rather frightening picture evoking Jesus' parable of the ten virgins, the five prepared bridesmaids and the five foolish ones who fell asleep and didn't have any oil left for their lamps. The artist was someone I'd never heard of, William Blake. My mom must have gotten a whole set of parable-themed cards, for the year before she'd given me one showing a lamb lost in the mountains and the shepherd scaling the crags to rescue it.

The ten virgins I found unnerving. I would have expected the prodigal son or the one about the talents, focused especially on that servant who just buried his and had nothing to show for it. Either parable would do, given how I'd been wasting my life. But no, I took the ten-virgins card as a chastisement that I wasn't prepared—not for the present moment, and not for Judgement Day. Possibly also a reminder to guard my precious virginity. Almost 18, I felt the full weight of it, especially given my recurring impure thoughts about Mar. Let me call them what they were— nothing but fantasies.

Inside the card was a quote from the parable: "Therefore keep watch, because you do not know the day or the hour." *Thanks for the reminder, Mom, but I've got enough on my plate right now.*

Dear Son, her letter began, *Happy 18th birthday! You're almost a man, but you'll always be my little boy. I remember well the day you were born. Remember, too, how we both almost died before that, while you were growing inside me, a little peanut? I do!*

From there, she recounted in her neat Dutch-schoolgirl handwriting her emergency appendectomy, as well as the tale of my infant illnesses that threatened to prevent me from having any birthday celebrations.

To this day, I carry a heavy burden of guilt over this, though I know you forgive me and have said so many times.

Like every year. She ended with, *I trust Mr. and Mrs. Logan are taking you to church and that through the service the Spirit is reaching your heart. Try hard not to be a foolish virgin. Your loving mother.*

PS Your father, brother, and sister wish you a happy birthday. They miss you too.

Lies, all lies.

I got up and stripped off my clothes. My skin was wrinkled and cold, in spite of the heat, as if I'd been swimming too long or soaking in the tub until all the heat had left the water. I had a snail's body. The words "you slug" came to mind.

I folded the letter and placed it back inside the card, then tucked the card back in the envelope. I looked for a hiding spot—under the mattress would do. Technically, my birthday was the Sunday coming up, but I was strangely content to let it pass unnoticed, with the Logans oblivious to the date's importance for my life. After all, wasn't the date and what the date celebrated insignificant to the universe? I'm ashamed to say that I also derived satisfaction from being alone and ignored, fantasizing that I was heaping burning coals upon the heads of my family who'd banished me here as my special birthday present. Cue the pity-party music. GOUDA.

When Niall and I came in for lunch on the Friday, Connie handed me another piece of mail. I excused myself, saying I'd be back in a few minutes. "What's the rush?" I heard Niall say as I hurried upstairs.

I sat on the bed and ripped at the envelope, tearing into the letter so that I had to piece it back together when I'd gotten it out. Jeff's forceful handwriting stared up at me.

Dear Milksop,

Let me start by apologizing profusely that I was unable to reply to your previous correspondence until this late date. Your missive caught me in the midst of my busy life: working at my highly rewarding summer occupations, preparing for my entry this fall into the highly esteemed, incredibly selective University of Toronto Pre-Med Program, and going to the beach with friends to frolic in the waves and lie in the sun. (My tan, by the way, is golden, positively golden.)

With respect to said occupations, they are crucial to my career pathway and therefore must take priority over your niggling concerns. I have been working in the St.

Joseph's Hospital lab (in air-conditioned comfort) helping determine illnesses and diseases — crucial to saving lives. In the evenings, I have been training to become a paramedic.

All of which is to say, soon but not quite yet, I shall be qualified to save your life. Until then, however, I am so sorry to tell you that you will have to endure your country suffering.

Is it so bad, dear little brother, to spend the summer in a rural paradise? My own summer working at Logan & Sons Dairy was indeed such a rewarding experience. It made me the man I am today. It could do the same for you, if you grow a set and stop whining. Try to uphold the family honour, will you? Please say hi to Niall and Connie for me. Same to Mar, if you see her. Such a fox with that red hair!

So, sad to say, you'll just need to suck it up, buttercup. My advice, Sunshine, is to take a chill pill and stop spazzing out. Catch my drift?

Ten four, little buddy — catch you on the flip side.

Your favourite brother,

Jeff

PS I've moved all your worldly possessions into the garage. I needed the space.

I ripped and ripped and ripped the letter until it was nothing but confetti all over the floor.

CHAPTER 21

hen I'd pulled myself back together, I got on my knees, picked up the inky confetti, and stuffed it in the torn envelope only to have much of it pour back out. Eventually, I shoved the envelope beneath the mattress with my mother's card and swept the rest of the confetti beneath the bed with my hand.

I pulled myself off the floor and sat on the bed. I stared at my untouched running clothes on the chair in the corner, then turned to the mess of clothes still sitting in a jumble in my open suitcase at the end of the bed. On the top of the dresser were my clothes that Connie had washed and neatly folded.

I leapt up and stuffed all of it in the dresser drawers, slamming them closed. I latched my suitcase and shoved it under the bed, out of sight.

I went down to lunch and found the kitchen empty. Niall and Connie had finished and were elsewhere; Finn and Jane were playing in the room off the kitchen. My lunch was on the table, covered with a napkin. I sat and chewed my homemade bread while chewing over what I'd done to deserve this life. It occurred to me that maybe I should hurry up and join Niall wherever he'd gone, but— bovine that I was—I couldn't escape my ruminations.

I heard footsteps on the stairs, the click and clunk of dress shoes on wood. Niall appeared in the kitchen wearing a suit, Connie the dress I'd seen her in the Sunday evening I'd been dumped on the farm. "Kids," she said. "It's time to go."

"Time to go?" I said. "Where are you going?"

Niall looked away and went to grab the car keys. Connie said, "We have an appointment in town at the bank." She turned back to Finn and Jane. "Come on, kids. We can't be late."

"Do we have to go?" Finn said. "Can't we stay home with Evan?"

"That wouldn't be fair. Evan's not your babysitter."

"We're not babies," Jane said. "We can look after ourselves—*and* Evan."

I studied in my hands the sandwich Connie had made me, feeling *myself* the big baby. I suppressed the ache in my throat. Something nudged me to say "I don't mind."

"I don't know," Connie said. "Ni, what do you think?"

"It'd be convenient, not worrying about the kids out in the car."

"You're sure, Evan? Please don't feel obliged to say yes."

I'd never babysat in my life, had never even taken a turn in the nursery at church—was totally unqualified to care for kids. But I said, "Happy to help."

"Finn, Jane, you know the rules. Don't give Evan any trouble."

"Let's visit all the animals," Jane said as soon as Niall and Connie's car was out of the laneway.

I took the last bite of my sandwich and finished my apple juice. "All of them?"

"Of course," Finn said, "We have to say hello everyday or they're not happy."

We started with the barn cats. Some tabby kittens had been born a few days before, and Jane wanted to make sure they were fine. We watched them feed from their mother. "Their eyes aren't open yet," Jane said. "But they'll open soon. Then they'll be able to play. It's kind of hard to play with your eyes closed, unless it's blind man's bluff." She smiled and seemed to be waiting for me to smile too. I gave it a try. She laughed. "Your face looks like you ate something sour."

Finn led us down to the calf pen, where we let the calves suck our fingers. "What a bunch of suckers," he said.

We left the barn and headed for the pasture fence. Jane said, "Let's climb the fence and visit the cows." Given the heat, most were lying in the pool of shade provided by the solitary tree in the far corner, chewing their cud; a few continued to graze just outside the shade.

I had visions of Jane and Finn getting charged by cows, me having to explain to Niall and Connie the tragic outcome. "I don't think that's a good idea."

Finn said, "We're not allowed, Jane. You know that."

"But they won't come over. I want to feed them some grass." She pulled up a handful from the fence line and started climbing the wire.

"It's not allowed, Jane."

I was contemplating having to extricate her from the fence when Finn said, "Let's feed it to the chickens instead."

"Chickens eat grass?" I said.

"They eat everything," Jane said as she climbed down and grabbed a second fistful of grass.

The chickens were outside in their run. No longer

small yellow puff balls, they were now full grown—white-feathered with gnarly yellow legs and blood-red combs and wattles. They raised a ruckus when they saw us, their heads turning and darting this way and that, their clawed feet scratching at the dirt, their beaks pecking at it. When Jane and Finn tossed the grass in, the flock attacked it. They pecked each other too, squawking and chasing.

"Crazy birds," Jane said.

"Birdbrained," Finn added.

"I guess with animals," I said, "it's all about their stomachs."

"Let's check the garden and see if anything's ready for picking," Finn said.

They led me around to the far side of the house. In the weeks I'd been on the farm, it was odd I'd never ventured there, not even to add any doors and windows from that side of the house to the total I'd begun the first evening. All those weeks, this enormous garden had been growing—row upon row of vegetables and fruit—strawberry plants, raspberry canes, blueberry bushes. Small apples beginning to redden hung from four trees beyond the garden.

The garden itself was surrounded with wire fencing. There were two scarecrows, one at either end. The first was made of old clothes from Niall stuffed with straw, the second an old dress of Connie's; each wore a straw hat at a jaunty angle, and from their outstretched arms hung tin pie plates that banged together in the breeze and reflected the sun. An owl perched on a tall pole in the centre. I had to look twice to realize it was fake.

Aside from tomatoes and corn stalks, I couldn't identify many of the vegetable plants, had little idea what food they produced. Finn and Jane led me through the rows naming them, but I was distracted by swarms of insects in the air and tiny creatures scurrying on the ground. When we got to the raspberries, Jane and Finn picked some and shared them with me.

"Your mom planted this whole garden?" I said, feeling the tiny raspberry seeds sticking in my teeth.

"We helped her," Jane said. "She says she's one of God's gardeners and we're her angel helpers."

God's gardener? Angels? I thought about the work this family put into producing food and felt keenly how ungracious I'd been. Had I insulted them when I'd rejected what they'd offered? If so, they'd hidden it well.

The sky was darkening in the west, the clouds building once again. "We better get inside," I said, "before we get soaked."

"Can we play in the puddles after?" Jane said.

"We'll see." I turned toward the house, noticing for the first time the flowers that bordered it. Vibrant red roses climbed on trellises, but there were so many others. Beds of daisies I recognized, but little else of the purples and oranges and yellows that spanned the full width of the house. As I got closer to them, I could hear a chorus of bees. From a safe distance, I watched them fly from flower to flower, collecting nectar and spreading pollen as they travelled.

The first drops of rain began to pepper us. Jane grabbed my hand, and we ran for the door.

Inside, Jane and Finn poured themselves a large glass of milk while I turned on some lights. By then it was raining heavily, the window in the playroom streaming with it. "Sure you don't want a glass?" Finn said. It had become their daily teasing.

"You've got a milk moustache," I said. They felt it above their lips, then like cats licked it off.

Jane put her empty glass in the sink. "Can you read me a story?"

I thought about how I'd come to see books as filled with lies. Reading one to Jane would feel like I was filling her head with them. "Wouldn't you like to do some math problems instead, maybe practice your times tables?"

"What's a math problem?" Jane said. She took me by the hand into the playroom and sat me in the rocking chair. She had a set of tiny illustrated books, tales by Beatrix Potter. She brought me *The Tale of Peter Rabbit* and climbed into my lap. The book looked harmless.

"Boring," Finn said. He pulled out a bin of Lego blocks and began putting them together.

I decided to risk it. "Once upon a time there were four

little rabbits," I began. A few sentences in, I was horrified to learn that Peter's father had been caught by Mr. McGregor in his garden and put in a pie by his wife. Peter seemed destined for the same dish but managed a lucky escape. Of course, he paid for his sins in the end with a sore stomach while his properly behaved siblings were rewarded with bread, milk, and blackberries. I closed the book. "So, Jane, what's the moral of this story?"

"I don't know. What?"

"Don't eat vegetables. They make you sick." I thought of clarifying not to eat fresh vegetables from a garden like her mom's—if you absolutely have to eat vegetables, buy them from the supermarket—but decided that was a step too far.

"No, they don't," Jane said.

"So, does your mom catch rabbits in her garden and put them into pies?"

"No," Finn said. "My dad catches them, and Mom puts them in stews."

"Read me another story," Jane said, sliding off my lap and returning Peter Rabbit to his spot in the collection.

She was still deciding on another book when Finn said, "It's my turn." Shyly, he presented me with one. "My mom's reading this to me. Could you read a chapter?" The rain was letting up a bit, but now lightning lit up the window, followed three Mississippis later by booming thunder.

I took *The Hobbit* from him, Smaug staring at me from

the cover while he lay upon a mountain of gold. All my nerd friends had read this book, along with *The Lord of the Rings*. Wanting to emulate their nerdiness, I'd started *The Hobbit* but had put it down a few pages in—short creatures with furry feet reminded me too much of myself; dwarves and wizards seemed childish, like fairy tales I was supposed to leave behind for the pursuit of grown-up knowledge rooted in mathematics and science. "Wouldn't your mom want to read this to you herself? She might be upset if we read ahead without her."

"She won't mind," Finn said. "She's read the book a hundred times. When she was a teacher."

"A teacher? Your mom?" The word gave me a jolt. Mr. Ashby came to mind.

"Of course, silly," Jane said. "Before she met Dad and fell in love and had us to take care of."

Finn sat at the table. He'd set aside his Lego and was folding a paper airplane. "I'm listening," he said.

"Just a minute." I got up, picked up a piece of paper, and knelt beside him. "Watch this." Curious, Jane came over. Fold by fold, I created the paper airplane David had taught me on the church balcony. I passed it to Finn. "Go ahead. Toss it gently. It doesn't need a lot of force." The three of us watched it swoop around the room until it glided onto the kitchen table.

"So cool!" Finn said.

Jane clapped her hands together. "Make me one too!"

From the rocker, I watched their planes flying around the room for some time as the rain continued to lash the house. Eventually, Finn and Jane settled into chairs still holding their planes. I opened the book and read, "Chapter 5, Riddles in the Dark." I cleared my throat and launched into the first sentence, Bilbo opening his eyes to find himself enclosed in darkness. On it went from there, Bilbo lost inside the mountain, fearful of goblins and wishing he was back home in his kitchen eating breakfast. His meeting of a strange creature at the heart of the mountain, a game of riddles his life depended on, the discovery of a magic ring. "Are you sure Jane should be listening to this?" I said to Finn. "It's pretty scary."

Jane said, "My mom lets me listen. She says it's a bit scary but it's a good kind of scary. It helps you not be afraid." I couldn't see how.

"Do you want to see pictures of my mom and dad?" Jane said. I'd gotten to the end of the chapter, Bilbo using the magic ring to escape not only Gollum and the mountain but the goblins as well.

Without waiting for an answer, she took my hand and led me down the hallway to the parlour, a room I'd only glanced in passing on my way upstairs. Finn followed, saying, "There's lots of neat old stuff in here, but we're not allowed to touch it."

I stood in the doorway and studied the dim room. It

felt like a museum at night. "Are you sure we're allowed in here?"

They didn't answer, just turned on some lamps; it was still dark and rainy outside. The room was filled with antique furniture that sat on a hardwood floor over which lay a wine-coloured carpet with an intricate design. At the end of the room on the far wall was a fireplace, and on its mantle sat a clock—the source of a chime I'd heard during the night.

On the walls hung paintings of rural scenes, one that seemed pastoral and peaceful with rolling fields bordered by stone hedges and a soft sky above it, the other a craggy coastline with a choppy sea and a tumultuous sky; a few sheep huddled in a field at the top of the cliffs. Other walls contained black and white photos, some of couples and others of families. Most were in formal poses, but one I recognized as having been taken in front of this house long ago, possibly when it was built in the previous century. Atop a small desk sat two portraits—a black-and-white wedding photo of Niall and Connie, plus a colour photo of them with Finn and Jane that looked to be from a year or two before. On an end table sat a snow globe with a little farm and countryside scene in it.

Jane and Finn sat me down between them on the sofa. Finn had a large Bible in his lap. He opened it to the front and showed me the family tree, pointing to his name and Jane's below Niall's and Connie's. The other names went back to the early 1800s. Niall's name appeared a number of times. "Those are all our people," he said, "all the way back to Scotland."

Jane placed a large photo album in my lap on top of the Bible. The first pages held pictures of Connie as a teenager in a rugged landscape by the sea. "Is your mom from Scotland too?" I asked. "Is that Scotland in the picture?"

"No," Finn said, "That's Nova Scotia, where my mom and her people are from."

Her people filled many of the early pages. Then followed a few photos of Connie graduating—first from high school and then from university, Dalhousie it was, one picture with her parents on either side, and finally one of her grinning, hamming it up for the camera and holding her teaching certificate below her chin. These were followed by some photos from her early years as a teacher, some in her classroom with students and others formal class photos.

Jane closed the album suddenly. "Look, the sun's out!" The storm had passed, and the sun had emerged from behind the clouds moments before, flooding the room. She turned to Finn. "Let's go jump in the puddles."

Before I could object or caution them, they were gone. I heard the screen door slam closed behind them and their laughter come to me as if from a great distance.

My curiosity got the better of me. Correction, my nosiness. I searched the drawer from which Jane had retrieved the photo album. There, I found a cream-coloured wedding album. I brought it back to the sofa and opened it to the first page—Niall and Connie hand-in-hand in a garden, followed by a photo of the wedding party in front of the church, several more posed pictures in the garden, plus less formal photos of the small reception in what looked like a restaurant. At the end were several photos of a honeymoon—she and Niall in Nova Scotia, some just the two of them in sunglasses with the ocean behind them, others with Connie's friends and family.

I was looking at these when Niall and Connie appeared in the doorway. Had I been so engrossed in the album I hadn't heard the door and their shoes? It was hard to imagine. I quickly shut the album and reddened. "I'm so sorry," I said. "I shouldn't have."

She walked over and took the album from me. She began flipping through it and smiled. "Ancient history," she said. Niall came and stood beside her, looking. Sitting on the couch, I felt small before them.

The kitchen door opened and slammed closed. Finn and Jane came running down the hallway and stood in the doorway. "Mom, Dad," they called out. "Look at us!" They were smiling—soaked and covered in mud.

Connie pulled herself away from the album. "Finley Logan! Jane Logan! Look at the floor. Go get yourselves cleaned up in the mudroom, now!" They ran off laughing while I contemplated my epic babysitting fail.

Niall glanced around the room as if he was remembering its contents. "Time for milking soon." He turned to leave the room; his shoes made a soft plunk as they climbed the stairs.

Milking and dinner were quiet affairs. Niall was more than commonly speechless, Connie limited herself to simple instructions, and when Finn and Jane were too chatty at the table, reminded them to eat rather than jabbering on and on.

I went upstairs early, around the same time Finn and Jane did, joking that taking care of them had tuckered me out. For a long time, I sat at the top of the attic steps eavesdropping. If I could, I wanted to find out what had happened at the bank.

It was quiet for a long time. I guessed Niall and Connie were waiting for the kids to fall asleep, maybe me too. Then I heard the murmur of their voices, at first just a few brief words exchanged. "Well, that's that." "There has to be a way." Then longer, more involved discussion, with sentences beginning "Maybe" and "What if," the words "help" and "books" and "accountant." Their talk trailed off with a brief exchange.

"There's no help for it. We may just have to sell to Jacob. At least we'd still have the house."

Connie raised her voice. "So you can look out the window at him farming your land, the land your people cleared a hundred years ago and have tilled ever since?

Maybe he'll hire you to work in his dairy. No, Ni, no. I won't have it."

I retreated to my room. By then, it was dusk. I lay on the bed studying the ceiling with its odd angles. Why the hell should I care? It wasn't my problem. It's not like they were my family, my people. I'd be out of here soon enough.

Survival of the fittest. The phrase from Biology came to me. What concern of mine was it if Niall was proving unfit, Jacob fitter? If it was a law, no one could change it anyway. Certainly not little me. Competition. It seemed to be the law that ruled life—not just the natural world, but farming too, competition for land, competition against insects and birds and the weather—and gophers, for that matter. Farming was a business, like others, the world where my dad survived by beating the competition. It was even there in my own little world of school and cross-country races, in my competition with my brother and sister—for grades, for my parents' approval and affection.

I turned on the desk lamp and began my nighttime ritual—turning Janus around, calculating the days and hours and minutes and seconds left in my sentence, counting the books on the shelf.

My count came up short. Each night, the books numbered 173. Now, there were only 172—no longer a prime number. I recounted them with the same result. A third time, the same number.

Einstein's definition of insanity came to me again. I stopped counting. Aside from numbering the books, I'd never paid attention to them, to their lying words, so I had no idea which book was missing. I began studying the titles, perhaps compelled by reading to Jane and Finn that afternoon. On the top shelf, a King James Bible and the *Book of Common Prayer*, *Pilgrim's Progress*, a book by Charles Sheldon titled *In His Steps*. *In whose steps?* I wondered. I pulled it down. The subtitle was *What Would Jesus Do?* I hadn't a clue. *Maybe*, I thought, *he'd put the book back on the shelf*, so I did.

The rest of the shelves were filled with novels and poetry collections and anthologies of literature. Some of the names I recognized—who didn't know Shakespeare and Dickens?—but others were unknown to me—Franz Kafka? Alice Munro?

A name caught my eye. William Blake, the artist who'd done the ten virgins painting on the birthday card my mom sent me. I pulled down the slim book, *Songs of Innocence and of Experience: Shewing the Two Contrary States of the Human Soul*. The cover image frightened me—a prostrate man and woman, nearly naked, below what looked like fiery vegetation. But the title spoke to me. I flipped through the book—a picture book like *Peter Rabbit*, but these pictures were different, and they contained poems inside the pictures.

I sat on the bed, directed the desk lamp onto the pages,

and began reading those poems and studying those odd pictures, with their sheep and wild vegetation circling the page, with people dancing and people bowed down, tiny figures peering out of branches, child cherubs and child chimney sweeps. I found annotations in the margins in a neat handwriting, words circled or underlined. That night, I read the whole book, understanding a little, confused a lot, strangely moved by it all.

Innocence and experience, good and evil—the joys of childhood, the mind-forged manacles of adulthood. Old, old poems reading my life too well.

Two poems struck me hardest, in opposite ways—the nurse's songs. I was confused at first, thinking the poems were about the kind of nurse Mar was training to be, but soon realized it was an old-fashioned word for a nanny, the other kind of nursing Mar did with her siblings. Mary Poppins came to mind, Maria in *The Sound of Music*. When I was younger, I'd had a crush on Julie Andrews.

The Innocence poem soared with the joy and laughter and play of the children in the summer, the peace of the nanny. These were all gone in Experience, play now whis-perings and disguises in a world turning to winter, the nurse bitter, so bitter at her lost youth.

It seemed to say, Growing up sucks, big time. I had to agree.

That night, I dreamed I was in a giant warehouse, dimly

lit, where workers were busy cutting up meat, opening boxes upon boxes filled with fruit and vegetables, with tinned goods, bottles, and jars. It was a vast warehouse behind some enormous grocery store, though I never made it into the store itself. The busy workers took no notice of me. They didn't seem to care that I was in a restricted zone. Perhaps they were too busy, run off their feet getting food into the store for hungry shoppers.

I was there with Mar. We were married with children, two of them Jane and Finn but many more. I needed to get into the store to find the ingredients for pizza, but I was filled with anxiety. The children ran around laughing and playing hide-and-go-seek, and I couldn't keep track of them—they could get lost or hurt. I was also worried about how I would find the ingredients in the store, so large and unfamiliar to me.

Mar left me. She had to do something else, I didn't know what exactly—something at home? Maybe nursing at the hospital? All the children ran off into the store. I needed to follow them, not to lose them, but I couldn't get into the store. I remained stuck alone in the warehouse.

I woke with a start, wondering, *Is she the woman of my dreams? Or my nightmares?*

CHAPTER 22

Daydreams and nightmares. Nightdreams and daymares. I'd spent the next day and night confused and troubled by it all, frightened by my feelings for Mar. It was too much—her magnetic pull on me, my mom's card, my brother's letter, the Logans' troubles. Jacob Van Dijck. Church. God. Dad. Cows calmly chewing their cud and chickens madly pecking each other. Children's stories and paper airplanes. Stupid poems about growing up.

When I woke on Sunday morning after another restless night, I was 18. An adult, more or less. *Time to act like one*, I thought, as I shut off my alarm and put my feet on the floor. I had no idea yet what that might mean, but I was determined to make a change this day. Janus seemed to be laughing at me out of both faces. I knocked him over.

"Donny, dear Donny, what happened to your groovy suit?" One twin shot this barb at me from the back seat of Mar's car. The other twin chimed in, "You should have at least worn a dress, Evelyn. It's church! But those are great shoes, man! I'm blinded by the light!"

I was wearing my yellow Nike Marathons, a button-up short-sleeved shirt with Mar's bandana around my neck, and clean jeans. Connie had promised my mom to get me to church each Sunday; my soiled suit proved ineffective against Connie's sense of obligation.

When I went to get in the back seat with the twins, Mar said, "You're in the front." She turned to her sister Sarah and told her to get in the back. "He's my guest. He rides up front."

Sarah shoved the door open and gave me a look of disgust. Reubeon said from the back as they let Sarah in, "Aw, sis, you spoil all our fun."

My Friday night dream was on my mind as Mar drove. I pretended to look out her half of the front window at the landscape, but I was studying her—her green eyes, the blush of her cheeks, loose wisps of her rust-coloured hair stirred by the breeze. Occasionally, she used two fingers to thread it out of her eyes and tuck it behind her ears.

She was wearing a sundress and sandals. I turned to look out my side window but was soon drawn back to the light grip of her hands on the wheel, her tanned forearms. I watched her shift gears, her hand maneuvering the stick while her feet worked the clutch and accelerator. I had it bad. She was definitely in the driver's seat. This wouldn't do, this wouldn't do at all.

Something small hit the back of my head. Sarah laughed. Her brothers started pelting me with spit balls. I could feel some sticking in my hair. Each one felt like a tiny hand grenade tossed into the pond of my stagnant, acrid feelings, stirring them up with each detonation, agitating me toward doing something, anything. But what?

I sat still as the pelting continued, thinking about turning 18 that day, supposedly becoming a man. What did it mean, to "man up"? It came to me that if I wanted this kind of abuse, I could get it at home from my own flesh and blood. Maybe it would be better to face the music with my dad and start the night shift at Cameron Confectionaries, to "man up" by getting on with whatever bitter dish life was offering me. At least there was a chance I'd be left alone working nights in the factory, sleeping all day.

All I had to do was walk away, to put one foot in front of the other.

Mar pulled into the church parking lot and brought

the car to a stop. I opened the door and decided to do it—
to leave behind my ruined suit and all my other clothes,
even my calculator and my Janus paperweight. To get far
away from beautiful Mar and her nasty siblings and her
clever father, from the Logans and their crisis too.

"Thanks for the ride," I said to her and turned to
leave. "It's been swell knowing you."

"What are you doing?" she said.

I turned back. "Walking away. It's a guy thing. You
wouldn't understand."

The twins pelted me one last time with spit balls.

I turned on them. "Listen, Rural Rube and Simple
Simon, knock it off." Before they could react, I grabbed
their straws and broke them in half. I boxed the ears of
one, then spun the other around, shoved my hand down
the back of his pants, grabbed the elastic of his underwear,
and yanked up as hard as I could. His yelp was partnered
with the sound of tearing fabric. The wedgie showed off a
good amount of his tighty whities. I'd become an expert on
wedgies, having been on the receiving end of several from
Jeff.

"See ya," I said to Mar. "*Au revoir,* Mary, *au revoir,* Jane.
(Madame Leblanc would have been proud of my French.)

I started running. Mar yelled after me, "You're nuts.
And it's not Mary-Jane."

"Whatever! No sadness, no pain. Until we meet
again."

I got some strange looks from cars pulling into the parking lot as I sprinted to the highway running south from town. One car contained the young couple I'd sat beside my first Sunday. They seemed unfazed by my sprint. The mother smiled at me; the father looked ahead stoically.

I knew if the twins didn't catch me in the first minute, they wouldn't. Though I hadn't been out running for weeks, I had reserves.

Clear of town, I slowed to a trot. Running in jeans proved hot and uncomfortable. I geared down to a speed walk and began pulling spitballs out of my hair. I could feel Mar like a magnet drawing me back, but I looked both ways, crossed to the lane heading south, and began hitch-hiking. Time to take the long way home.

Sunday morning traffic was slim, so I spent most of my time facing forward, only turning when I heard a vehicle coming up behind. I put my thumb out, resisting the urge to stick it in my mouth. My mother often reminded me I'd been a great thumb sucker, especially after I'd been weaned. She had to cure me of it before I started school. She tried brushing various terrible tasting substances on both thumbs, from lemon to vinegar to tabasco sauce and mustard. She got some product from the pet store that was supposed to stop dogs from chewing furniture—no luck. She covered both thumbs in bandages and then made me wear gloves. I chewed them off. She tried shame. "Your little sister has never sucked her thumb. You need to be a big boy now. Please be Mommy's big boy."

I stopped when Jeff said he'd cut them off if I didn't. He'd started school already and learned more advanced techniques for compelling my cooperation.

Now that I was 18, I'd stand up to him.

My speedwalk slowed to a stroll. Sadly, I was getting out of breath. This time last year, shortly after I'd turned 17, I'd been fit enough to run a half marathon. Mr. Ashby had taken me and three of my cross-country teammates to a road race in a small town outside London—training for it part of his plan to keep us running through the summer. We'd squeezed into his Civic hatchback, me on the hump in the middle back seat. At the course, he showed us the finish line and said, as he always did at cross-country races, "Picture the finish line, and from your first stride aim for it. Don't worry so much about the other runners. Just have the finish line in your mind."

It was the farthest I'd ever run, before or since. I kept that line in mind and pretty much collapsed across it, one of the volunteers helping me as my legs wobbled. I was the last of my teammates to finish, but I hadn't gone off course, hadn't gotten lost, hadn't quit. One year ago for one day I'd felt on top of the world.

On the way home, Mr. Ashby, always the teacher, had turned the race into a life lesson. "The secret to life is having a goal you're running toward. You can't just be running away from things or wandering aimlessly. You have to decide where you're heading. What the destination is isn't as important as simply having one. Then, half the fun is running the race, the challenge of getting there." When I'd gotten home, I recorded in my running log the distance I'd run (13.1 miles / 21.08 kilometres), along with this Ashbyism.

As I walked the shoulder of the highway and waited for someone to pick me up, I couldn't jive this advice with the blessed wisdom of Rick and Roger—take the long way home. They believed my life might need to become a catastrophe so that I—a boy—might grow. I felt the catastrophe, but when would the growth begin? Maybe today, now that I was a man.

Lost in thinking things through, I didn't hear the van come up behind me. As it passed, I thought, *Shit, too late to stick out my thumb.* But then it pulled over to the shoulder anyway.

From the back, I couldn't see into it, though I could tell from the paint job it might be a party on wheels, a shag wagon. My mother's warnings about hitchhikers disappearing, about abductions and murders, came back to me.

I approached the passenger window, relieved to see in the side mirror a young woman looking at me and smiling, motioning me forward with her hand.

She looked like Joni Mitchell. Across from her the driver, I swear, looked like John Lennon—at least the same hair and beard and glasses. Or maybe it was the flower power music pouring from the windows that made it seem that way. There was a large peace sign on the side of the van, a giant dove on its hood. The rest was covered in psychedelic many-coloured swirls.

The Lennon look-alike turned down the radio. "Hey man, you lost?"

I looked around. "Not really."

He said, "'Cause you look lost, man, really lost. But me and my lady can help you get found."

The woman held out her hand palm-up, her smile serene. "Need a friend? Looks like a lonely road you're travelling. We'd be happy to have you travel it with us. If you're tired, we've got a nice bed in the back."

"Sleeps three," the driver added.

"No strings," she said.

I considered their offer. Perfect strangers willing to be my friends. A fresh start in a wandering shag wagon. No strings—I was pretty sure that meant sex, but I was still a virgin, naive and alarmed at my impure thoughts. In this situation, what would a man do?

I opened the side door and got in.

"Yeah, man!" the driver said as he pulled back onto the road.

The floor and walls and even the ceiling of the van were covered in plush rich-red carpeting. I felt it. So soft. The back half had a wall-to-wall mattress neatly made up with a peacock design bedspread and covered with silky pillows fringed and tasselled.

I sat in the only other seat—a swivel chair slightly behind and between John and Joni. I looked for a seatbelt, but there wasn't one. *That's freedom,* I thought. "Thanks," I said. "Where are we headed?"

Joni turned to me. "We'll know when we get there."

"That's deep," I said, trying to pick up the shag-wagon vibe. "I was trying to get to London."

"Whoa," John said. "No maps allowed, man. We've got to just go with the flow, see where the road takes us."

"Nothing but the open road," Joni said. "But that's everything."

"Deep," I said again. "Sounds so free. I don't mind taking the long way." A phrase came to me from a poem I'd read in English class. "Even the road less travelled. But how do you pay for gas and food? I'd like to help out, but I'm afraid I don't have any money on me."

"Don't worry about that, baby," she said. "It's all co-pacetic." She smiled at me and pointed her thumb at the Lennon-look-alike. "Trust fund."

She opened the glove box and pulled a joint out of a bag. She lit it up, took a drag, and held the smoke in while passing the joint to John. When they exhaled, the open windows blew the smoke back at me. When he returned the joint to her, she passed it back.

I'd never smoked a cigarette, let alone pot. I thought

of the school patio and the smoke like a fog. Of a TV ad from some government agency: a picture of an egg. "This is your brain." The egg cracked and sizzling in a frying pan. "This is your brain on drugs." I thought of my runner's lungs and Mr. Ashby's lectures about running's power to keep body and mind healthy, in sync. I thought of how often I'd been told that my body was the temple of the Holy Spirit, and that I'd felt my temple emblazoned with a Vacancy sign for months.

I took the joint in my fingers, put it to my lips, and drew the smoke into my mouth so that the tip reddened. I didn't inhale. Unlike Bill Clinton, I'm not lying about this. (I haven't lied about my sex life, either.) I just couldn't do it. Even so, I started to cough and sputter as the smoke drifted up into my nose. "That's some sweet Mary Jane," I said as I passed the joint back to Joni.

As the joint went around, I tried a few more times without success, but I was beginning to feel mellow anyway, getting the smoke second-hand from the cloud filling the van.

When the joint was nothing but a tiny butt, Joni flicked it out the window and turned to a large purse she had between her feet, more a bag than a purse. It looked like it was made out of macramé, but the colours weren't brown; they were the colours of the rainbow. Slightly high now, I couldn't help thinking of Mar's bandana belt.

Joni pulled a plastic container out of the bag and

opened it to me. It was filled with pills of many colours, like candy, neatly organized by dividers. She smiled. "Help yourself. Take what you want."

I stared at all the choices, while her words registered on my foggy brain. Help myself. Take what I want. What did I want? I seemed to know what everyone else wanted of me, for me—my dad, my mom, Niall, even Mr. Ashby. I'd tried to please them all. But what did *I* want? What in God's name did I *really* want?

I wasn't sure, but I knew it wasn't this. I'd been born too late to embrace the 60s vibe, free love and sticking it to the Man. I was just too damned square.

I fingered the bandana at my throat. There was only one thing I knew I wanted for sure—Mar. It was so foolish, hopeless, and juvenile—this crush I had on her. I was afraid of it, afraid my attraction to her might prove fatal. My heart felt crushed by it, but I had to obey. It's what this boy-man needed to do. I needed to see it through.

"Stop the van," I said. "I need to get out."

John turned to look at me. "No can do, man. These wheels are in motion."

Joni twisted in the seat and held the case of pills closer to me, still smiling.

"Please stop the van."

"No can do," John repeated. "That'll ruin the vibe we're building together. You're in for some fun later. Just go with the flow, man. Go with the flow." He took his hands off the wheel and made wave motions with them.

I looked out the front window. We passed the cross-roads where turning right would go to the lake, going left back to the Logans' farm. The van was slowing as it struggled to climb the hill.

I smacked the bottom of the case, sending the colourful pills flying into the air. "What the fuck!" Joni said. I opened the side door and hesitated a moment, looking at the gravel shoulder flowing swiftly backward. I leapt out, catching the edge of the gravel and rolling into the ditch.

By the time I'd gotten up, bruised and scratched, the van had pulled over. Joni got out holding the empty pill case. In a tie-dyed dress she stood beside the open side door with its peace sign on it and yelled, "Fuck you!" She gave me the finger for good measure. I gave her the peace sign in return. For a moment, she looked annoyed, then leaned into the van, clearly searching the red shag carpet for all those capsized pills.

For a few moments I admired her bottom wiggling with the effort, then turned back to the crossroads. I brushed off my clothes, cleaned up the scrapes and scratches as best I could, and started running.

Chapter 23

I was sweaty and tired. I'd started at a run, but weeks of not running combined with the heat soon sapped me. I slowed to a walk but refused to stop. I'd never walked through this countryside. I was either on a tractor or atop a wagon or in another vehicle, whether Niall's pickup or Mar's Corolla—all of it moving fast and making noise. At first, walking was unnerving— the open space, the size of the fields, the green density of woods and their unfamiliar sounds as I passed them. Insect hum and birdsong—a language I didn't understand, except for the cries of red-winged blackbirds flying above my head, scolding me for invading their territory, telling me to move it along, stranger, to get lost.

When I passed Mar's house, I felt sheepish. Thankfully she hadn't returned from church yet. Soon after, I came in sight of the Logans' house and the gardens—the flower beds, the vegetables, the fruits—all of it guarded by those two scarecrows and that owl. It was as if I was truly seeing it for the first time, the glory of it.

I walked into the Logans' kitchen about an hour after I'd started. Connie was busy filling a picnic basket sitting on the table. "You're back, Evan. I didn't hear Mar's car in the laneway."

I didn't explain my morning walk. "Are you going somewhere?"

"We're going to the lake for a swim and a picnic."

"Would you like me to do anything while you're gone?"

She continued packing the hamper. "Don't be silly. You're coming."

"But I didn't bring a swimsuit."

"That's okay, it's a nude beach." She placed a table-cloth in the hamper and closed the lid. When she looked up, she must have seen my alarm. "Just joking. A pair of shorts will do."

The beach was crowded. Niall had driven us to a nearby

lakeside town in their family car, an old station wagon with fake wood panelling on the sides. Jane had given up her back-seat passenger-side window for me and sat in the middle.

Connie found a suitable picnic table above the beach in a grassy park with some shade trees. I helped Niall clip the tablecloth to the wooden top against the wind blowing off the lake. The breeze felt cool compared to the heat just miles inland.

"With all the rain and storms last week, this is a nice break in the weather," Connie said as she shaded her eyes and looked into the distance.

She passed around cold fried chicken, potato salad, and devilled eggs. She filled glasses with lemonade. After my walk, the food and drink she'd prepared were a blessing—in spite of the flies we had to fight off, the wasps hovering above our plates.

"We'll have to wait a bit before going in the water," Connie said to Jane and Finn as she poured coffee from a thermos for herself and Niall. "We don't want to get cramps. You two can play on the swings for now."

"Evan, come push us," Jane said.

As we walked over, Finn said, "I don't need a push. I can go really high by myself."

While I pushed Jane and Finn pumped his legs to show me how high he could get, I watched Niall and Connie sitting side by side at the table, their backs to us. At one point, he reached out and took her hand. They sat looking out over the lake, talking or not talking I couldn't tell.

After some time, they stood up and took off their shirts and shorts. Finn saw their mom and dad in their bathing suits and jumped off the swing. Jane begged me to stop her. They ran over and began shedding their clothes. I joined them and took off my T-shirt.

Finn beat his tanned chest. "Me Tarzan."

Jane looked at me and laughed. "You look just like my dad. You're both wearing a white shirt."

I glanced at Niall and then checked myself—tanned face and neck, tanned arms just past the elbow. Stark white shoulders and chest—almost reflective in the sun—ghost legs. At least Niall had dark hair all over. I was all ribs and knees and thin runner's legs, topped with a glasses-wearing, hairy knob.

"You're a real farmer now, with that tan," Connie said. "Here. You better put on some sunscreen. You might want to leave your glasses here too so they don't get washed out to sea."

We grabbed towels and walked down to the water, the sand burning my feet as we looked for an open spot to claim.

We set out our towels and approached the water's edge. With my glasses off, everything beyond a few feet was blurry. I felt awkward in my cut-off jeans among the crowd of swimmers and sun worshippers young and old in colourful swimsuits, me a white slug among tanned and glistening people who'd flocked here from towns and cities.

The water was choppy. Connie walked straight in without hesitating. When the water was up to her waist she dove in. Finn followed his mother's example. Niall carried Jane in his arms as he walked out, hesitating as each wave crashed against them.

I lagged behind at the water's edge. I wasn't a good swimmer, had never taken lessons. I moved forward, a surprisingly warm wave washing over my feet and sucking at the sand around them as it retreated. But the further in I went, the colder the water felt. I held my arms across my chest. When the water reached my groin, I turned against it and began walking out.

"Just jump in," Finn said. "It's the only way to do it."

Jane said, "You're not a chicken, are you?" She made squawking noises.

I turned back. She was now in the water, having been dunked under by Niall. I tucked my hands into my armpits, turning my arms into wings. I flapped them and started running into the lake, splashing and lifting my legs high against the waves. I lost my balance and capsized into the water, pummelled by a wave. I found my feet and came up spluttering and rubbing water from my eyes.

Niall said, "Try being a duck next time. Chickens can't swim."

Niall was helping Jane and Finn build a sandcastle. After

swimming, I sat at the picnic table with a towel around my shoulders watching them and studying the lake, water shining in the sun all the way to the horizon, so bright it hurt my eyes. Connie sat beside me drinking another coffee.

"It's good to get away, even for a few hours," she said. "I love it here, but it's not the same as the ocean." She talked about the east coast, about her family there. What with the farm and the kids, she hadn't been back since her honeymoon.

"Do you miss it?"

"Some days." She paused a moment, and said, "Most days."

"What about teaching?"

"What about it?" she said, laughing. "I miss it just a bit, though teenagers can be a real pain in the ass." She paused again. "No, when you've got your own kids, every day you're a teacher. Besides, I've got plenty to keep me busy, what with the house, the chickens, and the gardens. When I got married, I discovered I loved gardening. The soil here is so rich, so different from the rocky land where I grew up. I can't keep my hands out of it." Then, as if talking to herself, she said, "Don't know what I'd do without it."

I mentioned I'd been looking at her books and asked if that was okay. "Of course," she said. "Books are for reading. They've been some of my best friends. Come to think of it, a book is kind of like a garden too."

"One's missing." I confessed I had a thing about

numbers and had counted them each night.

"*Great Expectations*," she said. "My bedtime reading right now." She told me about some of her favourite books, and her days in university and teacher's college, her decision to come out here where she knew no one and had no family, then meeting Niall at a Legion dance—what a gentleman he'd been. By then, his parents, whom he'd taken care of for years, had died and he was alone on the farm, their only child, the last of the Logans.

"It's good for him to get away from all the work and worry for an hour," Connie said. She took another sip of coffee and seemed to study her husband, either him or the horizon, I couldn't tell which. The wind had picked up and the waves grown stronger, washing further up the beach. Niall was helping Finn build a sand wall to keep the waves from washing away the castle Jane continued to build.

The largest wave yet came crashing up the beach, washed over the three of them kneeling there, over the wall as well, and sucked much of the sand back with it.

They were too far away for us to hear what they said. Jane stood and threw down her pail. Finn tried to stop the castle from melting and retreating.

Niall stood and put his hands to his head. I couldn't tell if his distress was real or play acting. Then he seemed to be laughing.

During the afternoon milking, I thought about holding

back waves. How could it be done? My ancestors were famous for doing it with dykes. But the financial wave Niall and Connie were facing—that would require a different kind of dyke. Would it be possible to build one?

The dinner table was quiet to begin with, an aftereffect of a day in the sun at the beach. At the centre of the table stood the pitcher of milk Niall had brought in. I sipped my water and studied the pitcher. I glanced at Jane's and Finn's half-empty glasses, their milk moustaches.

I drained the water from my glass and set it before my plate. "Connie, could you pass the milk, please."

A moment of silence followed, forks and knives pausing in midair. Only chewing continued. If I'd farted, they couldn't have been more surprised. Connie said, "Certainly."

The jug was sweaty with condensation. I filled my glass and brought it to my lips. A sip became a swallow became a gulp. Had I ever tasted anything so rich? It was the milk of human kindness, of bovine kindness also, filling me— and I thanked those cows out in the pasture for it.

I put down my empty glass. Jane clapped. Finn said, "Told you it's the best."

Niall's face wore a smirk. "Finish your dinner, you two. Leave Evan to enjoy his."

I filled my glass again.

Before I headed for bed that evening, I said to Connie and Niall, "Thanks for today. I enjoyed it." I wanted to add that it had meant a lot to me, but then I'd have to explain why and might blurt out that it was my birthday. It would feel like begging for attention as the clock wound down to zero.

In my room, I stood in the middle some moments and looked around, unnerved at how familiar it was feeling. I didn't dare use the word "home" for it.

I turned to the dresser and emptied each drawer onto the bed. As best I could, I sorted and folded my clothes— not very neatly, given that my mom had always done it for me, but good enough. I returned them to the drawers, all except my running clothes, which I put back on the corner chair.

I looked at my running log on the desk. Without picking it up, I flipped it open using one finger to an early page. There it was in black and white: 13.1 miles / 21.08 kilometres, and Mr. Ashby's wisdom on destinations. From afar, the man was still being a pain in my ass. Maybe it was time to write him another letter giving him a piece of my mind.

I parked my backside at the desk and stared out the window into the dark, listening to the leaves rustling in a breeze that had travelled here off the lake.

Instead of another letter to Mr. Ashby, I decided it was time I wrote back to my brother. I slid open a desk drawer and rummaged for more paper and an envelope. What I pulled out were piles of invoices and bank statements and tally sheets, plus a notebook filled with numbers and jottings. The previous fall, I'd taken Business Math, one of my efforts to please my dad. Without thinking, I started reviewing and organizing all the paperwork.

After about fifteen minutes, though, I stopped. I was nosy, but this felt like an invasion into territory that wasn't any of my business. I found a piece of paper and an envelope, then put the financial records back in the drawer—now just a little neater than they'd been before.

I picked up the pen and stared at the blank sheet for some time.

Dear Putz,
I don't need to be saved by the likes of you.
Evan
PS Mar's too good for the likes of you too.

Not terribly eloquent, but it would have to do.

I undressed and pulled Blake's *Songs* off the shelf, not bothering to count the books anymore. Tonight, I'd leave the book on the desk when I finished reading it through. The night before, I'd reread it and would again tomorrow and for several more days. At odd hours in the coming weeks, lines from the poems would come to me. Maybe it was years of memory work in Sunday School, but I discovered a knack for storing the words inside until they were needed, when of their own volition they would surface.

I slid into bed, careful not to knock off the wet shorts draped over the footboard to dry, and began studying the book's cover, those figures I now knew were Adam and Eve cast out of the Garden of Eden after their fall. I opened to the first poem.

When I was done, I felt as if I understood my life, myself, even less than when I woke up that morning. Like Rick and Roger, I asked, "Please tell me who I am?" I thought I might find some answers if I performed an inventory of the day. Why I'd done what I did, how I'd come to choose to stay—I couldn't tease it out. My attraction to Mar, what I was beginning to feel for the Logans and their farm—it was all uncertain, troubling. *Thanks, Mr. Blake. You too, Rick and Roger—the question is still hanging in the air. Mr. Ashby, where would I be without you and your damn finish lines? Oh yes, thank you, Canadian government, for your anti-drug ad. Thanks too, God.*

Dammit, Mar. Most of all, you and your bloody magnetism. Thanks a bunch.

Such a big help, all of you.

Mr. Ashby came back to school the September after that road race, born again and filled with the Spirit. The Frozen Chosen, even Chilly Sillies like me, were wary of Born-Agains. I found it hard to understand his conversion, his joy, given his logical, mathematical mind. When I asked him about it, he said, "Not everything in life adds up." The words were there in my running log. After, I'd written "Why not?"

I hadn't found an answer yet.

Chapter 24

Something awoke in me that day. What the something was, I didn't know yet, but the next day, I started asking questions, and day after day I kept peppering Niall and Connie with them. I didn't let up. Often, my questions were asked wearing a milk moustache.

For Niall: Why do the cows need hay and grain when they're eating grass in the pasture all day? What's in the grain you feed them? What's the deal with corn silage? Kinda nasty stuff! Why do you add that in sometimes, and why in the world do the cows like it? The fermentation? It's kind of like booze, then? Why are cows chewing like that nonstop when they're lying down? How long does a cow give milk before she dries up? When do you breed them, and how do you breed them with your bull? Sounds dangerous! How long is a cow's pregnancy? Nine months? Just like a woman's! How do you know when a heifer is ready to breed? What about male calves, what happens to them? How does the quota system work? How do you get quota? What if your cows produce more milk than the quota you have? Can I spend some time helping Connie in the garden?

For Connie: Can I help you in the garden? What's this plant? What's that one? How do you know potatoes are ready to harvest if they're hidden underground? What are those flowers? What's the difference between a perennial and an annual? I mean, the flowers are pretty, I guess, but what's the point? Okay, they're good for the bees, but why would you want bees? They sting! What? The planet wouldn't survive without bees? That's crazy! What was God thinking? Could we survive without chickens? They're kind of smelly and creepy, like feathery little raptors. What's your favourite book? *Jane Eyre*? Never heard of it. So you named Jane after Jane Eyre? Jane Austen too, a writer? Has she written anything good? You also have an aunt down east named Jane? That's a lot of Janes for Jane to live up to. What about Finn? So it's really Finlay? Niall's middle name—that's neat. And Huck Finn too?

I made a nuisance of myself. I wanted to know the

answers to these questions and so many more. I wanted explanations that made sense of things.

Here's what I asked Niall and Connie near the end of the week, Jane and Finn having gone to bed, me thinking of those papers in the desk: Are you going to lose the farm? Will you sell it to Jacob, or is the bank going to take it? Is there anything I can do to help? They explained. I said, "I'm good with numbers."

By midweek, it's possible Niall was tired of being peppered with questions. After the morning milking on the Wednesday, he said we were going on a field trip to get some answers from the experts.

I was surprised when Mar pulled into the laneway as we were getting ready to leave. Apparently, she was coming along. It was the first time I'd seen her since my aborted farewell on Sunday. I'd dreaded seeing her again, all the while fruitlessly concocting plans to do so, thinking what I might say to her. Now that she was in front of me, I was flushed with embarrassment and filled with hope. People talk about butterflies in the stomach. Well, mine was filled with bees.

"I've got a friend in Guelph I want to say hi to," she said. "Plus, I'm doing some scouting for my brothers, you know, Rural Rube and Simple Simon, 'cause my father will likely send them there to get some farming sense knocked into them."

"You can lead a horse to water," I said. "And those two are senseless asses."

"I'll tell them you said that. They're still smarting."

"From what?" Niall said. Mar explained the drubbing I'd given to them, spinning out the story so she had Niall laughing. She exaggerated quite a bit, I have to confess, but my name in her mouth made my heart swell. "About time," Niall said. "Didn't think you had it in you."

"Is it safe to ride in the truck with you?" Mar asked.

"I'll be as meek as a lamb," I said, thinking all the while I was the one in danger, Mar being a tiger.

We climbed in, me in the middle, both legs to the right of the gear stick so Niall could work it. My right leg might as well have been tied to Mar's left leg, ready for a two-legged race at a fair, it was that snug in the cab. I was wearing a short-sleeved button-up shirt, she a short-sleeved blouse. The skin of our upper arms was touching. I kept my forearm turned away from her, my hand in my lap. Our heads were close enough that loose hairs tickled my ear as wind flowed in through the open window. Given my mop of hair, it's possible mine was tickling her.

She wore a bandana loosely tied around her throat, the knot ends drawing my attention to her cleavage. I was wearing the bandana she'd given me, not nearly as attractively tied; it certainly wasn't drawing attention to my chest, not that there was much to look at. Most of the time, I pretended to be looking out the window at the landscape, but I was really studying her in profile—the line where her hair met her forehead, all the curves of her face—her eyebrow and eye, the point of her nose, her lips and chin, her cheekbone with the blushed skin over it. I noticed she was wearing makeup, which I'd only ever seen on Sundays. Just above her bandana, I could see her pulse working the skin.

At one point, she said, "It's rude to stare."

"Just admiring the view." When she turned to look at me, I added, "Out the window. You know, the beautiful countryside." I shifted my attention forward and thanked God I'd put on an extra layer of deodorant after milking—and could cover my crotch with my hand.

Niall and I parted from Mar at the agricultural college's parking lot, arranging to meet for lunch before heading back.

He clearly knew the place and some of the people there. As we toured it, he explained the type of training it offered in modern farming methods, techniques such as low-till or no-till, along with the research it did. We toured test sites for crops where scientists bred and cross-bred for productivity and drought resistance and protection against diseases. All this would be needed as the world's population grew. Genetics was the newest frontier, he said, and was proving a game-changer. There was also a strong movement to better environmental practices, less fertilizer, less pesticide. Organic farming he was a bit skeptical about, but it was becoming popular—something of a European import, he said.

I'd never seen anything like the dairy research facility. It seemed space-age and sci-fi, even more so than Jacob's farm. I wasn't sure it could be called farming anymore. In one building, we came upon an enormous Holstein bull. He was in a large room on the other side of observation glass. His handlers had inserted a device into his butt, an electro-ejaculator Niall called it, and were collecting semen from his bull-sized, highly stimulated penis. Impressive, but scary. "That's likely worth thousands of dollars," Niall said. "Liquid gold." He said Holstein semen was shipped around the world, Canadian Holsteins were that good. He explained artificial insemination, along with the value and importance of good and careful breeding to get quality cows with high milk production. "That's my goal," he said. "More of a dream, maybe just a pipe dream. Slowly change over my herd to purebred Holsteins with better production so I can afford to purchase a bit more quota and make enough profit to keep the farm for Finn and Jane."

When we got together later for lunch in the cafeteria, Mar had a large stack of papers, forms, and flyers in a plastic bag bearing the name and crest of the college.

"How was your visit with your boyfriend," I said after swallowing a bite of my sandwich.

She'd just taken a bite of hers. She stopped chewing, but didn't answer until she'd swallowed. "Not my boyfriend."

"Oh, right," I said. "That's Gerrit." She blushed at his

name. I pushed harder. "Of course, you could have more than one boyfriend, like one in every city."

"Nope, just a friend. Of course, you wouldn't know about that, would you, having none."

Touché, I thought. A hit, a palpable hit. "Okay, so what's her name then, this so-called friend?"

"Shasta, not that it's any of your business."

"Like the daisy?"

"Since when do you know the name of flowers, City Slicker?"

I wiped some mayo off my chin with my paper napkin. "I happen to live for flowers. Always have, Marigold."

"Connie taught him the name yesterday," Niall said. "He's started helping her in the garden, making a right nuisance of himself, she said, peppering her with questions. Said she felt like she was back in the classroom."

It was my turn to blush.

"Marigold, huh?" Mar said. "Wrong again. I bet you wouldn't know a marigold if it bit you in the ass."

"I didn't know they were carnivorous, but I would recognize one. Connie taught me."

"Carnivorous. Look at you, using a big word. Did you learn it in school? You deserve a reward." She tossed a cherry tomato from her salad at me. It bounced off my forehead into my lap.

"Children, children," Niall said. "Get along or I'll have to put you both in timeout." He took a sip of coffee.

"Connie taught me that parenting technique." After a moment, he said to Mar, "How's the nursing program going? Looking forward to going back in the fall?"

Mar finished chewing, and said, "Good, good." She speared some salad with her fork and studied it. "The program's tough but good. I learned a lot last year, about nursing, about myself. You know, being away from home for the first time."

She'd sounded cheerful, but I sensed a note of sadness in her voice, a note she was struggling to hide. Mr. Blake's lines surfaced in my mind. "The days of my youth rise fresh in my mind, my face turns green and pale."

When we got back to the farm, another letter from my mother was waiting for me. It was in a large envelope, and within the envelope was a second envelope with my name and home address neatly typed on it. The envelope bore the return address and crest of William Lyon Mackenzie King Secondary School, a lion-head in profile roaring. The envelope bore the marks of having been steamed open and then resealed.

I read the note from my mother first.

Dearest Evan,

I hope you're eating right and drinking lots of water. It's very dangerous to let yourself get dehydrated when you are working in this heat. I hope, as well, that Mr. and Mrs.

Logan don't make you work outside in storms. We have had some terrible storms here with dangerous lightning. Make sure you aren't touching any metal if you must work in the rain.

This letter from the school arrived for you. I will leave you to open it since it looks official and is addressed to you. Besides, now that you are 18 (did you have a great birthday? did you like the card I sent?) I think it would be a federal crime for me to open mail addressed to you. Your father and I are still your parents, but you are now an adult, and I must respect the laws of this land. Your father and I sacrificed so much to come to Canada so that our children, you included, could have a better life. I don't want to ruin those chances by getting a police record, which would be a dark stain on the whole family.

I'm eagerly waiting for your return home.

Love,

Mom

PS I hope your soul continues to be fed at church each Sunday. Your body and soul must both eat regularly or they starve together, so closely were they knit together by God in my womb.

I paused for a moment on that PS. My body seemed to be doing better, now that I'd started drinking milk again and dousing my cereal with it. My soul? That was still up in the air.

I opened the letter from the school. Below the date was

"Mr. Evan Mulder" and my home address typed in full, then the letter proper.

Dear Evan:

Re: Judgement Regarding Admittance into Grade 13

The senior administrative team has met to discuss your academic performance in the winter term of the 1978-1979 academic year. Said team deliberated long and hard on the merits of barring you from the university preparatory year versus the benefits of allowing you to take it. We sincerely fear that allowing you to do so would risk further difficulty and possible failure, an event that could become a potentially catastrophic stain on your permanent academic record, which we hope to avoid for your sake at all costs.

However, given the events that transpired this past winter term, it was a particularly difficult time for you. We see that now. For that reason, the team has made a decision to allow you entry into Grade 13. We took into account your academic record prior to that term, and we will put into place supports that will help you rebound from the difficulties you experienced.

It is our heartfelt hope to see you succeed! The week prior to the beginning of school, please contact Ms. Turnbull in the Guidance Office in order to make actionable the supports designed to ensure that success.

Yours sincerely,

Principal Philip Stickley, BA, BEd, MEd

I tucked the letter back in the envelope and placed it in the larger envelope, along with my mother's letter, then put it with my other letters under the mattress. Combined, they were now the thickness of a pea. It was time for the afternoon milking.

Later that evening, I reread both letters. I'd been readmitted. I felt torn about that judgement. It gave me a choice, but I wasn't sure it was a choice I wanted to make. Did I really want to go back to school? For what? What was waiting for me there except that sense of being in a sailboat on a perfectly calm sea, no wind to move me, no land in sight—just adrift on invisible currents.

I flipped open my running log and looked for some Ashbyism to help me decide. Instead, he gave me another Einstein nugget: "As far as the laws of mathematics refer to reality, they are not certain, and as far as they are certain, they do not refer to reality." I was definitely mired in an uncertain reality.

I pulled out a sheet of paper. *Dear Mr. Ashby,* I wrote. *I'm not sure what to do...*

When I was finished, I undressed and lay in bed trying to read Blake's *Songs* again. A dream began floating to the surface of my mind. At first, it was just a small bubble. Why couldn't I stay here on the farm, escape the city and all my troubles, leap out of my old life and land in this new one? I was alarmed at first at the thought. Until then, I'd struggled to get away from this place or simply endure it until my sentence was over.

The dream began churning. Mar surfaced in the turbulent vision, a source of agitation. We were married, together on a farm just like this one. It was a picture that disturbed me, leading to lovely impure thoughts. Mar was tying my hands and feet with bandanas to an iron bed frame. I was naked. She was in uniform, and she was nursing me back to health.

A pup tent formed beneath the sheets covering my groin. I tried to banish the vision—and failed miserably.

That night, a cow gave birth. When Niall discovered it the next morning, we went out to the pasture, me with a wheelbarrow. He led the cow into the barn where for the next ten months or so she'd offer up the milk generated by her pregnancy for Niall and his family instead of for her calf.

I picked up the calf and placed it in the wheelbarrow. The calf was a heifer. "Lucky you," I said to her. "You're not a bull calf. Lucky for Niall too." As I wheeled her to the barn, I chanted, "Little calf, who made thee? Dost thou know who made thee? Gave thee life and bid thee feed, by the stream and o'er the mead?" I knew the cow and Niall's bull had something to do with it. Indirectly, Niall too, for he was the matchmaker. Beyond that, it was a mystery to me. Born-again Mr. Ashby might have had an answer.

CHAPTER 25

"**H**old the body snug with both hands, keeping the wings pinned," Niall said to me. "Place the head there on the chopping block. Whatever you do, don't move and don't let go."

At breakfast that morning—about a week after I'd received my get-out-of-jail letter from school—Connie had said to Niall, "The chickens have reached market weight. Can we take care of them this afternoon?"

I imagined a truck coming to transport them to wherever chickens got turned into packaged meat sitting on grocery refrigerator shelves or deep fried and deposited in a bucket.

Those yellow puffballs I'd met that first Sunday evening had grown into the white Leghorns I'd seen in the run for some weeks now. That afternoon, we were butchering them and putting them in a large freezer. It was one of the ways Connie supplemented the farm's dairy income—raising chickens for themselves but also selling them to neighbours.

Mar had been enlisted to help with the operation, which was set up in a large room in the coop. I'd bring the chickens out one door alive, Niall would chop off their heads, and Mar would bring the headless chickens in another door to the room where a large vat of boiling water waited. She and Connie would dip the carcasses in the vat, hang the birds by their feet on hooks and, using gloves, rub and pull all the feathers off. Connie would carefully gut the birds, bag them, and hand them to Finn and Jane, who would put them in the freezer.

I wasn't keen to witness the journey a chicken made from clucking, scratching, pecking bird to packaged meat, let alone lead them on their walk to the guillotine. The phrase "Off with their heads!" came to me from a book I had to read in grade school, a book about a girl named Alice who rather carelessly fell down a rabbit hole. The day was beginning to feel like one.

After lunch, Niall sharpened his axe on the grindstone

in the machine shed. I felt edgy waiting for the cauldron of water to boil. When Connie gave the signal, everyone went to their stations. Finn and Jane helped me catch a bird and showed me how to hold it with its wings pinned.

I brought it to Niall, waiting at the chopping block. I followed his directions and laid the head on it. The bird's eye darted about.

The axe came down and the chicken's head fell to the ground cleanly. As blood poured from the neck, I felt the body convulse and the legs kick. I held tight until the body went limp, then passed it to Mar. I felt shaky as I went to fetch the next bird from death row.

The axe came down again and again. The bloodied heads piled up at the base of the chopping block. Sweat or tears or some combination of the two was beginning to blur my vision, to stain my glasses. I laid the next bird's head on the block. The axe came down and severed its head from its body. As the head fell, I lost my grip.

The bird flapped and flapped its wings and kicked its feet. I managed to grab one of its legs before it got away. The bird flapped wildly at the end of my hand, blood spraying from its neck—all over me, all over Niall, all around the chopping block. Finally, I let go. The bird fell to the ground, ran a few paces, and fell over.

My first thought was, *it's true; chickens can run with their heads cut off.*

I looked at Niall through drops of blood on my glasses.

Splattered, he held his arms wide, the axe still in his right hand, and looked at his clothes, stunned. He looked up, pointed the axe at me, and started laughing.

I started laughing too. Or rather, I was laughing and crying. Someone should invent a word for laughing and crying at the same time. Crauphing or laurying, maybe, though they don't quite capture the spirit of it.

Laughing and crying, I looked at the limp, headless bird on the ground and saw again Mr. Ashby's body.

It came back to me in a wave that washed over me and threatened to pull me under, what I'd held back or pressed down for so long in hopes I wouldn't ever see it again. I felt my knees weaken and I collapsed onto them in the bloody dirt.

Mr. Ashby came to school early every morning to run the three-mile circuit we used as part of our training. He'd invited me to run it with him any time I wanted to, and most mornings I did.

That morning, I hadn't made it on time—late because I'd overslept, having stayed up the night before finishing homework I'd procrastinated doing.

I thought perhaps I might catch up to him, or at least when I'd finished the circuit I could meet him at the school to show him I'd completed it, kept up my training.

There had been a late-winter melt. The roads were wet. Slushy, dirty snow was receding into ditches and melting into curbs and rushing into drains. I came up to the scene on a stretch of the busy main road that cut through our subdivision. I slowed to a walk and looked for a way around the police cruiser and ambulance, both their lights flashing. An officer was directing traffic, two paramedics working on a fallen body. The road was too busy to cross. I'd have to go into the ditch off the shoulder, still snowy, to skirt the accident.

As I dipped into the ditch, slush beneath the top layer of snow filled my shoes with icy water. I could see the limp body clearly—Mr. Ashby in his school track suit. His head lying there looked strangely heavy.

I felt a weight descend on me, both outside and inside. I kept moving, trying to escape the weight. I started running again. I completed the circuit, but the weight was still there. I'd been running with it ever since, running in place, running even when still, running away.

That day and the ones that followed remain a blur—the principal coming to our homeroom, the announcement of Mr. Ashby's death over the intercom, like just another morning announcement after the recording of "Oh Canada" and the Lord's Prayer. Classes followed each other in their planned succession. A day or two later, a special assembly. I skipped it.

I'd presumed at first he'd been hit by a car, possibly hit-and-run since there was no car at the scene. It seemed inconceivable that a marathoner like Mr. Ashby could suffer a heart attack while doing a simple three-mile run.

Then we were told what happened, an explanation for what seemed inexplicable. He'd suffered a brain aneurysm, had died more or less instantly there at the side of the road. Mr. Ashby, who'd praised the human brain, one of the mysteries and marvels of the universe, he'd called it, his brain had killed him. "Off with his head" the universe, that crazy Queen of Hearts, had cried.

I went to the visitation at the funeral home. There in the casket lay the body of Richard Ashby, in a dark suit I'd never seen him wear, eyes closed and hands folded across his chest. I couldn't jive the body with the man I'd seen in homeroom every day of school, in Math class teaching us the wonders of numbers.

Born again the summer before, now dead—John the Baptist, his head on a platter.

I shook the hands of his parents, of his children and his wife, and could offer nothing but "My condolences."

What I should have told them is that I loved him, that I was in love with him, whatever that means.

I loved my parents, even my brother and sister—with a family love. But I loved Mr. Ashby in a way I didn't and maybe still don't understand.

From the moment of his death, my life was turmoil. I found no rest. I kept running, running sometimes filled with rage and bitterness, sometimes sadness. I'd run over the spot where he'd fallen. I'd run against the traffic on the road rather than on the sidewalk or shoulder. I'd dare cars to hit me, giving them no grace. It came to me that all I needed to do was leap further into the road and it would be over. Other times, I'd run with the traffic, sensing cars and trucks coming up behind me, blind to them but feeling the rush of sound and wind hit my back—my body just another machine heading down the road, lungs pumping air, heart pushing blood through pipes, brain sending electrical currents to muscles contracting and relaxing like elastic bands.

Since his death, I'd been a chicken running around with my head cut off—the rest of the school year, so far this summer. Running around and running away, running on empty—the well of myself empty, or filled with emptiness.

Rick and Roger, I asked, *is a time of sadness truly a time to understand?*

"O!" said Mr. Blake the poet of lost innocence, "He gives to us his joy, that our grief he may destroy. Till our grief is fled and gone, he doth sit by us and moan."

Was that to be believed as I knelt there covered in blood, laughing and crying?

Mar came to fetch the next dead bird and found us in this state. "Are you guys insane? Looks like the set of a horror movie out here." She picked up the bird and took it to the finishing room. Moments later she returned with towels for Niall and me. Connie and the kids followed to survey the scene of the crime.

Niall and I wiped the blood from our arms and faces. I cleaned the blood, sweat, and tears from my glasses as best I could with my Supertramp T-shirt, then went to get the next chicken for Niall's axe.

Chapter 26

That night I retrieved from beneath my pillow the four letters I'd written to the ghost of Mr. Ashby since arriving at the farm. I re-read them, then tucked them inside the front of my running log.

Nowadays, in the wake of such a tragic death, an army of psychologists and counsellors would descend upon a school to heal the students through talk therapy. If they had back then, a squadron of them, like military police, might have tracked AWOL me through the city from the hospital to the university to that industrial park. They would have transported me back to the school, sat me in a comfortable chair in a small room, and encouraged me to spill my guts—to share my feelings, then ask me what my feelings were about those feelings. All very touchy feely. At the time, that simply wasn't done—certainly not at working-class WLM-KSS. Even if counselling had been available, I doubt I'd have talked about what I'd seen on the road, the grief I felt for a lost love. I'd closed down. I talked to no one, had no one to talk to.

I drew apart, and I ran—away, or around and around in circles, chasing my tail. Thinking that with enough spinning, I could both contain and hide the pain—until, too late, the teachers and my family learned I'd fallen apart.

When I look back on that time, I'm struck now by an act of generosity from my parents, both before and after Mr. Ashby's death, a decision they may not even have realized was a gift. It must have frightened my mother especially. Though my infant illnesses had left me with a heart murmur, my parents never once stopped me from running. Perhaps my dad thought the running would toughen me, even strengthen my heart and help me grow a set of bootstraps. Maybe unknown to me, my mom had checked first with a doctor to ensure it was safe.

With the chicken butchering, I finally faced what had happened, even if I didn't yet understand all these things. In the early afternoon of the following day, I was hoeing in the garden, sweating, my back sore. It occurred to me that when my parents found out about my collapse and failure, they didn't know how to deal with me except through what they themselves knew. Children in Holland during the war, they'd experienced hardship and suffering I couldn't comprehend. Had they also witnessed death? As immigrants, they'd risked much, left behind so much. Work was their therapy, maybe especially for my dad; sending me to the farm was his idea of therapy for me. I was caught unaware by the thought that this was love. Overwhelmed, I struggled with it clutching at my throat and chest. I looked around to make sure no one was watching. I let the tears come; I hoed them into the ground as they fell.

That night in my room, I pulled the piles of papers out of the desk drawers and went back to sorting them, Janus finally coming in handy.

My thoughts and feelings were somehow mixed with casting about for a way to help Niall and Connie save the farm. Part of it, I have to confess, was my desire to thwart Jacob in his plot to buy their land and milk quota. I didn't fully understand my antipathy to him, but it was real. Perhaps it had something to do with his greed for more land when in the end we all end up like Mr. Ashby, six feet under in a tiny piece of real estate.

When I'd asked about their troubles, Niall was reluctant to open up, saying I needn't concern myself about them. Connie was more forthcoming, saying they were between a rock and a hard place. Jacob's persistent pressure with his offer was the rock, the bank's loan requirements the hard place—they needed to look at the farm's books and they wouldn't extend more credit without a solid business plan for making the farm profitable.

It turned out all that paperwork had been sitting in the desk in my room—out of sight, out of mind, I guess. Neither Niall nor Connie, it seemed, had a head for that side of things and used the desk drawers to put off dealing with it.

I searched the drawers for bills, receipts, and bank statements. During my digging, I came across binders and folders filled with the paperwork of Connie's earlier life—lesson plans for the novels and poems and plays she taught high school students, grammar exercises she'd used, essays she'd written herself in English classes at university. I confess I was a terrible snoop, but I was curious to understand the words she'd written, to read her thoughts from school days and study the red-ink comments from her professors, mostly praise, A grades. An essay that earned an A+ comparing Blake's two Nurse's Songs.

Late into the night, I sat sorting and calculating. On the surface, it seemed simple. They needed more revenue coming in than was going out. I hoped I could somehow help them tip the scales in the right direction. It felt good to bring order out of that chaos, to make sense of income and expenses so they could get a picture of how money was flowing, or not, as it were.

Doing these calculations, hoeing the garden—in ways I

didn't understand they offered some solace against the loss I now felt keenly.

After the next morning's milking and breakfast, I brought all the sorted paperwork down to the kitchen table.

"What's all this?" Niall said, looking at me through the mudroom door. He'd been putting his work boots back on. Connie paused in doing the dishes, began drying her hands on the towel, and turned to hear my answer.

I looked down at the table and began placing the papers in neat piles. "I thought I'd help get things sorted out."

They were silent for a few moments. I looked up. They were studying each other. Connie was the first to speak. "You did this for us?" She folded the tea towel and placed it on the counter.

"Okay, then," Niall said, slipping off his boots. "Show us what you've got."

We sat at the table and went through the numbers. I showed them the tallies I'd made and the simple bookkeeping system I'd set up for them, the single-entry system I'd learned in my Business Math class. They could use it to track the flow of money through daybooks—records of sales, purchases, receipts, and payments. As they listened, I could sense their concentration and relief.

"This is so helpful," Connie said.

"You're really good at these numbers," Niall added. "You could do something with this."

Do something? Sitting there, it came to me how orderly finances, even if they're meagre, could offer solace, build courage and resolve. Perhaps small consolation, but consolation nonetheless.

Though we discussed possible futures, Niall and Connie were still no closer to a business plan that would satisfy the bank—and their deadline was looming.

Later that week, Niall said the barley was ripe and would be coming down in the next day or two. To get ready, the granary had to be emptied of last year's remaining barley. He called in Mar and put her in charge of getting it done, made me her sidekick.

The granary was a tall metal cylinder with a door at the base and a hatch in the cone at the top that could be reached by a ladder running up its side. Mar explained that we needed to shovel all the grain out the lower door into an auger that would carry it up into grain wagons. When we'd cleaned out the granary, we'd take the wagons to the grain elevators in town.

"But first," she said, "we have to climb up into the granary and break the crust on the top. This sometimes happens with stored grain, along with a buildup of gases. Very dangerous. We'll have to be careful. Grain can be like quicksand. Plus the gases can knock you out. Farmers have suffocated in minutes."

"We both have to climb that ladder?"

"Afraid of heights?"

"No. Just of falling."

"I need you to spot me while I go in, so you'll need to suck it up, buttercup."

"I know now what a buttercup looks like. I'll take that as a compliment."

Mar clambered up the ladder with a rope looped over her shoulders and opened the hatch. While she tied the rope to the top rung, I followed slowly, making the mistake of looking back down when I reached her.

She dropped the rope into the granary, swung herself through the hatch, and looked back at me. "You keep a watch on me in case anything goes wrong."

"And what the hell do I do if it does?"

"You'll think of something. Yell 'help' like the little girl you are." When she saw my face, she added, "Nothing's going to happen. I'm just messing with you."

The moment after she said that, the knot she'd made gave way. She yelled out. A thud reverberated throughout the bin. "Shit, Evan! Help, I'm sinking."

I climbed up and looked in. I saw her prostrate body below. "What do I do?" My voice echoed through the dim, hollow space. She looked spread eagle, as if she was floating on her back.

She didn't answer. I hesitated. There wasn't time to get help. She could disappear in moments. A metal bar ran vertically up the inside of the bin—if I could somehow retrieve the rope and tie it around my waist and then to the bar, I might be able to pull Mar out. I entered the hatch and hung from its edge. So that I would land in reach of the rope but also the bar, I swung wide and let go.

I landed and felt myself sinking. I reached for the bar, grabbed it with my fingers, and stretched my other hand for the rope. I'd sunk past my knees. The rope was getting farther away. It was looking hopeless.

Laughter rang through the bin, an echoing bell. I held the bar and turned to the voice. Mar was standing up, covered in dust, grain just above her waist, grain filling her hair. "Gee, Evan. I didn't expect you to leap to my rescue."

I let go of the bar and felt my feet sink to the granary's cement floor. I looked at the sea of grain and at Mar, a ghost in the dim light. I noticed then behind her the granary door only half covered. "Dammit, Mar, not funny," I said. "I thought you were going to die." I wiped at grain dust turning to mud on my face.

"It was just a joke, Evan. Lighten up."

"Some joke. You're just like your turd brothers."

"No I'm not. That's not true." Before I could argue the point, she said, "And what about that stunt you pulled just walking away that Sunday?" She waded over to the door, unlatched it, and pushed it open. She stepped out. Moments later she reappeared holding two shovels. "Start digging."

Chapter 27

I still wasn't talking to Mar the next day when the barley came down. She didn't seem terribly bothered by the silent treatment. Maybe she preferred it.

Since Niall didn't have his own combine, he'd made an agreement with Jacob to take down the field. Niall appeared not to find this arrangement awkward; at least, he didn't show it. But as Jacob ran the combine through the field—the front attachment like an enormous paddle wheel cutting down the barley and gathering in the stalks, the interior of the machine magically separating the grain from the chaff and spitting the chaff and straw out the back—I couldn't help feeling that with each circuit of the field Jacob was thinking, *Soon all this will be mine!*

Niall manned the grain wagons. After Jacob filled them with barley, Niall pulled them to the granary. He opened a chute at the bottom of the wagon, and the barley would spill onto the same augur we'd used the day before to empty the granary. This time, though, the auger drew the barley to the hatch at the top of the bin, spitting it down to where Mar had played her practical joke on me.

Mar and I followed in the wake of the combine to bale the straw and load it on wagons, which one half of Reubeon took to the barn, where the other half worked to stack it separate from the hay.

I found it easy to avoid talking to Mar. I was driving the tractor while she built the loads. That doesn't mean I wasn't able to send her messages. Each time we started a new load, I jerked the tractor forward so she lost her balance. Twice I managed to land her on her ass.

We exchanged words only once. We'd finished a load and were switching wagons. When she'd hitched the empty wagon to the baler, she marched forward to the tractor, climbed on the running board, and throttled it down. "I'm driving," she said. "Get down."

I smiled. "No can do. I don't know how to build a load. No joke, I swear. That's your thing. Sorry, but you'll have to get back there on the wagon."

She stared me down. "Listen, Einstein, it doesn't take a genius to figure it out." She explained how to build the load up and forward. "Now get your ass out of this seat and do some real work, you putz." She grabbed the wheel and used it as leverage to give me a hip check out of the driver's seat. I managed to keep my balance and jump off the tractor; otherwise, I would have done a face plant in front of the back tire, offering Mar a huge temptation to run me over.

I climbed aboard the wagon. As Mar started up the baler and the wagon jerked forward, I spread my legs and struggled to keep my balance. I untied the bandana from around my neck and retied it around my forehead. She gave me the peace sign looking back from the tractor. I flipped her the bird.

As I pulled the first bale from the chute, I fell over backwards with the bale on top of me. I'd forgotten that straw was lighter than hay. When I got up, I could see Mar laughing.

Jacob had finished combining the field. He and his machine were gone. The barley was in the bin, the straw in the barn, and it was only early afternoon—several hours before the next milking. "I think it's time for a little celebration," Niall said. We were up at the barn—Mar and the twins, me too, keeping a wary distance from her.

Niall was clearly pleased with how smoothly the harvest had gone, how much the field had yielded. "Evan, you're driving."

"Me? But I don't have a license."

The twins laughed. "What a dork," one of them said.

Niall said, "License? This is the country. Farm kids learn to drive as soon as their feet reach the pedals, sometimes sooner."

"That's great for them, but I don't know how to drive a stick."

"What do you think you've been doing all summer on a tractor? Don't worry, I'll show you how." He tossed me the truck keys. I fumbled the pass and they tumbled to the ground.

"Nice one, Evy," said one twin. "Yeah, like spaz out much?" said the other.

"You want another wedgie?" I said as I rose from picking up the keys.

"Shut your traps and get in the truck," Mar said as she climbed into the bed. It wasn't clear to me whether or not I was included in her command.

I slid into the driver's seat and turned to Niall. "It doesn't seem safe, me driving with them in the back."

"Nothing's going to happen," he said. "We'll take it nice and slow."

"Where are we going?"

"To the pub."

I'd watched how Mar drove on the way to church, so I had a basic sense of what was involved driving a stick. Of course, I'd been distracted by her legs and arms and all the rest of her.

With my first effort, I let the clutch out too fast. The truck jerked forward and stalled. I could hear Reubeon laughing. "Jeepers creepers, Evy, you're breaking my back."

I restarted the truck. "Gently," Niall said. "Clutch up, accelerator down until you feel the gear catch." I pressed the accelerator more than needed. The engine roared, but the gear caught and we shot forward. I ground the gears going into second, as I didn't have the clutch in far enough. But from there, Niall guided me through the archway of trees and out onto the road. I geared up to cruising speed.

I thought he'd take over when we got to the highway, but no. I had to get us to the pub or there'd be no drinks for anyone.

Keeping it slow and under control, I had vehicles whizzing past me. As we approached the church, I said a little prayer—and thanked God when Niall guided me into an angled parking spot in front of the pub. I jumped the curb, apologized, and backed it up. Reubeon congratulated me with mock clapping as they stood in the bed. When they climbed out, they gave me some heavy and hearty claps on the back too.

I was about to hold out my hand to help Mar down off the bed, then thought better of it, remembering I was giving her the silent treatment, along with the cold shoulder.

After hours of working in the sun, the pub felt cool and dim. Niall led us to a table in the middle. I tried for a chair far from Mar, but I wasn't fast enough—the twins shoved me aside. The only chair left was beside her. I went to pull the chair out, but she hooked her foot around the chair's leg. "There's an empty table over there."

"Very funny," I said, and yanked it off her foot. "The jokes just keep coming."

Niall ordered a couple of pitchers of beer and pop.

I'd never been in a bar. I'd never even had a drink. It wasn't that my parents didn't drink—my mom took sherry or wine for medicinal purposes, my dad beer and wine and occasionally something harder after work. It's just that I was underage.

The pitchers arrived. Before I could pour myself some pop, Niall filled my glass with beer. Apparently the pop was just for Reubeon. I mentioned to Niall I was also underage.

"How old are you?"

"Just 18."

"Close enough," he said. "It's more a suggestion around here." Reubeon protested they were close enough too. "Nice try," Niall said. "I'm not buying what you two are selling. I've got plenty of that in a pile at home."

Niall raised his glass. "Thanks for your hard work to-day—and all the other days." We clinked glasses. Mar avoided mine. *So petty,* I thought.

"What did you say?"

Had I said it aloud?

"I think he said 'you're so pretty.'" *Thanks for your help, Twin 1.* The awkward silence that followed was a still pool surrounded by sounds echoing through the space—the click of pool balls, the laughter of other conversations.

How could I deny it without (a) insulting Mar or (b) confessing what I'd really said? I kept quiet. I brought the beer to my lips, filled my mouth, and swallowed. I started coughing. My nose stung.

Mar smacked me on my back, and Niall passed me some paper napkins. She grabbed one from me and started wiping her arm. "Can't hold your liquor?"

"Up your nose with a rubber hose," said one half of Reubeon. The other half added, "Don't flip your wig, Evy."

When I could speak again, I said, "That tastes like cow piss!"

Mar said, "You're familiar with the taste, are you?"

"Well, it looks like cow piss."

Niall said, "The taste grows on you."

After that, I sipped the rest of my first glass more slowly. By the time I finished, I was feeling lightheaded and thick-tongued. "The taste is growing on me, Niall." He poured me a second glass.

I drank it more quickly. As I drained my glass, Niall got up, excusing himself to use the washroom. "Pour yourself another," he said. "If you think you can handle it."

I felt bubbly with confidence, and filled my third glass. Some splashed onto the table. I took a napkin and wiped at the spill in wobbly circles. My tongue had loosened, my thoughts flowing to it without their normal filters. I held up the soggy napkin and turned to Mar. "You are beautiful."

"You're drunk," she said. *Was it my hearing that was slightly slurred, or was it her voice?*

"No, I'm not," I said. "I'm happy. For the first time in a long, long time, I'm happy."

Reubeon snorted. "Groovy," said one. "Nifty," said the other.

I dropped the napkin on the floor. "I should pick that up." Instead, suddenly inspired, I rose from my chair and climbed onto it unsteadily. I leaned over, picked up my glass of beer, and raised it. "Dear Mother, dear Mother, the Church is cold," I yelled out, "But the Ale-house is healthy and pleasant and warm." I pointed to the bartender and said to him, "That's poetry, and your beer is a poem."

Mar stood and grabbed my hand. "Get down, Evan. You're making a fool of yourself, and you might get hurt."

I looked down at her. "*I'm* making a fool of myself? Listen, you, you university chicky-poo. You might have gotten hurt."

"I'm no chick, you turd."

"You should NOT have played that joke on me. You pretended to be a DAMSEL in distress. To a KNIGHT in shining armour like me, such MOCKery is UNforgivable. It's INconceivable."

"I'm no damsel, and I'll never need rescuing from the likes of you. Get down."

"I thought you were going to die," I said. "I've seen someone I love die. Let me tell you, it's not pretty, and it's definitely not funny." She looked alarmed as I tottered. She snatched the beer from my hand, placed it on the table, and grabbed my free hand to steady me. "You think your joke was pretty funny," I continued, "but last night I kept seeing your face sinking below the barley. I couldn't sleep because your face is so beautiful, you know. Your hair is the colour of rust, and you have such rosy cheeks." They turned rosier. She looked angry. I turned to Reubeon, who were snorting. "Did I say something wrong?"

Mar said, "My hair's not rust-coloured. It's auburn. And for your information, my cheeks are this way because I have rosacea."

"That sounds serious," I said. "I'm sorry you have rosacea, but it still looks beautiful, like a lovely red flower on each of your lovely cheeks."

The twins laughed. One of them said, "Oh, Evelyn, aren't you the poet! What a sissy!"

She helped me down off the chair. I felt the wet napkin beneath my right shoe, making me feel unbalanced. She looked in my eyes and hesitated a moment, as if she was looking for words. She grabbed me by the bandana around my neck, drew me to her, and kissed me.

I was shocked. My eyes widened and I tightened my lips against hers. I'd never been kissed like this before. Soon enough, I relented, closed my eyes, and relaxed my lips against hers. I opened my mouth to her searching tongue. Like my tongue, hers tasted of that lovely, poetic beer. By that point, she had me in a firm embrace, her breasts pressing against my chest.

"You can't do that," one of her brothers said. "She's my sister." Said the other, "Get your grubby lips and paws off her, you fucking city-slicker milksop."

I began to get hard.

When I'd started getting erections in adolescence, I'd discovered that my penis was a most troublesome piece of flesh. Until then, it had simply been a useful tool for emptying a full bladder, occasionally for writing my name in a snowbank. But then it became this noisy organ, saying loudly, frequently, and at inconvenient moments, "Look at me! Look at me! Pick me! Oh, please pick me!" There was no reasoning with it.

As the years passed, I came to think of it as my badly behaved and erratic divining rod. Where it pointed I couldn't help but follow. It took charge of me, misbehaving or rather behaving as it was designed to do, in ways my mind couldn't fathom, leaving me often embarrassed and ashamed.

As Mar and I kissed, my divining rod was doing what

it was designed—possibly destined—to do: point in her direction. I was sure she could feel it. She loosened her embrace and brought her hand to the front of my jeans. I raised a hand to her breast. I was beyond alarmed.

She squeezed my crotch and bit my lip. I drew back and opened my eyes, astonished. There was blood on her teeth. Reubeon were jumping up from their chairs, knocking them over. She said, "That was a holy kiss." Then she grabbed my glass of beer and poured it over my head. "I baptize you in the name of the holy cows and the little chickens and the great big horses." The beer splattered my glasses and stung my lip.

As first, I was stunned that she was capable of such sacrilege. I'd been baptized as an infant, and my thought was that it was theologically incorrect to be re-baptized, especially in the name of animals. But then, perhaps she was baptizing me into some other aspect of the faith I didn't understand and she did. We would have to discuss it later. I grabbed the half-full pitcher of beer from the table and doused her beautiful auburn hair.

Reuben and Simeon were on me like flies on shit, as the saying goes.

Looking back, I'm sure they used the kiss and the dousing as an excuse to revenge the wedgie and the boxed ears I'd given them. After all, Mar was the one who'd kissed me first, touched me there.

I fought like a drunk, enraged milksop. I roared and

lashed out at them. I grabbed one by the hair and poked the other in the eye. I bit the thumb of one and scratched the arms of the other. In the middle of it all, I heard one yell, "Jeepers creepers, you ain't fighting fair," the other whining, "You're fighting like a girl." I got one in a head-lock until the other pulled me off. I kneed him in the nuts for his trouble.

But it was two against one. Eventually I tired and felt them piling on my back. "Get off," Mar yelled as she pulled at them. I felt the weight lighten and started lashing out with my elbows.

I smacked Mar right in the face and she fell backward to the floor.

By then, Niall was back from the washroom and the bartender had worked his way through the crowd that had gathered around us egging us on.

I stood up unsteadily. My glasses were bent and crooked, barely held in place by the elastic band around my head, but I could see Mar holding her face, her nose bleeding. The bandana knot was sitting in my mouth, the two ends protruding like fangs.

"Oh shit," Niall said.

Chapter 28

y that evening, I'd sobered up from the beer. Whether I'd sobered from Mar's kiss was another matter.

I'd stepped battered and bruised out of the cool gloom of the pub into the brilliant afternoon sunlight and was momentarily blinded. I'd never felt so alive, bathed in warm rays, a child of the earth with a bleeding lip and bruised ribs.

Connie was there by then with the station wagon, Jane and Finn too. Niall had called her using the phone in the pub, the bartender insisting he wasn't sober enough to drive. His pickup would have to sit there until morning.

The ride back was quiet—Connie driving, Niall beside her in the front, neither of them talking to each other. Reuben and Simeon sat in the back seat, Mar between them to make them behave, holding a bloody tissue to her nose. I was laid out in the back of the station wagon where Finn and Jane were playing "I spy." The car's movement made me woozy, and I was dazzled by sunlight coming through the windows, the light occasionally filtered in a strobe effect through roadside trees whizzing by the window.

Connie stopped at the Van Dijck laneway to let out Mar and her brothers. "Apologize to your parents for me, will you, Mar?"

"I'll explain everything."

At home, I sat at the kitchen table with Niall and Connie while she used some small sewing tools to repair my glasses. The room was blurry without them, but her words were clear. "How could you, Niall? What will Jacob do now? You know he'll find a way to use this against us. His children involved in a barroom brawl."

"Frankly, Connie, I don't give a damn." It was a fairly good if slightly slurred imitation of Rhett Butler.

"You should. This is serious. Mar's an adult, but those twins are seriously underage and shouldn't have been there without his permission. This gives him leverage, if only moral leverage."

"He can take his leverage and shove it up his tight Dutch ass, as far as I'm concerned."

I considered whether I too had a tight Dutch ass.

Connie passed me my glasses. "And what about Evan here? Getting him drunk when we're responsible for his care."

I tried to take one for the team. "Don't blame Niall, Connie. We were celebrating, and I got carried away. He didn't force me to drink all that beer."

"Nice try, Evan," Connie said, "But Niall was the adult."

"I'm an adult, more or less," I said. "Probably less. But I am almost 19."

"You are?"

"I will be in eleven months and a little bit."

"Oh, Lord. What will your parents think?" she said.

It occurred to me in my drunken state that if they found out, they might come get me right away. My mom would insist on it, with my dad blaming his bootstraps philosophy for making me vulnerable to such immorality.

In that moment, I realized I didn't want to go, not anymore. I had unfinished business. More grieving, more loving, maybe more math. Niall, Connie, and I had been going over the books, making sure they were in perfect order for their meeting at the bank; they were still searching for the right plan, and I hoped I might be of help if they found it. "On today's events," I said, "I shall remain as silent as the grave." I pretended to turn a lock on my lips and throw away the key. I'd intended to bring my thumb and finger to my mouth but hit my nose instead.

Connie rose. "I guess I'll have to do the afternoon milking. You two are in no state to be working around cows, let alone attaching a milking machine to them."

I'd been dismissed and forgiven by Connie, Niall not so much. In my room that evening I set aside any thoughts of coming up with a scheme to save the Logan farm. My thoughts were all of Mar—that kiss, her touch, that bite. My foolish words.

Among Connie's books was a volume of Romantic poetry. Until then, I'd ignored it, thinking it likely filled with sappy love poetry. I had no idea then that "Romantic" was a period, a movement. That evening, in Saint Augustine fashion, I heard a voice, this one in my head, not outside the window, telling me to take down the book and read it. I did so, hoping I would find words pointing to my salvation.

I sat on my bed and placed the volume in my lap. I let it fall open to a page, trusting the gesture to lead me to what I needed to hear. The name looked promising. William Wordsworth. With a name like that, he had to be a great poet. I read,

My heart leaps up when I behold
A rainbow in the sky:

So was it when my life began;
So is it now I am a man;
So be it when I shall grow old
  Or let me die!
The Child is father of the Man;
And I could wish my days to be
Bound each to each by natural piety.

I'll be honest. At first I was confused and disappointed. This was no love poem, nothing I might recite to Mar while tossing bales of hay together or cleaning manure from the stalls of her father's prize purebred Friesians. I re-read the poem silently, then read it aloud.

Perhaps I wasn't as sober as I thought. "Or let me die!" Tears blurred my vision. I held them back, lifted my glasses, and wiped my eyes with my T-shirt. I read the poem aloud again, then glanced at the papers held down by Janus, my calculator sitting beside them. I turned sideways with the book still in my lap and looked out the window into the canopy of trees. A leaping heart, a life filled with natural piety. Was it even possible? I thought about where loving Mr. Ashby had gotten me, what wound it had inflicted on my heart. I read the poem aloud once again.

I opened my running log to the last page with an entry: 5.2 kilometres, around the pond. And the last Ashbyism, a gift the day before he died: "Mathematics is like love; a simple idea, but it can get complicated." On the next page, I carefully copied out the poem, and wrote after it, *Rest in peace, Mr. Ashby.*

I closed the log and placed the volume of Romantic poetry under Blake's *Songs* sitting on the desk. My thoughts wandered from rainbows back to Mar. To the problem of Mar, to my feelings for Mar. I recalled another title I'd seen on the shelves, a title that seemed to promise insight and understanding. I found it and pulled it off. *Lives of Girls and Women* by Alice Munro, a writer I'd never heard of; but then again, I'd heard of few.

I brought it back to the bed and studied the cover. The wistful woman on the front reminded me somehow of Mar, though they didn't have the same appearance. Possibly it was the expression, the eyes. I read the blurb on the back. *Cosmopolitan* recommended the book for its portrait of "the sexually awakening female." That could be useful. I liked Mar sexually awakened. Maybe the book would give me some clue about how to respond to her.

There was a quiet knock at the door. I turned the book over and covered it with my hand. "Come in."

Connie stood in the doorway. "I thought I should just check how you're doing before I turned in for the night."

"Better, thanks."

"I've brought you some aspirin and a glass of water. You might wake up in the night with a bad headache." She placed them on the desk and glanced at the book in my lap. "I'm not sure your parents would approve of that book

—the sex and some of the stuff on religion. She's a local writer, but some people have raised a stink about it, tried to get it banned from schools."

I moved my hand and turned the book back over to reveal the full cover. I could feel myself blushing.

"It's Mar, isn't it?"

I shook my head.

Connie smiled. "She's something else, isn't she?"

I shook my head again.

That night, I dreamed Mar and I were in church together sitting in the back row. As soon as the service started, though, we remembered it was our turn for Nursery. We were supposed to be downstairs. We rushed down and kept searching for the right room but they were all empty. In what seemed like a large boiler room we found an enormous gopher hole at the very root of the building. In it was a set of stairs. Mar was afraid to go first, they were so steep. She followed me. The stairs went deeper and deeper, got narrower and narrower. They seemed to be going nowhere; the sense of depth became oppressive. We turned around to go back, but for some reason Mar couldn't move. I tried to coax and coach her to move, but she couldn't. Claustrophobia in that windowless space overwhelmed me. The opposite of a fear of heights, a terror of depths.

Chapter 29

After the morning milking on the following Sunday, I sat at the breakfast table waffling in my mind. I wanted to see Mar, and I didn't. Could I face church with her?

I looked at my glass of apple juice and considered what to do. I brought it to my lips, took a sip, and yelled "Ow!" For added effect, I brought my left hand to my mouth, scrunched my eyes closed, and tried to squeeze some tears out of them.

"Still smarting?" Niall said.

"Doesn't seem to be closing up," I lied.

Jane was sitting beside me. She patted my right hand. "Do you want me to kiss your booboo better? That's what my mom does."

"No, no!" I said. "That's sweet, but I don't think it will help."

"Maybe if Mar kissed it better," Finn said, "You'd like that, wouldn't you?" For good measure, he rattled off the rhyme. "Evan and Mar sittin' in a tree, k-i-s-s-i-n-g. First comes love, next comes marriage, then comes baby in a baby carriage!"

I felt myself redden, my eyes watering for real now. For cover, I said, "Very funny. Ow!"

"Finn," Connie said, "that enough teasing."

"That was a good one though, Finn," I said and offered a fake laugh. I cut it short and grabbed my side. "I think my ribs are still badly bruised, maybe even cracked."

"If they were cracked," Niall said, "you wouldn't be able to lift hay bales or milk cans. I didn't notice you having any problems during milking."

I ignored his medical assessment and turned to Connie. "I don't think I should go to church today. There's no way I'll be able to sing or even sit for long on those hard pews. I better skip it, just this week."

Connie lifted her cup of coffee and held it by two hands in front of her, studying me for some moments. Eventually, she said, "Well, I guess your mom won't mind just this once, given the circumstances." The corner of her mouth lifted slightly. "It's not like you don't *want* to go. You just *can't* in your current condition. I can see you're hurting." She took a sip of coffee, then closed the subject, saying, "I'll call Mar and let her know."

The day after, Niall and I completed a second cutting of hay. He'd sent me back to that first field, giving me a second chance. I now had a map of gopher holes in my mind and completed the field without mishap.

When done, I paused at the edge of the field to raise the sickle-bar mower to its vertical position and lock it in place. I looked at the neat pattern of cut grass and thought of the winter day months from now when the cows would feed on it, when feeding on it would sustain their lives and become milk to sustain other lives.

At the edge of the field a fox appeared. It stood still, alert on the ground ahead. It leaped and snapped at something on the ground when it landed. It lifted its head, a tiny body in its jaws, and looked at me. It chewed briefly, swallowed, and trotted away.

Later in the week, I was sitting at the top of the attic stairs once again listening. We would be baling the second cut the next day. My nosy self was wondering if Niall and Connie would say something about the farm's future, given their bank appointment was drawing near.

"You need to put Mar and Evan together in the mow

tomorrow," Connie said.

"I'd rather have them in the field with me. They know the rhythm. The twins are too easily distracted, and damn careless."

"No, they have unfinished business. Evan and Mar."

Almost a week had passed since I'd seen Mar. I'd given her a black eye along with the bloody nose. A week later the bruise was a sickly yellow. "Oh, Rose," I thought, "thou are sick." Was I the sickness, the invisible worm that flies in the night? *Thanks for the thought, Mr. Blake.*

She was wearing her rainbow belt; her auburn hair was in a ponytail that stuck out the back of the kerchief atop her head. I'd rehearsed what I'd say to her when we met again, but all I could manage was, "How's your nose?"

"Better." She cleared her throat. "And your lip?"

"Better." I felt like a damn echo, a parrot. "The ribs are still a bit sore, though."

"That's to be expected," she said. "They're slow healers."

Kinda like a sore heart, I wanted to say, but didn't.

We sat in the mow waiting for the first load to arrive, and kept our distance. We were high up, the first cutting having filled the barn almost to the height of some massive beams. Far below was the pile of last year's hay I'd cleaned up, beside it the few remaining bales from the year before.

I didn't see how the barn could hold much more hay.

When I mentioned it to Mar, she said, "The second cut is much lighter than the first. There's plenty of room still."

The air in the upper reaches of the barn was hot. I was sweating and hadn't lifted a bale yet. I took off my bandana, wiped my face with it, and retied it around my forehead.

The elevator came to life. Mar and I stood and waited for the first bale to tumble in. If I were a gentleman, would I let her go first or would I step in and grab it? In my moment of indecision, Mar stepped forward.

Back and forth we went, passing each other, avoiding each other's eyes. Aside from our breathing and the sound of the bales falling and being lifted and shifted into position, we might as well have been in a silent movie, the clickity clack of the elevator the musical accompaniment to the scene.

The elevator shut down. As we put the last few bales in position, we heard Simeon driving away with the wagon. "We'll get a good rest now," Mar said. "Because the second cut is lighter, it takes longer to build a full load."

I sat on a bale. She took the bale next to me, drank some water from a jug, and passed it over. While I was drinking, she said, "So you saw someone you love die? That sounds heavy."

I kept drinking. Water slipped from the corners of my mouth and ran down my chin onto my chest. I brought the jug back down and placed it between us. I felt my throat tighten in spite of the water. "His name was Richard

Ashby." The story began leaking out of me, then spilling. Mr. Ashby's life and death and my life at school and home tangled up with it.

"The whole thing screwed me up," I said. "I screwed up. That's how I got here." I passed the water back to her.

She took a long drink before saying, "Here's not so bad, is it? Maybe, this is where you need to be, right now, to get things sorted."

"If you'd told me that six week ago, I'd have said you were crazy. Now, I'm almost ready to believe you."

She passed me the jug. As I drank, she said simply, "I'm sorry."

For what? I thought. Mr. Ashby's death, my grief, her joke in the granary, what happened in the pub? I wasn't sure, but her words seemed to cover everything. "So am I."

I took another sip and held out the jug.

More silence filled the space between us. She took a quick drink, then said, "It's Marijke."

"Mah-rye-kah? What is?" I said dumbly.

"My name."

The sound of the tractor interrupted us, followed shortly by the elevator starting up. We stood and waited for the bales to begin tumbling in. "Marijke," I said again. "I like it."

The first bale fell, and she grabbed it. "Yeah, if you like bitter things." She walked the bale over and shoved it into position.

I grabbed one and passed her returning. "Bitter?"

"My name means 'a drop of the sea, bitter.'" She grabbed another bale and passed me as I hurried for the next one. They were starting to pile up. Simeon must have been working double time to get them end to end on the elevator. Smart ass. "Mind you," she said. "It can also mean 'beloved,' so figure that one out for me."

I picked up a bale. Without looking at her as she returned, I said, "Maybe it means some day someone will call you 'beloved' and you'll no longer be bitter." I went to put the bale in place. I was sweaty and flushed. My heart was beating with the effort to move the bale, but there was a drumming on top of that.

When I turned back, Mar was standing with her hands on her hips. The bales kept tumbling in, but she ignored them. "About that kiss."

I walked to the pile and went to grab another bale. "It was more than a kiss."

As I picked it up and passed her, she tucked some loose hair under her bandana. "I was over the line. Plus, I was drunk. We were both drunk, so it doesn't count."

Doesn't count? I shoved the bale in harder than necessary. I turned back. "It counted for me. Maybe you've kissed someone else like that before. I haven't." I went to grab another bale while she continued to stand there. "I'm glad you did it. A cut lip is a small price to pay for…" *For what?* I couldn't finish the sentence, possibly even the thought. For the pleasure of her mouth and tongue on mine? For passion erupting in my poorly managed life? For —did I dare think it—love?

"Simeon, slow the fuck down," she yelled out the hay door.

"Take a chill pill, sis," he shouted back. "What's the hold-up in there? You two need more time to make out?"

"Fuck you," she said.

"Spaz out much?" he replied. After some moments, the bales stopped falling.

"I'll let you know when we're caught up," she said.

We worked silently, passing each other back and forth until the pile was gone.

"Okay," she shouted. "We're ready." Nothing happened for a minute. "I said 'We're ready,'" she yelled. A single bale dropped in. I grabbed it. "Come on, Sim. Get moving."

"Oh," he said, "Thought you needed me to slow down."

"Asshole! Send up those bales or I'll come out there and stick *you* on the elevator."

The elevator starting shaking with him piling the bales on as fast as he could. Mar and I seemed to understand each other without speaking. We went at the bales as fast as we could, refusing to give Simeon the satisfaction of getting another rise out of us.

Eventually, the bales stopped coming. "Catch you on

the flip side," Simeon yelled. He throttled up the tractor and headed off for another load.

Mar grabbed some water and sat on a bale. I came and made to sit beside her. She resisted at first, but moved over when I gave her a hip check. My heart was still thumping, sweat covered me. As she drank, I removed the bandana from around my forehead and wiped my face, my neck, and my arms, scratched and covered with hay. The bandana was soaked and dirty. She passed me the jug. I put my lips to it, thinking of her lips having been there a moment before—almost like kissing, but not. The water filled my chest cavity.

"So why 'Mar'?" I said as I passed the jug back to her.

"When my brothers were little, that's what they started calling me, and it stuck. All my brothers and sisters call me that. The only one who doesn't is my mother." She took another drink. "I actually don't mind it. 'Marijke' hasn't been an easy name to live with. I prefer 'Mar' now."

I thought of Naomi in the Bible, who after losing her husband and sons, says, "Call me Mara," bitter. But Mar hadn't lost a husband, didn't have one or any sons to lose. Why bitter?

"It was a hard name to live with in school. The teachers couldn't pronounce it. 'Mah-Ridge-Key,' they would say at the beginning of the year until I corrected them. But it would stick as a taunt from the other kids. They'd say 'Mah-Ridge-Key Van Ditch-Key," and try to come up with rhymes for it. Their efforts usually ended with 'pee.' That and the rosacea made me an easy target."

"Kids can be cruel." I held out my hand.

She looked surprised. "I'm okay. You don't need to hold my hand. It was a long time ago. I'm over it."

"I can tell." I kept my hand out. "Water please."

"Dork." She passed it over, and I put the jug to my mouth. "I'm named after my aunt, my dad's oldest sister. She was in the Dutch underground and died during the war. My mom chose my name to honour her. She did it for him, but I think it actually makes it hard for him, for both of us."

"Is it ever easy?" I said.

She picked up some loose hay at her feet and began breaking it. "I'm a disappointment to him." There was the bitterness. She dropped the hay and laced her fingers together. She leaned over and looked into the empty cup her hands made. "He wanted his firstborn to be a son."

"You told me that before. Is that it? That's a bummer for you, but it seems to me it's really his problem."

"It's the tip of the iceberg." She went on, almost as if she was speaking to herself. "I've failed his expectations, and my mother's too—you know, get married young to a nice Dutch boy, produce many grandchildren for them."

"I'm a nice Dutch boy."

"No you're not. At least not the kind my dad would want me to marry. A Dutch farm boy, someone who will inherit his father's farm so that my father's empire would grow through me." She looked at me. "Sorry. I didn't mean that about you. I'm glad you're not."

"No worries." I felt that electrical current again, but I couldn't tell if it was one direction only, from me to Mar, or whether it was alternating, moving between us.

"They're disappointed I've broken it off with Gerrit, my first boyfriend. His family has a large farm near the lake. And they're pissed I've gone to university to study nursing."

"Pissed? You're kidding. Why? My dad is all over me about school and going to university."

"It's complicated. If I'm not going to get married right away, then second best would be going to a Bible college, maybe training to work in a daycare or be a kindergarten teacher. But what they'd really want me to do there is find a husband. My dad might be happy to be rid of me. My mom would be sad at my leaving, since I've been her help all these years."

"The oldest girl."

"Momma's little helper from the time I was 5 or 6." She looked up at the hay door. "I'm sick of kids. I know that's a terrible thing to say."

I thought of Mr. Blake. "But isn't nursing sorta like taking care of kids?" She kept peering out the hay door at the blue sky. When she didn't answer, I took a different tack. "I don't get why your parents are against you being a nurse. It's a noble profession and pretty traditional for women."

She cleared her throat and looked down at her hands. "My dad doesn't want me seeing men's bodies, taking care of them. He thinks it will coarsen me, ruin my chances."

"I would think it would improve them, or at least let you know what you'd be getting into with the male of the species."

She seemed to mull this over. "I really don't know." Moments later, she said, "I can't remember anymore if I went into nursing because I wanted to do something good with my life or because I wanted to irritate him." She turned to look at me. "Anyway, after one year I'm not sure. To be honest, I'm sick of nursing too. I feel like I've been a nurse my whole life, helping my mother take care of all my brothers and sisters, most of them from the time they were babies. Am I a monster for saying I'm sick of kids? For not wanting to take care of other people?"

I thought of the nurse from *Songs of Experience*. "You're not a monster," I said simply. "You have to take care of yourself too. To find what you're meant to do with your life, the one life we're given. You need to tell your parents." It struck me as the words came out of my mouth what a fool I was—naïve milksop me offering Mar advice I couldn't follow myself.

"Like you're taking care of *yourself*? Like you're standing up to *your* dad?"

"Fair enough. But I'm trying now. I'm looking for

something to do, for someone." How far could I push it? How obvious could I be? Where was the courage I needed to say it out loud? I fumbled for the words, reaching for her hand.

She folded her arms across her chest. "Have you ever had a roll in the hay, Evan?"

I let my hand drop. "I'm from the city—not a lot of hay there."

"Very funny. You understand me, don't you? You're not that naïve."

Innocent me, always late to get a clue. Still a virgin. I couldn't bring myself to say the word. Clearly she wanted someone more mature, more experienced.

She looked straight ahead. "It was in a place like this it happened, my roll in the hay. Sounds fun, doesn't it, a roll in the hay? It wasn't. It was with Gerrit. He wouldn't take no for an answer. I think you understand me now. Like you guys say, he popped my cherry, and was proud of it. I broke it off with him after that."

"You're not together?"

"No! What made you think that?"

"The two of you at church. And when he visited you at your farm…" My voice trailed off.

She reddened. "It's over. He just doesn't seem to know it."

I studied her face. Along with her words, it put a wall between us, a protective wall around her. A tractor sounded in the distance—the next load. I looked away, sorry for Mar, sorry for myself.

We worked the next load silently. The awkwardness had returned, this time tinged with sadness and confusion, at least for me. What to do with these feelings, which, if anything, had grown stronger from what Mar had told me, feelings that now included some wish to protect her, along with a touch of hope now that I knew she was unattached, all of it mixed with some shame over the desire I felt for her. Was it any different than Gerrit's?

The load finished, she found more water and sat drinking. There was no room for me, and I couldn't push her over with a hip check. Not now. I moved a bale so it was across from her. She passed me the jug and I tasted again her lips on the rim. Strawberry girl.

"You'll laugh," she said, "but what I really want to do is farm, to spend my life growing things, taking care of things."

I tried a smile. "You like spending your time in hot hay mows?" Her face darkened. *Roll in the hay*. Stupid me. "Sorry, that's not what I meant." I regrouped. "So a different kind of nursing, caring for plants, tending flocks. I can see you as a shepherdess."

"Very funny. Do I look like Little Bo Beep to you?"

"No, not exactly." I came back to her original wish. "So why don't you do it?"

"I told you, the farm's going to my brothers. That's my

father's plan." She looked around at all the hay. "It's why he wants Niall's land and quota—there are two of them."

I thought of Niall and Connie, of the land and quota passing from them, from their children Finn and Jane, to Jacob and his sons. Where I was sitting felt under siege. I imagined Niall, having lost everything but the house. Diminished. How could he survive that? I thought of his operation, all the aspects of it—the cleanliness of the milking parlour and the purity of the milk in the tank, the orderliness and efficiency of his milking operation, his cleverness and care for his tools and equipment, his quiet but profound care for his creatures. All of it lost. To Jacob.

"But I'm just a girl," Mar continued, "and girls are okay working on the farm, but they'd never be able to run the whole operation. That's his thinking." She held out her hand for the water. "Anyway, his farming isn't the kind of farming I'd want to do." She took a drink. "To be honest, that's the real reason I went to the Ág college. I wasn't checking it out for Reuben and Simeon. I was looking into programs for market gardening and organic farming. I want to grow good, healthy food that I can sell directly to people. I want to know the people who eat what I grow." She looked at me. "But getting started is overwhelming, the costs involved scary. It's nothing but a pipe dream, really."

It came to me. Connie's garden. "Maybe not," I said.

"How would you feel about doing something to stop your dad from getting the Logan farm while making your dream real?"

She looked skeptical but said, "I'm listening."

I told her about Niall and Connie needing help with their books and a business plan. "They need some ideas for making the dairy more efficient and profitable. Maybe you could help there. But what might be really exciting is you and Connie becoming partners in market gardening."

She looked worried. "Do you really think Connie would be interested in that?"

"I don't know, but there's a chance. Maybe she and Niall are ready to take one."

We started spit-balling ideas and possibilities as we sat. We continued as the last load of hay started falling through the door. When we were finished stacking it, we had the outline of a plan—not a formal business plan, but a blue-print for a dream.

The hay was now up to the rafters. I was looking for a safe way to climb down to the floor, but Mar said, "Come on," and took me by the hand to the edge. I looked at the pile of loose hay below. It had to be a twenty-foot drop. I pulled back, and Mar let go of my hand. She looked down, looked back at me a moment, then leapt.

I moved to the edge. She was spread-eagle in the hay, smiling up at me. For a moment, I saw Mr. Ashby's body splayed at the side of the road, until Mar jumped up and climbed down the far side of the pile. She turned and looked up. "Go for it, Evan!"

I looked around for some other way. An easier way. A way out. A way back. I looked over the edge. The bale felt wobbly beneath my feet, as if it could slide out and fall at any moment. I thought of my dream, Mar and I entering the gopher hole and descending the staircase. I saw myself landing in the hay and falling right through, going down and down and down, never reaching bottom. It came to me there was no way back—to a time before any of it had happened. What "it"? Everything, from the moment I'd become that soft animal nestled in my mother's womb.

"Come on," Mar said. "I'll be here when you land. Live a little!"

Live a little? Live a little. "Give a little" came to me. *Give a little bit of your love to me, and I'll give a little bit of my love to you. Thank you, Rick and Roger. As always, the right words at the right time.*

I brought my right foot back and pushed off, throwing my hands in the air as I leapt. It must have lasted only a second or two, but I fell through barred sunlight coming through cracks in the barn board. The hay caught me. I'd overshot the middle, so I rolled down the side, coming to a stop at Mar's feet. I looked up at her.

"Hello, Sunshine. Nice jump." She put out her hands to me. I held on, as if for dear life.

CHAPTER 30

I'd spent hours in the hot mow with Mar, and needed to get outside. To run in the wide open. When I'd arrived seven weeks earlier—a span I could hardly fathom now—I'd intended to run every day—a temporary jailbreak, if nothing else. At the end of the first day, though, I'd found myself exhausted. Day after day exhausted. And when I'd finally gotten used to the work, I was held back by fear—of open space, of gravel roads and pickup trucks, of strange fields and forests, of wrong turns.

That evening, after milking and dinner, I realized I still had unspent energy. Was it possible my dad was right about bootstraps and grindstones? I didn't want to admit it, let alone accept it. Farm labour wasn't simply any hard work, it was something more.

In my room, I opened my running log to the page where I'd copied out the Wordsworth poem. After reading it again, on the next blank page I wrote the date, my location in the universe, my intended route, and the approximate distance. Grabbing them off the chair, I slipped on my black short shorts and yellow tank top. I noticed for the first time that my legs were more muscled, and so were my arms and shoulders—though my farmer's tan meant I still glowed ridiculously in spots. I attached the elastic to my glasses and tied a bandana around my forehead. Last, I slid my feet into my Nike Marathons and tied them tightly with double knots.

"I'm going for a run," I said simply when I came downstairs to the kitchen. Niall and Connie, sitting at the table with coffee cups in front of them, looked stunned. Finn and Jane paused in their playing to stare.

Jane laughed. "You look like a bee."

"Didn't you know, that's what I am?" I replied.

"Gotta run?" Niall said. "Something chasing you? That's the only time I run, when a bear's after me."

"Bear?"

"Happened years ago. I'm sure it's long gone."

Connie said, "You won't get lost, will you?"

"I'll just head out a certain distance and then retrace my steps. What can go wrong?"

"Bears, coyotes, cougars, snapping turtles, escaped cattle, chickens crossing the road for some unknown reason, pickup trucks filled with drunk teenagers."

"Ni, enough."

Jane said, "Can I watch you run?"

"There's not much to watch. You can watch me leave, but I don't know when I'll get back."

"I'll wait for you in the yard."

She came and held my hand, and walked me outside. Finn followed. I did some warm-up stretches, starting with neck rolls and working down to my ankles. Jane and Finn copied me.

"Okay," I said, "I'm heading out."

Finn said, "On your mark, get set, go!"

I began at a jog, and they followed me beneath the canopy of leaves to the road. "Be back soon," I said, as they waved me on my way.

At first, I ran west toward the sun. I passed the side yard with its gardens. I passed the barley field, stubble now. As I came up to Mar's house, I half hoped, half feared she was watching from somewhere—her bedroom window, the front of the horse barn, the calf pens.

There she was, standing by her Corolla, talking to the girl from church, Lily. I felt a jolt in my stomach. They must have heard the crunch of my shoes on the gravel, for they both turned their faces toward me. I waved, which broke the rhythm of my limbs. I tripped but recovered quickly enough to see them wave back and hear Mar laugh and say, "That's Evan." At my name in her mouth I felt my face redden, my heart rise up.

My limbs found their familiar rhythm, heart and lungs too. I glanced at the fenceposts, pushing back the urge to count them. I looked at the fields and the woods and the sky. Mostly I focused on a spot on the road in the middle distance, a spot that advanced as I ran toward it. But I listened to the birds of the evening and tasted the air, ripe and sweet and sour. I found a quiet space emptied for a brief time of my worries and griefs and hopes. Yes, hopes. Within that space, I searched for some measure of natural piety.

I ran out to the distant hayfield I'd worked my first day. Brer Fox wasn't there, but I said a blessing for him nonetheless. I stopped short of offering one for the gophers.

The sun was low now. I turned back. I felt its warmth on my back until it dipped below the horizon. When I turned into the laneway, dusk had fallen. I pushed myself to sprint beneath the archway of trees. Jane and Finn were flying the paper airplanes on the lawn. When they saw me, they abandoned the planes, picked up flags they'd made, and waved me across the finish line.

"The winner," Jane shouted.

"First place," Finn said.

The only race I'd ever won. It felt like the crown of life.

It was Saturday evening. I'd had dinner and showered and put on clean jeans and a button-up shirt. Looking in a mirror, thinking of Mar, I'd tied and retied a bandana loosely around my throat. I hoped it added a little colour to my personality, the jaunty angle suggesting I didn't take myself too seriously. Fake it 'til you make it.

Mar was picking me up. We were going to a coffee shop in town to put on paper the ideas we'd dreamed up in the mow. I considered it a date. She didn't seem to know that and was treating it like a business meeting. I'd dug through Connie's books and found some love poems—Elizabeth Barrett Browning's *Sonnets from the Portuguese*—and was hoping to slip some lines into the conversation, possibly between developing a marketing plan and calculating financial projections. "How do I love thee? Let me count the ways"—my kind of poem. Clearly I'd become a hopelessly romantic but clueless dork.

I came downstairs and surprised Niall and Connie for the second evening in a row. My calculator was in my back pocket; I carried a pad of paper and a pen. "Mar and I are just getting coffee," I said. "I wanted to talk to her about university. I really don't know what I want to do and thought she might help." Connie wore a satisfied smile.

I hoped Mar would wear a sundress, a sign there was an alternating current of attraction, if not love, running between us, but she wore jeans and a tank top—equally attractive, but not a date-night outfit. She had a bandana around her throat. We were matching, and as she drove to town I had a vision of us in old age wearing matching clothes, possibly bib overalls, sitting on a porch in matching chairs, rocking in rhythm.

"Do you mind if I call you Marijke?" I said. "I like it better than Mar, and it is your name." I wanted to tell her it was lovely like her, that I didn't care if her feelings for me were bitter, she was beloved. Some Romeo.

She looked at me skeptically but said. "Just don't wear it out."

"Marijke, Marijke, Marijke." I could have gone on saying it for hours. I'd been fool enough to whisper it as I drifted to sleep the night before.

She gave me an elbow. "Enough, Evelyn."

At the coffee shop, I tasted my first cup of coffee. I was a virgin in so many ways, it was embarrassing. "The taste grows on you," Mar said.

"What?" I replied. "Like fungus?"

I kept thinking of firsts. I'd never sat across from a girl —a woman really—in a booth in a coffee shop or restaurant, just the two of us. I'd never before talked with a girl for any length of time, never felt so vulnerable—wanting to say so much, fearing I'd say too much. I felt a novice at conversation, the art of love.

I worried my way through the evening while Mar was

all business. She left me no opening for poetry or song. *Sorry, Rick and Roger, I tried. Sorry, Mr. Blake, Mr. Wordsworth, Ms. Barrett Browning—you Romantic fools—your poetry had little chance against business strategies and implementation plans.* By the end of the evening, we had an outline, a map of how the dairy might become stronger, how it might be partnered with market gardening, how Mar might become a partner with Connie and Niall.

It was dark when Mar pulled up to the Logans' side porch. She kept her feet firmly pressed on the brake and clutch, but grabbed my hand as I opened the door. "This is a great plan, Evan. I think they'll love it." She seemed to be searching for words. "*I* love it." Not *I love you.* "I can't tell you what this means to me. Thank you so much. I'll never forget this."

What could I say to that? Her words expressed a gratitude that pulled me closer to her than to anyone else I'd ever known—even Mr. Ashby—while setting a wall between us I wasn't sure I could breach. I looked at her searchingly. "Happy to help" was all I could manage. I squeezed her hand and let go. I got out the door and shut it. Without looking back or waving, I turned to the house, a lump in my throat.

Chapter 31

I couldn't skip church again, and maybe now I didn't want to. Mar assumed I'd come, saying the night before that right after the service we'd come back to the farm and present the plan to Niall and Connie. If nothing else, I would be near her in her Corolla, could watch her sitting among her siblings.

I didn't wear my suit, even though Connie had managed to get it more or less clean. Jeans and a button-up shirt would have to do, dress code be damned.

Mar was alone when she picked me up. "I told my

mother it was Reuben and Simeon's turn to take care of their brothers and sisters. They're riding the family bus."

I followed Mar into the sanctuary. She slipped into the back pew beside the young couple, greeted them, and rubbed the cheeks of the baby with her forefinger. Wasn't she sick of babies? Did she know this was the designated breast-feeding pew? And was she aware that sitting alone with a guy in the back pew was as good as an engagement announcement to the congregation?

I sat beside Mar and looked for refuge from my impure thoughts about her. But were they impure? Might they be part of the natural piety I was looking for, sitting on these wooden pews crafted from once-living trees, a forest shaped for worship? The thought seemed sacrilegious, but still.

It came to me, the possibility that their feelings for women, like mine for Mar, drew many men to church—and perhaps kept them there, kept them coming back Sunday after Sunday. So be it.

The service began, and I tried to find my long-silent singing voice, holding the hymnbook with my right hand, Mar holding it with her left. "Morning has broken like the first morning." A hymn? I'd thought it was a Cat Stevens song. Maybe it was both.

I hadn't imagined this congregation capable of singing one of this decade's anthems. It didn't add up. Was it a sign or just coincidence? Could coincidences become signs if you knew how to read them? As Rick and Roger might say, "Oh Lord, is it mine?"

"Ask the animals," the minister's voice boomed through the sound system, "and they will teach you, or the birds in the sky, and they will tell you; or speak to the earth, and it will teach you or let the fish in the sea inform you. Which of all these does not know that the hand of the Lord has done this? In his hand is the life of every creature and the breath of all mankind." Wise guy, that Job, even if unlucky. Who was I to argue with him?

I'd asked for a sign, but things were getting out of hand. The minister had paired this Old Testament reading with one from the Sermon on the Mount, the passage about the birds of the air and the flowers of the field. "Each day," the pastor finished, "has enough trouble of its own." *Ain't that the truth, sweet Jesus?*

I didn't hear the sermon. I was sitting beside a bird of the air, a flower of the field, myself a worry wart. I muddled over the two passages, trying to make sense of what the animals were saying to me, how sowing and reaping and putting in barns, what I'd done all summer, was different from the lives of the animals, yet somehow necessary for people, for Niall and Connie, for Mar's family. Was it?

Worry could not add one single hour to my life. What was Mr. Ashby's dying thought as he fell to the ground? No worry would have prevented what happened in his brain, to his brain. If I'd been there when he fell, it wouldn't have made a difference. I couldn't have saved him. Evolution and revolution intersecting at that moment in his life, revelation in a moment of extinction. Then what? Kingdom come? Born-again to be born yet again at some distant resurrection?

He'd had his come-to-Jesus moment. When might I, if ever?

It came to me that this persistent and pesky book, the Bible, would hound me, haunt me, console and frighten me throughout my life, as would the man at the centre of it.

Stop worrying! I made the attempt, Mar beside me, me thinking, a lily of the field clothed in all her splendour. Me, just a buzzing, bumbling bee.

Niall and Connie were surprised when Mar stepped into the kitchen with me, but were happy to have her stay for lunch. Connie seemed especially pleased. "That's a lovely dress, Mar. Don't you think so, Evan?"

"Yes," I said, "it goes nicely with her auburn hair."

After lunch, Mar explained that we'd been doing some thinking and we wanted to share with them some ideas. "Oh?" Niall said. Connie sent Jane and Finn outside to play.

We cleared the dishes and Connie put on a pot of coffee. The four of us sat at the table, Niall and Connie at either end, Mar across from me. Before Mar got started, Niall said, "I mean no disrespect, Mar, but how did you get involved in this business?"

Her rosacea deepened. "Evan and I got talking when we were in the mow."

Fool that I was, until that moment I hadn't realized I'd broken a confidence. "I'm sorry, Niall, it just kind of came out."

Connie said, "What about your father, Mar?"

"My father?" she said. "It's simple. I don't want my father to get your farm. I'd like to help stop him if you'll let me."

Connie looked at Niall and poured coffee for him, Mar, and herself. I held out my cup. Connie looked surprised but filled it for me. I put a lot of milk in it to counteract the taste.

Niall glanced at Connie, leaned forward, and folded his hands in front of his cup. "Okay, we're listening."

"When we went to the Ag college," Mar said, "I wasn't just visiting a friend or checking out programs for my brothers. I was there for myself. I don't want to be a nurse. I want to farm."

"I don't understand," Niall said. "If you're hoping to farm with your father, what does that have to do with us?"

Mar stumbled for words. "It's complicated."

Connie studied her a moment and said. "*He* doesn't want to farm with *you*, does he? It's not that *you* don't want to farm with *him*."

"That's part of it. He's preparing Reuben and Simeon to take over."

"Sons, not daughters," Connie said.

"I don't want to do the kind of farming he does," Mar said. "It's large-scale, more like factory farming. There's a place for that, I know. So many people in the world need to be fed. But at the college, I was checking out programs for small-scale, family-focused operations. There's a trend back to producing locally-grown food, more organic and environmentally friendly practices, as well as creating artisan products. There's a growing market for these healthy alternatives." She took a breath, looked across at me, then looked at Niall and Connie in turn. "If you'll have me, I'd like to partner with you in this kind of farming."

Niall put down his cup. "I'm still listening."

Mar knew dairy practices, and she talked about equipment upgrades and new techniques that would lighten Niall's workload and make his operation more efficient. On top of that, she suggested he divert some of his milk into making artisan products such as cheese and butter—simply an expansion of what Connie was already doing for home use. The second prong of our two-prong plan was to expand Connie's garden into a full market garden operation—fruits and vegetables, including strawberries and sweet corn, the most popular items. All of this could be sold from the farm itself, or, even more profitably, at local markets. The towns along the lake were filled with tourists all summer, the whole area with cottagers and campers—all of them needing to eat, all of them with money to spend. And this was on top of all the locals in area towns. Artisan milk products, free-range chickens, fresh fruits and vegetables—all supplementing the income from the dairy. Mar made it sound like a winning proposition.

"To expand the garden, you might give up some acres from the barley field to the west of your house. But I would also lease some acres from my parents and bring that into the partnership, along with my savings and the training I'll get at the Ag college. I have to talk to my mom and dad about switching from Nursing to Ag, anyway, and I'm going to tell them they owe me for years of taking care of my brothers and sisters. I'll see if I can get some acres in the wheat field across the road. It might be a tough sell with my dad, given that it's the opposite of what he really wants. But I won't back down on this."

Connie and Niall looked at each other. "Ni, what do you think?"

He took a long sip of coffee. "It sounds like a nice dream, Mar, but the truth is we've been running on empty here for a long while now, barely getting by. Your plan sounds like it'll cost a lot of money to even get off the ground, let alone run. I'm sorry to say it's just a pipe dream."

"It's not," I said. "We've run the numbers. There's a good chance the bank will like them. I'll show you."

I brought out the paperwork Mar and I had put together. "Your books are cleaned up now. The bank will see that your finances are in good order, and they're not as bad as you originally thought. But with this plan, you can also show them how a modest investment will pay off."

I went over the calculations Mar and I had developed based on the research she'd done—talking with her contact in the Ag program, snooping in her father's records, consulting seed catalogues, and phoning Ag suppliers. I presented the numbers as objectively as I could, but found myself growing excited as I did. We discussed and debated the numbers, talked about the assets Niall and Connie could leverage, the government funding they and Mar might apply for. I could sense Niall and Connie beginning to grow excited.

Finally, there was a pause. Mar and I waited. Niall looked at Connie. Some silent message passed between them. He said, "I'm not sure this will work, but we must move forward somehow."

Mar smiled at me. Her eyes were brimming. My heart was aching.

Connie retrieved her electric typewriter from the bottom cupboard of the bookshelf in my room. That afternoon, she and Mar typed up the formal business plan for the bank.

While they did that, Niall went outside. I joined him, helping him sterilize the milking equipment and give the parlour a thorough cleaning. He tried to rest on Sundays but wasn't very good at it. The agitation created by the plan didn't help.

We went to the machine shed and tidied the tools. He got a grease gun and began servicing his tractors and equipment. He showed me how and gave me a turn. "Take care of your machines, and they'll take care of you," he said.

After, we went into the pasture. He wanted to check a pregnant cow whose time was getting close.

He talked to her while rubbing his hands over her, and it came to me what care he took of what was under his care—not a shepherd to a flock, but a cowherd, a pastor of another sort. To everything he did he brought a kind of tender skill, skills he'd likely inherited from his father, skills that were threatened by the present and might be judged useless by the future—unless the plan we'd come up with worked. I thought of the moment he'd lost it in the barn. My hope was he'd never be pushed to that again. It was so easy to lose it, to get lost.

"Dad, Dad, come play catch with us." It was Finn and Jane, calling over the fence.

As we walked over, Niall said, "Maybe we need new ways to go forward, but God help me I don't want to lose what's good in the old ways."

While Connie and Mar finished the plan, we tossed a ball around the yard. Soon it would be time for the afternoon milking.

That evening, I sat at the desk in my attic room, paper and pen before me, feeling a fool. From the first day, I'd wanted to get away. I'd written to my brother for rescue. I'd even tried to run off on my own. But now, as the time to go was getting close—just a week away—I feared leaving.

I looked out the window at the canopy of leaves descending into darkness. A faint glow was on them as they shook in a light breeze. Was I afraid of what I would leave behind, or what I had to face at home? It wasn't clear to me yet what I needed to be running toward, what I should run from.

It hadn't occurred to Mar, to Niall and Connie, that I might want to become a partner, as well. But why would it? A green city kid on a working vacation from his real life would want this? No way! Then again, did I? Or was it just an escape I was looking for from my family and decisions I needed to face at home, from that other possible future?

I'd caught a glimpse of what that future might be in Niall and Connie's relief and excitement, in working on the plan with Mar. Numbers used to order at least some small part of life's chaos, to buttress dreams and possibilities. Calculations not just for their own sake but to liberate people to find and live their full lives, to guard their dignity, to show them a way forward. I'd always loved pure mathematics—elegance and balance, rules and formulas, solutions to problems, correct answers—but I could see now how such math might apply to life. Applied math.

Perhaps I could become a mild-mannered accountant, the Clark Kent of the spreadsheet? Would Mar be my Lois Lane? Or would she find me a citizen of Dullsville, no Superman in disguise?

Was such a modest vocation the best I could do? *Rick and Roger, you wanted me to be a child of vision, to do something right, to find myself a new ambition. Was this pedestrian path the one?*

I turned from the window to the paper before me on the desk. I picked up and fiddled with the pen for some moments, then gripped it and wrote *Dear*.

I stopped and looked around the desk, seeing if I could find the right words there. I put down the pen, turned on my calculator, and punched 7734 into it. I turned it upside down and studied the word made by the numbers—a silly trick, a sophomoric joke, but it seemed apt to my feelings.

I turned to Janus. Like him, I felt my face pointing in two directions—in and out, toward and away, farm and home. Niall and Connie and Finn and Jane; my mom and dad, Jeff and Annalise. Pulled toward Mar and lost to her forever. Looking back at Mr. Ashby's death, carrying it with me, and propelled into an uncertain future.

I picked up Janus and felt his heft in my hand as I held him beneath the lamp. It was black now outside the window. Each day was a new door to go through. One day, near or far, would present me with my last door, the one to death, the door through death—to what? Extinction of this one silly, beautiful body of mine among billions? Or revolution, revelation, resurrection? Too much to hope for?

I returned Janus to his spot—facing the dark window, poised also to look down at me when I slept, if I slept this night.

I picked up the pen again.

Dear Jeff,
I've faced the manure this summer. Now I need you to do me a favour. If you need me to beg, this is me begging...

CHAPTER 32

It was Tuesday morning, and I was once again babysitting Jane and Finn. I'd watched Niall, suited-up, and Connie and Mar in dresses head down the laneway for their 10:00 a.m. appointment at the bank, their financial books and business plan—containing all the calculations I'd made—safely tucked in an old leather satchel.

Soon it would be afternoon, and there was no sign of them yet. I'd tried to keep calm by busying myself with Jane's and Finn's requests—visit the animals, check the garden, eat snacks, read stories. Through it all, I remained jumpy.

We were outside flying paper airplanes when the station wagon finally drove up the laneway. Was its slow speed a sign of victory or defeat? I stood with a plane in my hand until Niall, Connie, and Mar emerged from the car.

Connie was smiling. Niall was trying hard not to smile. Mar raised her arms in the air and let out a whoop. I tossed the plane into the sky and watched it twist and turn. I didn't notice until she was right in front of me Mar coming in for a hug. I held her as long as she would let me.

Inside, at a celebratory lunch, they filled me in on how the appointment had gone, praising my calculations I think a little too enthusiastically, exaggerating their importance to the bank's positive decision. Maybe they were trying to console me for not being there.

When lunch was done, Finn and Jane brought their dishes to the sink and headed outside to play.

Niall watched them with affection as the door closed behind them. "A new start," he said, "calls for a new name. It was my granddad who named this farm Logan & Sons Dairy. It doesn't seem a perfect fit now."

We threw around names until Connie said, "How about Bonnie Farm? We'll call our partnership Bonnie Farm Foods."

"Bonnie," Niall said. "Yes, it is bonnie, isn't it? I've thought that my whole life."

Connie retrieved a bottle from the pantry, along with four glasses from a cupboard. "This is a wonderful plan, a new dream that's going to take a lot of work to make it a reality. But no one here's afraid of work. I think we should drink to it."

"What is it?" I said.

"Strawberry wine." She poured the glasses. As she passed me mine, she said, "Take it slow."

We joined Niall as he stood and raised his glass. He turned to Mar and me. "To you, both of you. Thank you." He turned to Connie. "To us, dearest, and our little ones." He brought his glass to the centre of the table. "To all of us, whatever the future brings, and to Bonnie Farm."

We clinked glasses. I took a sip. "Holy cow," I said. "Bonnie Farm has to sell this wine. What other fruit wines do you make, Connie? I'd love to sample some."

It was my last day, my last Sunday. My ride would arrive sometime after church, shortly after lunch.

When Mar's Corolla pulled into the laneway, she stepped out wearing a bathing suit and cut-off jeans. On her head was a kerchief made from a many-coloured bandana. "We're celebrating," she said.

"What?" I said, standing on the porch.

She waved her arm in an arc. "Everything. Nothing. Go get your bathing suit."

"I don't have one."

"Shorts will do."

I went and changed into my cut-off jeans and my Supertramp T-shirt. Since the bank appointment, Niall and Connie and Mar had met daily to set their plan in motion. I'd sat in on the talk, sitting at the kitchen table with them and drinking coffee, but truth be told I felt like a fourth wheel on a tricycle and tried to keep my sad envy in check.

Mar pulled out of the laneway. "Where are we going?" I asked.

"You'll see. It's a surprise."

She drove to the highway. To the right was the town and the church. To the left was the road south that ran to the small towns along the lake—the road I might have travelled in the shag wagon, the road that led eventually to cities—Sarnia and Windsor, London, even Toronto. To the ends of the earth.

Mar crossed the road onto gravel, the Corolla kicking up a dust cloud. Soon, I could see the lake in the distance from a hilltop. We descended into a valley, and Mar pulled into a farm laneway.

"Whose farm is this?"

"Gerrit and Lily's family's."

I turned to her. "Gerrit? Lily? They're related?"

"Yeah. Brother and sister. You didn't know?"

"Why would I? Do they know we're here?"

She glanced at me, then turned back to the laneway.

"Their farm has lakefront and a great private beach. We've got about an hour, maybe an hour and a half before they're back from church."

She followed a track and parked where it ended at a small bluff. We climbed down it, then up over a dune to get to the beach. She pulled two towels out of a beach bag. I helped her spread them on the sand side by side. I pulled off my T-shirt as she shimmied out of her shorts.

"Nice tan," she said.

"You're one to talk." While her shoulders were tanned and mine weren't, her tank tops had left plenty of white skin, and her legs had tan lines from shorts. In the white skin of her cleavage, a silver necklace hung with a small cross at the end.

She smiled. "Guess I'm not much of a beach bunny." She pulled off her kerchief and turned toward the water, shielding her eyes with her hand. The wind blew her hair back. There was so much I wanted to say. The words churned inside, spinning around and around a rotary, refusing to find an exit.

I followed her gaze. The water was calm and bright, just small waves washing the sand. "Come on," she said, walking to the water's edge. "We don't have a lot of time." I followed her but stood at the verge as she ran in. As the water splashed up, I saw little rainbows refracted in the spray. When the water was up to her thighs, she dove in. She came up, stood, and ran her hands over her hair, pushing it back. The water turned it an even deeper red.

She turned toward me. "What? Do you need a written invitation?"

I wanted something in writing, words fixed on a page, promises. "I forgot about my glasses and watch." I walked back across the hot sand and placed them on the towel. The sand, the sky, the water, Mar—my world turned fuzzy. I walked straight into the water, feeling my feet sinking in the cool sand, the water pushing and pulling at my legs. When it reached the top of my thighs, I twisted and flopped into the water backwards.

"Nice dive. You're ready for the Olympics."

I splashed water at her, windmilling my arms for full effect. She fought back but eventually swam away. I followed her out to deeper water. We were up to our necks, arms out for balance. "Marijke."

"Do you ever feel like walking away, leaving it all behind? Or swimming, in this case?" She began swimming into deeper water.

Months ago, I might have said yes. Not anymore. "Marijke, that's not funny."

She turned toward me, treading. "Come save me, then."

"I'm not falling for that again."

"Then come out and I'll save you. I've taken swimming lessons and have my first-aid certificate. You're in good hands."

I pushed off, performing something that approximated a breast stroke. When I reached her, she showed me how to tread water, then turned to the horizon. "It's so big and so beautiful."

So wonderful, magical, Rick and Roger would say. Maybe miraculous. "Yes, and so blurry with my glasses off."

She laughed. "Sometimes it's good to feel this small, this vulnerable. A drop in the sea."

"Marijke."

"Okay, let's turn back. You go ahead and I'll follow you."

We climbed out of the water and gathered sand on our feet as we walked to the towels. While Mar squeezed the water out of her hair, I found my glasses and checked my watch.

We sat propped on our elbows, legs stretched out, and studied the horizon. The world was beautiful, beautiful and scary. Mar was beautiful and scary. Was I somehow beautiful and scary too? "Marijke," I said again. If she looked, I was sure she would see my heart thumping through my chest. It was beating a tattoo against my ribs.

"I shouldn't have kissed you," she said.

"You've already said that. You don't hear me complaining, do you?"

"No, Evan, I really, really shouldn't have kissed you."

At the very same moment as I leapt at last and said "But I think I love you," she said, "Because I think I'm gay."

"What?" we said together.

"You think you're gay?"

"No. I know I'm gay. I've just had a hard time accepting it. Until recently."

Was I that bad a kisser? was the thought that came to me. But I said, "Was it what happened with Gerrit?"

"It doesn't work that way. I've been struggling with it a long time, as long as I can remember. I haven't told anyone. Can you imagine my parents' reaction, the people in church? What I did to you in the pub was wrong, maybe unforgivable. I don't really understand it, but it was like I was testing myself, seeing if I could want a guy. If any guy, I thought it'd be you. That's why I'm sorry. It wasn't fair to you. And now that you've said what you said I feel even worse. God, I'm so sorry."

My first kiss, my first love, my first heartbreak—with a lesbian. I felt like such an idiot. Zero to sixty in my feelings, all the time, what a dork. A milksop. Why hadn't I just asked her if she'd like to go out for coffee again some time, maybe have another business meeting. I could have simply asked her if I could write her a letter after I got home, like we might become pen pals. But no, I had to use the L word. I turned to face her, and she looked at me. "So that's all I was? An experiment?"

"That's not fair. It wasn't really like that. If I'd known. I didn't think."

I struggled to make sense of what she said, what I felt.

One of Mr. Ashby's sayings came to me. "Life's an experiment. It hurts, but I don't regret it, and, strangely, I do still love you, just it's different knowing."

"You're okay with it? Most people aren't."

Dyke. Butch. Words I'd heard at school. They felt shameful as they came to mind. A name came to me too. Milk. Harvey Milk, murdered last fall, no milk of human kindness shown him. "I can't pretend to understand it, but I'd like to." More words came to me. "'We are put on earth a little space, that we may learn to bear the beams of love.' A poet said that."

She looked out over the water. "'Bear the beams of love.' I like it." After a moment, she turned to me. "Friends? That would mean a lot to me."

I hesitated. Wounded as I felt, was it even possible? I met her gaze. "I'd like to think of you as more than that."

"I thought you understood. That I can't."

"I meant we could be bosom friends."

"You mean like Anne Shirley and Diana Barry?"

"With your rust-coloured hair, you'd obviously be Anne. That would make me Diana."

She smiled. "Smart-ass. I had no idea you were a fan of *Green Gables.*"

"Closet fan. If it got out that I'd read all the books, it would definitely cement my milksop reputation."

"Embrace it, Evan. It makes us kindred spirits."

"Kindred spirits?" I thought about it. "Kindred. That

means family. Like brother and sister. I'd like to think of you as a sister."

She smiled and reached for my hand. "I've already got too many brothers, but yeah, I'd like that. Maybe if you really had been Evelyn, it might have been a different story."

I think I hid the pain pretty well. Underneath, I knew I'd probably never see her again, but I wanted to make the effort, to imagine a life in which we could be brother and sister, kindred spirits, even if it seemed impossible in that moment.

A thought came to me. Mar and a girl at church, arm in arm, heads together. Mar blushing at a girl, not at Gerrit. "It's Lily, isn't it?"

She looked surprised, even afraid. "Is it that obvious?"

"No, no. But now that you've told me, the penny just kind of dropped."

She looked out over the lake and swiped at her eyes with her free hand. "I've got it bad. Problem is, I don't know what her feelings are, and I can't risk asking. So I'm stuck. It'll never be anything but a pointless crush."

I squeezed her hand and smiled. "Now *that* I understand." After a moment, I said, "Does she know about Gerrit, what he did to you?"

"God, no! How could I tell her that?"

I laced my fingers in hers and looked out at the immense sky and the vast lake. I seemed to see there my past and future converge. I would never be a man's man, maybe always a momma's boy. I could be among men, but there would always be a part of me that was acting, a round peg in a square hole. I would feel most comfortable in the company of women, them with me because I was no Romeo, no Casanova. But only just comfortable. I felt the line between affection and friendship on the one hand and a passionate attraction on the other to be razor thin, that the line could so easily blur, like the world with my glasses off. A leap across it was filled with risk. Was there room in it for platonic love? Love God, love your neighbour—five words it could take a lifetime to work out.

I knew then I needed to love and be loved, the only antidote to my loneliness and grief. I asked Rick and Roger, Is there really a reason I need to be alone?

If all this need made me a milksop, so be it. It came to me sitting beside Mar that this *was* my better nature. I was soft, but so what? My softness might be my strength, my superpower, foolish as that sounds. It was time to embrace it. A weird joy and peace came over me, and I thought, is this what it feels like to be born again?

Mar squeezed my hand. "Thanks, Evan."

"For what?"

"I don't know. For listening. For everything. For being who you are."

I hesitated, thinking these might be some of the last words I said to her. "I just want to tell you you're amazing.

I thought so from the moment I met you. And I hope some day you can be your whole amazing self, nothing to hide."

She leaned her shoulder against mine. I leaned my head against hers. We sat like that for a long time. At last, she said, "One last swim?"

I looked at my watch. "We're cutting it close."

"Live a little."

When we got back to the farm, Jeff had already arrived on his motorcycle. He was sitting on the porch with Connie and Niall. They rose and came down the steps as Mar rolled to a stop.

"Mar!" Jeff said as she exited the car. "Looking good." He walked toward her with his arms open.

She ignored him and met me in front of the hood. She kissed me on the cheek and embraced me. "Goodbye, Sunshine," she said.

When we let go, Jeff was staring, looking puzzled and amazed, his arms still wide. I said, "Big brother, your mouth's hanging open. You're gonna catch flies if you don't shut your trap."

"Mar," he said. "Remember me? Jeff."

"Of course, Jeff. You know you're absolutely unforgettable." She turned away from him to Niall and Connie. "What time do you want to get together tomorrow?"

Jeff dropped his arms and stared at me. I came close and whispered, "Have you got it?"

He tousled my mop of hair, then squeezed my biceps. "My, how you've grown, little brother. Told you farm work would make a man of you."

"Just give it to me."

"Take a chill pill, Milksop." He pulled a thick envelope from an inside pocket of his leather jacket and passed it over. "You owe me."

Mar had started her car. I waved to her, my throat tightening, and watched until her car disappeared, leaving behind dust and the sound of its receding engine. "I'll go pack," I said.

Upstairs, I sat at the desk and opened the envelope. Inside was $2,325. I pulled a second envelope out of the drawer. Inside were all my earnings from that summer, $2,800. I added them to the envelope.

I'd written to Jeff, asking him to lend me the money until I got home. There, I'd go to the bank and repay him, the funds exactly half of all the money I'd saved, starting with my grade-school paper route. I wrote to him begging him to bring it when he picked me up, to show up on his motorcycle with the cash and an extra helmet. I didn't want Mom and Dad coming to get me.

I pulled out paper and a pen.

Dear Niall, Connie, and Mar:
Please accept this seed money for Bonnie Farm. It's a small amount compared to the

debt I feel for what you've given me this summer.

Evan

I folded the paper in half and slid it beneath the envelope. To hold it all down, I balanced Janus on top of it.

I finished packing, remembering to pull the card and letters from below the mattress, looked around once, and headed for the stairs. My suit still hung on the nail. I left it there.

Connie was waiting in the kitchen. A bottle of strawberry wine and a loaf of bread sat on the table. "Here, for you. Just pack it safely among your clothes." I wrapped the wine in my bandana, and made it snug inside a pant leg. The bread went inside a clean T-shirt. When both were safe, we stood awkwardly facing each other. "Thanks for taking care of me," I said. She hugged me. "Could I have one last glass of milk?" She poured the largest glass she could find. I drained it, forever imprinting on my brain that glorious taste.

Outside, Finn and Jane were flying their paper airplanes with Jeff. They ran up to me. "For you," they said.

"Are you sure?"

Finn said, "I know how to make them myself now."

I thanked them with a hug and tucked the planes in my suitcase. "Every time I fly them I'll think of you." I passed my suitcase to Jeff so he could strap it to his bike.

I turned to Niall and held out my hand. He went in for an awkward man-hug instead. I felt his hands on my upper back. "Take care of yourself, kid. And get that license, will you?"

I donned my helmet, climbed up behind Jeff, and held him around the waist for my virgin bike ride. For the last time, I passed beneath the archway of trees, dappled with light. I looked back as we left the laneway. The whole family was waving. I lifted my hand in a salute until they disappeared from view.

CHAPTER 33

It was a strange homecoming. Perched aboard Jeff's bike as he rode into the city, I found it overwhelming after eight weeks in the country—big and busy, bossy and loud, yet so crowded that everything felt small. The heat radiating off the pavement and buildings was intense; any wind from the countryside was blocked, the city itself muffled and landlocked.

We landed in the driveway of our townhouse midafternoon. The house seemed to have shrunk, pressed in a vice grip by the houses on either side. I climbed off Jeff's bike and stood staring at the garage, at the window of the room above it that my brother and I shared, the tiny globe-shaped shrubs and the bed of petunias in the yard. I was untying my bag from Jeff's bike when my parents and sister filed out the front door.

My mother I knew would be happy to see me and hugged me to herself as if I'd just returned from climbing Mount Everest or fighting in Vietnam. But apparently I'd been missed even by my father and my sister.

"You look different," Annalise said. "Taller, not so sickly, Runt." My father cleared his throat. He patted me on the back, grabbed my hand, and pulled me into a sideways hug.

They felt like strangers to me, my family still, but there was a small fissure in the land between us. Perhaps it was an eight-week-sized gap. Maybe I was now the stranger. Or perhaps I was now finally myself.

Inside, I unpacked in my room. Either Jeff had lied about moving all my stuff out, or he'd thought better of it and put everything back where it belonged. I unwrapped the strawberry wine and tied the bandana Mar had given me to my bedpost. I took the loaf of bread out of my T-shirt and smelled them both. I looked at my shelf and dresser covered with paperweights, then took them down and placed them in the bottom drawer of my desk, leaving just the one on the desktop, the Expo 67 biosphere. On the shelf I put the paper airplanes Finn and Jane had given me.

I brought the bread and wine downstairs, saying they were gifts for the whole family from the Logans. It was a little white lie, but I wanted to share what Connie had grown and made. Perhaps I also wanted to soften up my dad for the interrogation I knew would follow dinner.

"Homemade," my mom said. "Is that safe?"

I said, "Better than safe. Real."

Ahead of supper, I walked to the store and bought real food, including a carton of whole milk. When I unpacked the fruits and vegetables on the counter, my mother looked worried. I studied the colourful display a moment and said, "I want to eat real food. I want to learn how to cook real food."

"Well," she said, "I don't know. That means I'll have to try to remember how my mom cooked. So no processed cheese, even? It's a flavour saver."

"Real cheese." I cleared my throat. "If you want to, Mom, we can go together to the farmer's market on Saturdays to get the good stuff. All the good stuff. I'll even drive when I get my license."

I went to the fridge, got out the jug of powdered milk my mom had made up, and poured it down the drain. I replaced it with the carton of whole milk. She didn't protest.

For dinner, I cut up the loaf of bread and the vegetables, doing a hatchet job on them, my knife skills being what they were. I brought them on platters to the table, along with butter and dressing and the milk.

Jeff pointed and laughed. "What's this mess? You've murdered those poor vegetables and maimed Connie's loaf of bread. She'd be horrified."

I poured myself a glass of milk and considered it. "If that's what you think, Big Brother, then you don't know Connie at all. And maybe you don't know me."

"I know exactly what you are. Once a milksop, always a milksop."

"What I am, maybe, but not who I am." I stood and raised my glass of milk as if to do a toast. Instead, I reached across the table and baptized my brother with it.

He jumped up wearing a cap of milk flowing down his face onto his chest. "Evan!" my mother said. Annalise jumped back so she wouldn't get wet, and started laughing. I waited for the scolding from my father, maybe even to be sent from the table. He said simply, "Jeff, you had that coming. Evan, get your brother a towel."

Jeff spent the rest of the meal giving me the hairy eyeball. When my plate was empty, I retrieved the bottle of strawberry wine and poured a glass for everyone, including Annalise and myself, though we were still underage. My parents didn't object. "Delicious," Dad said after a sip. "Now, son, let's talk about the summer and your future."

I felt myself redden. "Not yet, please. That can wait. I just want to enjoy this wine, which is exactly what my summer was like."

My father looked as if he was about to object, but my mother headed him off. "Yes, it can wait. Isn't that right, dear?"

To further delay my interrogation—my father's opportunity to judge whether I'd passed his test—I got up when I'd finished my wine, cleared the table without being asked, and helped my mother with the dishes.

When they were done, it couldn't be delayed any longer. I sat with my parents in the living room, and before they said anything, I said simply, "I know what I want to do now." When I explained, I'm certain my father was congratulating himself that his plan had worked. I let him believe it. Maybe in some strange way it had.

Then I said, "Let me tell you about my summer." It came spilling out, everything I'd done, the mistakes I'd made, the lessons I'd learned. But I kept much to myself— the pub, my feelings for Mar, an hour spent with her at the beach.

When my words were spent, I said, "I'm going for a run now."

"What? You just got home," my mother said. "Don't you want to rest?

How could I explain to her that being home made me restless?

I didn't follow my old route, the three-mile circuit that would take me past the spot where Mr. Ashby died. I didn't feel the need to punish myself with it anymore. As I ran, I remembered instead being packed with my teammates in his little yellow Civic on the way to the road race, and then coming home with him.

I ran east until I was out of the city. There, as dusk fell, I found the smell of fresh-cut hay.

It's early September, after Labour Day. I'm back walking the halls of WLM-KSS for the first day of school. I feel the ghost of my brother striding ahead of me, though he's left for university. I've just been to my homeroom, where we've been introduced to our new homeroom teacher, Ms. Bond. She's fresh out of teacher's college, still a bit green judging from her nerves. She broke the chalk when she wrote her name on the board, saying she preferred "Ms." and joking, no, she wasn't secret agent 007; that was her sister, Felicity. It's possible Ms. Bond is a fellow milksop; I recognize the signs.

The ghost of Mr. Ashby lingers in the room. The pi banner still circles the walls where they meet the ceiling, but Ms. Bond has removed other posters and made it her own with ones about acid rain, the greenhouse effect, endangered species. (Gophers aren't on the list. I checked with her.) She wants to save the planet, and she's aiming to make us her conscripts. On her desk sits the small model of the lever and fulcrum; the wisdom of Archimedes remains to be pondered each day. I guess, like Mr. Ashby, she too believes in moving the world.

After school I have cross-country practice. I'm heading to my first class, English, when I see Annalise walking toward me, by her side a friend I've not met before. Students slam lockers and mill about me on their way to first period, while I stare at the girl—brunette hair in a bob, like dark chocolate, tortoise-shell glasses with beautiful brown eyes behind them, milk chocolate. She's wearing cut-off jeans and an army-green tank top, carrying a binder and books pressed to her chest. She's bronzed by the summer sun.

"Ignore him," Annalise says as they approach. "That's just my runt brother." She gives me the finger, double-barrelled, pumping them up and down, "pew pew, pew pew." The knapsack on her back jiggles with the effort of it.

"That all you got, baby sister?" I give her the finger in return.

The girl looks at me, smiling as we pass.

I turn, walking backwards, and stare at her. I don't know if she senses my eyes on her, but she turns back to look at me. I stumble and fall, books and binders scattering. She laughs and walks on. I leap up from the floor, embarrassed.

My heart leaps up too, the same way it leapt up to Mar. I recognize it now, the booster-rocket lift of it.

That night, I ask Annalise the name of her friend. "Mae," she says simply.

"Mae?"

Mae? Mar? *How bizarre,* I think, their names sounding

so similar, the first two letters identical. Is the universe playing a joke on me? Are those letters a message from God? Is it those letters that attract me to both of them, so different in appearance? Or do those letters somehow confirm the attraction I feel?

"Yes, Mae," my sister says. "Don't get any ideas. She's mine."

CHAPTER 34

At the beginning, my much-loved children, I said this was the story of how I fell for your mother. Quite literally, you see. It's been a roundabout journey to get here. That hallway encounter was our first sighting of each other, brought about most serendipitously by my annoying, brilliant sister and all the people of Bonnie Farm who'd saved me, who helped me get past my grief and leap into life, despite the risk and the likely pain, the certain failure, the inevitable end.

The money I left behind at Bonnie Farm, sitting in

that envelope with Janus on top, was the first investment I ever made, more of a gift, really. I didn't expect anything in return. Since then, I've had a soft spot for underdogs, though there's always a fine line between an underdog and a lost cause. I thought about Mar and the Logan family, about Bonnie Farm, and I knew there were some dividends that couldn't be calculated. I'm collecting them still. Would I have done anything different knowing the train of the farm crisis was barrelling down the track at them? Not on your life.

And yes, I stole your aunt's girlfriend to be mine. Until then, I didn't know I had such good badness in me. Mind you, in telling my tale I've lied to you about one thing: that Janus paperweight. You see, Mr. Ashby didn't give it to me as a gift. No, I stole it. The day after he died, I walked into my homeroom, a room now changed forever, picked it up off his desk, and slipped it in my knapsack. I couldn't bear to tell you earlier, just as I couldn't bear to part with it then, maybe because I couldn't bear to part from him— not until the end of the summer, when I passed on my stolen goods to Niall, Connie, and Mar.

Since I'm confessing, let me add this *mea culpa*: I've never told your mother this, that she was my gay rebound girlfriend. Rejected by Mar, I was ready to fall for your mom, to fall hard while my heart leapt up to her. If you think about it, you owe your existence to Mar. Our whole family is in her debt.

And what of Mar? Well, you know her as Auntie Jo. Had you figured it out, caught the clues? I left a trail of bandanas rather than breadcrumbs.

Years after that summer, when she came out, she dropped the name Marijke and took on her middle name, Johanna. She changed her last name too, adopting her mom's maiden name, Terpstra, a strong Friesian name.

Coming out cost her much. Not me, her adopted brother. Not everything, but much. Surprisingly, Reuben and Simeon stood by her. I'd so wanted them to be asses about it, my tormentors, those twin pricks.

Speaking of pricks, I'm sure Brice Barrow will recover from the drubbing I gave him at my retirement celebration. After all those years of slaving for him, coddling the wealth of London's many millionaires at Wheel and Barrow Chartered Accountants, all I get from him is "milksop"? The way he said the word disgraced what had been my lifetime badge of honour, my lifelong membership in U-MAW—the United Milksops Association of the World.

Standing that close to the mic, about to offer a speech in my honour, Brice must have known I would hear, that everyone would. Right away, I smelled a conspiracy. I looked around for your Uncle Jeff, and there he was by all the nibblies, filling his face, as usual. With his cheeks puffed out with canapés, he grinned at me and raised his glass of champagne. The bastard. As he had been our whole lives, he was one step ahead of me, still mussing me up.

That's when I saw red. It was a tough choice who to go after, Jeff or Brice. Jeff being blood, I went for the man who was now my ex-boss. I no longer gave a damn. I rushed him with my one-two combination, boxing his ears and giving him the wedgie of all wedgies while he tried to recover his hearing. Imagine my surprise when I discovered the undies beneath his leather pants were green silk, bikini briefs covered with dollar signs. I got a good look before Bunny, that trophy wife of his, pulled me off him. I do feel bad that the effort split the seam of her leather miniskirt, exposing her thong, and much of her ample buttocks. I got a good look at those too, when your mom and Auntie Jo pulled her off me and dragged me out of there.

I don't expect your mom and I will be receiving an invitation to one of their famous pool parties anytime soon. Even if we did, I suspect your mom still wouldn't be speaking to me. I'm not sure anymore whether she's banished me to this attic room, what she calls my man cave, or whether exercising discretion, that better part of valour, I simply retreated to it. Probably a bit of both. Perhaps sharing this tale with all of you will get me back in her good graces. Either that or forking out for a second honeymoon. I hear Cancun is the perfect spot to rekindle romance— and apologize for the very many errors of one's ways.

Whenever I could, children, I tried to tilt the numbers for the little guy, the underdogs like Niall and Connie and Mar. Not often enough or well enough to make me a superhero, Captain Accountant rescuing lost causes, just plain old Mr. Milksop in a muddle. Don't I know it, but I need you to understand I've tried each day since that summer to live a life the people I love and who have loved me wouldn't be ashamed of, might even be proud of. To me the world has often seemed filled with too many people trying to be big, their bodies unable to contain egos that spilled over and flooded the land around them, making a mess others had to clean up. People bloating by devouring the earth, Pac Men chomping everything in their path. I've had enough trouble managing my little self. If that makes me a milksop, so be it.

Dear children, I've come to believe that the world is a strange and marvellous place. Bloody marvellous, Rick and Roger would say. And we are in it for a short time as bloody marvellous creatures. In the brief span I have left with you and your mom, I so want to make the most of it, this magical planet, our miraculous lives.

ACKNOWLEDGEMENTS

When the idea for *Milksop* began taking shape, I knew I needed some guidance and structure around turning it into a novel. Until then, I'd written short stories, a tight and demanding form, but the longer form of the novel posed new challenges. That's when I discovered The Novelry. Their motto? "We grow writers." I wanted to grow! Their program? "Tools, not rules!" While I like some rules, I needed tools!

Milksop would not be the novel it is without The Novelry. I'm grateful to Louise Dean for creating this program and the thriving community of writers that exists because of it. In particular, I had three wonderful coaches who guided me toward completing the first draft of *Milksop*: primarily Mahsuda Snaith, but also Emylia Hall and Rachel Joyce. Further in the process, I received immensely valuable feedback from two editors: Lily Lindon, who provided an "ultimate manuscript assessment" of *Milksop*, and Francine Toon, who reviewed my query package to ensure it was ready for the eyes of agents and publishers. Finally, I'm grateful to the Literary Fiction group at The Novelry, who listened to me read from the opening chapters and provided encouraging feedback.

In between that first draft and the editorial review, I shared *Milksop* with my longtime mentor, Hugh Cook. Implementing his advice made me look to Lily and Francine a much better writer than I actually am.

I owe a huge thank you to Larry Link for reading my manuscript to ensure I didn't say anything wrong or foolish about farming. For many years, Larry's been my supplier (not of drugs but of hay for my horses).

I wrote the first draft of *Milksop* in 2023 while I was on sabbatical from my professor duties at Redeemer University. To all my former colleagues in the English Department and the administration, thank you for encouraging and supporting me in this adventure of a scholar-turned-creative-writer. My sabbatical was also supported by a Professional Development for Artists Grant from the Canada Council for the Arts, which had designated me a New and Emerging Artist—at the age of 61. (Apparently, I spent decades in my artistic chrysalis before emerging as the writerly butterfly you now see.)

I'm hugely grateful to my publisher, Alanna Rusnak, for answering a message in a bottle from an old-dog writer with the query blues. It's been a joy to work with her on bringing *Milksop* to life as a real book that readers will hold in their hands or on their e-reader. (Dear Reader: My hope is that this tale brings you or already has brought you some pleasure.)

Without my supportive family, *Milksop* would not exist. First, to my brother Nick and my sisters Tracy and Wendy, thanks for the childhood we shared and which partly inspired this story. To my children and their partners, you are a joy that motivates me. Matt, Beth and Ren, Tony and Kaleigh, Charlie and Evy: thanks for all the crazy! And, above all, thanks to my wife April for more than forty years of beautiful chaos: writers need a mess to work with.

Many sources of inspiration and imagination have gone into the making of *Milksop*. A major one was a summer I spent on the dairy farm of Melvin and Barbara Knox. I'm grateful to them for what was an amazing, formative experience. They are gone but not forgotten.

John Van Rys is no longer young, he hasn't been urban for about thirty years, and he's never been hip. That makes him old, rural, and pretty square. That said, when he was 61, the Canada Council for the Arts designated him a New and Emerging Artist. Go figure!

John lives on a hobby farm outside Dunnville, Ontario, with his wife April, dogs, cats, horses, free-run egg-laying hens, and Cayuga ducks, as well as two of his adult children, their partners, his two granddaughters—and, just to keep things interesting, his mother-in-law. This life has supplied much of the inspiration for his fiction. People tell John that he has a thing about chickens, so he's been given chicken mugs, chicken boots, chicken T-shirts, a stuffed chicken, and a chicken lunch bag. Chickens do appear all over the place in his fiction, but he's convinced that doesn't mean he has a weird obsession with them.

Until his retirement on July 1, 2025, his day job involved being a mild-mannered English professor, but his passion since late 2016 has been writing stories. He's had short stories published in *The New Quarterly, The Dalhousie Review, Agnes and True, Blank Spaces,* and *Solum Literary Journal.* His story "Excavations" won the 2022 Prairie Fire MRB Short Fiction Contest. His first book-length collection, the story cycle *Moonshine Promises*, was published in 2021 by Wipf and Stock. He has drafted a second collection of stories, *The Healing Arts*, through the support of the Canada Council for the Arts and a mentorship at the Humber School for Writers Graduate Certificate. He completed his first novel, *Milksop*, through The Novelry. You can find out more about John's writing by visiting his website, johnvanrys.com. If you wish to stay up-to-date with his writing shenanigans, you can follow him at his Facebook page and at his Substack newsletter, Old Dog Dumps (ODD): Dispatches from a Journeyman Writer.

www.ingramcontent.com/pod-product-compliance
Lightning Source LLC
Chambersburg PA
CBHW020902060726
47591CB00004B/1048